HIDDEN KILLERS

"Get back inside!" Nate bellowed, giving Winona a push as he heaved to his knees and swung to confront their unseen attackers. A rifle flashed in the dark, spewing smoke. A bullet slammed into the wall at his shoulder.

Taking a hasty bead, Nate fired into the center of the smoke, then backpedaled into the cabin as an arrow cleaved the crisp air. It narrowly missed his head.

Winona had flung herself indoors. Darting to their table, she procured a pair of pistols and dashed to her man's side. "Here," she said, taking his Hawken and shoving the smooth stocks into his brawny hands.

Nate King pressed a shoulder to the jamb and peeked out, seeking signs of their attackers.

The woods were unnaturally still. All the wildlife in the valley had gone quiet.

WILDERNESS

SPANISH SLAUGHTER
David Thompson

LEISURE BOOKS   NEW YORK CITY

To Judy, Joshua, and Shane

A LEISURE BOOK®

September 1997

Published by

Dorchester Publishing Co., Inc.
276 Fifth Avenue
New York, NY 10001

Printed in the United States of America.

SPANISH SLAUGHTER

Chapter One

Nate King sat up with a start. Alarmed, he scanned his family's cozy cabin. Bathed in the rosy glow of tiny fingers of flame dancing in the fireplace were the sleeping forms of his son, Zach, and his daughter, Evelyn. Each lay in an opposite corner, bundled in thick bear hides.

Beside Nate, his wife stirred and muttered. Nate glanced down at Winona's beautiful features. She was still asleep, her long raven tresses framing her head like a luxuriant dark halo.

What had awakened him? Nate recalled having a bizarre dream about strange, bloodthirsty creatures. One had the body of a man but the head of a bull, and was nearly impossible to kill. The thing had charged him, snorting loudly, wicked horns gleaming. Although Nate emptied his guns, the creature just kept coming. The monster had been almost on top of him when Nate woke up.

Nate smiled sheepishly. So that was the reason, a

stupid nightmare. It served him right for eating a late snack of pemmican and wild onions. Relieved, Nate lay back down, idly scratching his bearded chin.

Gradually, his powerful body relaxing, Nate drifted off. He was almost sound asleep when a series of thuds and a high-pitched nicker snapped him bolt upright again. His piercing green eyes swung toward the window, paned with precious glass brought all the way from St. Louis.

When the whinny was repeated, Nate quietly slid from bed and padded in his bare feet to a chair. Over it were draped his buckskin shirt and leggings. Under it were his moccasins.

Despite the chill at that altitude at night, Nate donned only the leggings. If something was after their horses, he would have to get outside right away.

Propped against the doorjamb was his prized Hawken, crafted by the famous brothers of that name. Grabbing it, he cracked the door and listened. Wind whispered in the pines. To the north, in the distance, a wolf howled. It was answered by another far to the west.

Nate slipped from the low cabin, keeping his back to the wall as he cat-footed to the right toward the rough-hewn corral. In it were their four mounts and three packhorses.

At the corner, Nate paused. The horses were clustered in the center, ears pricked, staring intently at the inky forest that ringed the homestead. Something must be out there, stalking them, he figured.

Nate frowned. He had cleared their secluded valley of big predators years ago. From time to time, however, a painter or a grizzly would wander into the pristine paradise and take up residence. Whenever that happened, he tracked them down and disposed of them. They were simply too dangerous, especially the grizzlies, to be allowed to live in close proximity to his loved ones.

Nate's razor-keen senses probed the murky woods. Whatever prowled the night was not making any noise. With the limitless patience of a true hunter, he waited, watching the horses. They would tell him when the beast was near.

Sure enough, in under a minute Nate's black stallion stamped a hoof and tossed its head. It was a signal for the others to act up.

In among the trees, a twig snapped. Nate instantly crouched, his thumb curling back the Hawken's hammer. He wished that he had thought to bring his pistols, as well. A single shot seldom dropped a charging grizzly, if that was indeed what lurked in the darkness.

A broad-shouldered, powerfully built man, Nate King was not the least bit scared. He had tangled with grizzlies before. So often, in fact, that he was known as ''Grizzly Killer'' by the tribes who inhabited the region.

Still, grizzlies were never to be taken lightly. Enormous brutes, some five to six feet high at the shoulders and weighing up to a thousand pounds, they were the lords of their domain. Notoriously hard to kill, they sported claws over four inches long and teeth that could crush the thickest bones, or a human skull, with frightening ease.

The big stallion stomped again and moved a few feet toward the rails. It peered intently at a thicket fifty feet away.

Nate did the same. He trusted the stallion's hearing, which was vastly superior to his own. A hint of vague movement stiffened him. He pressed his cheek to the rifle and sighted down the barrel. Fixing a bead in the dark would be a challenge, but he must not miss.

Something flitted from the thicket to a tree. Nate

was startled to see a two-legged silhouette. It wasn't a wild animal, after all!

Nate's mind raced. Who could it be? He had made peace with all the neighboring tribes, even the Utes, who claimed the valley as part of their territory. It had been ages since any Indians gave him trouble.

Maybe it was Blackfeet, Nate speculated. Or one of their allies in the Blackfoot Confederacy, the Piegans or the Bloods. All three tribes hated whites. For years now they had made wolf meat of every mountaineer they came across.

It was rare, though, for Blackfoot war parties to rove this far south of their usual haunts. Rare, but not unprecedented.

Nate prayed it wasn't the case. His deepest, abiding fear was that one day his family would be caught unprepared by hostiles, and slaughtered. The fear was not unfounded, since many whites, some friends of his, had suffered just such a grisly fate.

The figure moved again, to another tree. Whoever it was, the man was circling around to the front of the cabin.

Holding his fire, Nate eased onto his belly. Stygian shadows at the base of the wall effectively hid him. The nocturnal stalker was in for a nasty surprise.

Then another form, much nearer, separated itself from a large boulder. Nate shifted to fix a bead, but the man went to ground behind a log.

A faint noise sounded. To Nate's utter dismay, it came from *inside* the cabin. Someone must be up. Maybe Winona had woke, found him gone, and noticed the door he had foolishly left open. Knowing her, she would immediately rise to investigate.

An awful mental image of his wife being transfixed by arrows as she stood framed in the doorway galvanized Nate into rising into a crouch and backing toward the door.

Neither of the figures was visible.

Maybe it would be all right, Nate told himself. Maybe Winona had not made the noise. Maybe she was still sound asleep. Maybe—

Hinges creaked. The door swung wide. "Nate?" Winona King whispered. Moments ago she had rolled over in bed and sleepily reached out to drape an arm across her husband's muscular chest. Only, he had not been there.

Concerned, Winona had roused herself. Discovering the door cracked sparked more worry.

Now, rifle in hand, Winona stared into the benighted woodland, her hair fanned by a gust of wind. She took a cautious step. Common sense dictated that she be extremely careful. As her people, the Shoshones, had learned the hard way, in the wilderness mistakes usually proved fatal.

Out of the corner of her eye she registered motion. Someone was slinking along the base of the cabin toward her! He sprang! Pivoting, she brought the muzzle up.

Nate King, fearful for his wife's safety, tackled her around the shins, his shoulder brushing against her gun. It was well he bumped it, for the rifle went off in her ear, discharging a ball into the earth.

Too late, Winona had recognized who it was. As she fell, a whizzing object flashed overhead and embedded itself in a log. She landed flat on her back, a quivering arrow in the space her chest had occupied a heartbeat ago.

"Get back inside!" Nate bellowed, giving her a push as he heaved to his knees and swung to confront their attackers. A rifle flashed in the dark, spewing smoke. A bullet slammed into the wall at his shoulder.

Taking a hasty bead, Nate fired into the center of the smoke, then backpedaled into the cabin as another arrow cleaved the crisp air. It narrowly missed his head.

Winona had flung herself indoors. Darting to their table, she procured a pair of pistols and dashed to her man's side. "Here," she said, taking his Hawken and shoving the smooth stocks into his brawny hands.

In the far corner, young Zachary King jumped up out of his bedding and rushed to his parents. "What's happening, Pa?" he cried. "Who's out there?"

From under a pile of bearskins in the other corner rose little Evelyn. Where city-bred girls her tender age might have screamed or cringed in terror, she took in the situation at a glance and promptly ran to her mother's side to be of what help she could.

Nate King pressed a shoulder to the jamb and peeked out, seeking sign of their attackers.

"Who the blazes is out there?" Zach repeated anxiously.

"I don't rightly know," Nate whispered. "Now, hush."

The woods were unnaturally still. All the wildlife in the valley had gone quiet.

Winona, bent at the waist, moved to the wall where their ammo pouches and powder horns were suspended from pegs. She began reloading the Hawken and her rifle, measuring how much black powder to use by the feel of the grains in her palm.

Winona took great pride in her ability. Few Shoshones owned rifles; those who did were all warriors. And few of them were as skilled as she was, thanks to her husband's tutelage.

It had been Nate who insisted she learn to shoot. As in everything else, she had proven to be a fast learner. On occasion, she even outshot him, and he was accounted a first-rate marksman by the mountain-man fraternity.

Fighting alongside him came as natural to her as

breathing. From an early age, Shoshone girls were taught to stand by their men in a crisis, to be brave in the face of adversity. It was essential if the Shoshones were to survive, for they were a warrior society at heart.

Warriors garnered positions of leadership and prestige by counting coup in battle. Women were required to master crafts necessary for the upkeep of a lodge and the welfare of their families, but they were also expected to show as much courage as their mates when the need arose.

Nate was mystified by the silence. War parties usually made all sorts of racket to intimidate their enemies. Where were the wild war whoops, the frenzied screeches, the lusty yips of adversaries eager to take scalps?

In the midst of the dense foliage, a rifle boomed. The ball smashed into the jamb inches from Nate's cheek. Flying slivers stung him as he jerked back.

"Watch out, Pa!" Zach cried. Eager to do his part, he glided to his rifle, which he had leaned in the corner before retiring. A Hawken, like his pa's, it was a .40-caliber instead of a .60-, but it shot just as true.

Zach looped to the other side of the doorway. "Anything?" he whispered.

Nate shook his head. It proved a mistake. The movement drew a buzzing shaft, which passed a finger's-width from his ear, missing his startled daughter by a cat's whisker, and shattered against the stone fireplace.

"Whoever it is must have eyes like an owl," Zach commented.

Nate nodded. "Get down," he told Evelyn, and after she obeyed, he sidled to the window and placed an eye against the lower edge.

"Too bad Shakespeare isn't here," Winona said.

The man she referred to, Shakespeare McNair, was

13

a fellow free trapper and the best friend Nate ever had. Most of what Nate knew, his vast knowledge of woodlore and wildlife, he owed to McNair, whose fondness for the English bard had earned him the unusual nickname.

That very morning, Shakespeare and his wife had left after an extended visit. Nate mused wryly that the two extra guns would sure come in handy right about now.

"Maybe they'll give up once they see that they can't get at us," Zach remarked. The log walls were too thick for lead balls and arrows to penetrate. Fire might drive them out, but anyone foolish enough to rush the cabin with a burning brand would be picked off before he got close enough to fling the torch.

Winona finished reloading and brought the heavy Hawken to her husband. "Here."

Nate tucked the two pistols under his wide leather belt, accepted the rifle, and said, "Keep your eyes skinned out front." Hurrying to a narrow slit carved at shoulder height in the north wall, he lifted a flap of deer hide that covered it and gazed at the thick foliage beyond the clearing in which the cabin stood.

The slit was a new addition, one of a half-dozen gun ports patterned after those at Bent's Fort. Nate had carved them six months ago, with Zach's help, prompted by dread that one day a war party might trap his family in the cabin and burn it down around them.

The tops of trees bent to gusts of wind. If anyone was out there, they were well concealed.

Nate stepped to the next port, and the next. "Not a sign," he grumbled.

"Fat lot of good it'll do the vermin, Pa," Zach declared. "At first light, let's rush on out. We can hunt each and every one down and give them a taste of their own medicine. What do you say?"

Nate King sighed. He couldn't fault his son for being impetuous and overconfident. Typically, most youths his age were. The young always rushed in, where wiser heads exercised caution. "We'll wait and see," he responded.

In the gloom, no one noticed Zach's disappointment. It was not the Shoshone way to wait meekly to be slaughtered. When a village was raided, the warriors always carried the fight to their foes.

Many an evening, Zach had sat around a roaring campfire, listening with other Shoshone boys to seasoned warriors relate their exploits in war.

There would come a day, Zach had vowed, when he, too, would be a great warrior, just like Touch The Clouds and Drags The Rope and Buffalo Hump. And his father.

It pleased Zach to no end that his pa, an adopted Shoshone, was reckoned among the bravest. On numerous occasions he had heard how his father once rallied the entire tribe against a marauding band of Blackfeet. How his pa once saved countless lives, and risked life and limb in the bargain, to arrange a crucial truce between the Shoshones and the Utes. And how his father had slain the largest grizzly ever encountered in the central Rockies, a monster that had terrorized the Shoshones for years.

Yes, sir! Zach proudly reflected. He would make his father proud of him, or he would die in the attempt.

Nate returned to the door. Winona was at the window; Evelyn was huddled under the table. For the moment they were safe enough.

Their mounts and the pack animals were another matter. Among some tribes, a warrior was accorded as high a coup for stealing a horse as for slaying an enemy. The war party was bound to try to sneak into the corral. Nate mentioned as much.

"I will keep watch over them," Winona volunteered, and moved to a slit in the south wall.

It was the best they could do. Nate hunkered, cradling the Hawken. Closing the door would offer more protection but deprive him of an unobstructed view of the area in front of the cabin, so he left it as it was.

"Is everyone's mouth as dry as mine?" Zach asked.

Evelyn took that as her cue to go to the water pail kept on a counter under the window. Taking a dipper off the wall, she brought a drink to her brother, giving the entrance a wide berth when she crossed the room. It was not much, but she was helping out, which she yearned to do more than anything else.

"Thanks, sis," Zach said.

Nate smiled at them. For siblings, they got along well. None of the bickering so common among the children of his kin back in New York. None of the constant spatting that drove a parent to distraction.

Nate could not get over how much his daughter had grown in the past year. It seemed like just yesterday she had been a chubby little cherub in a cradleboard. Except for her curly hair, Evelyn was the spitting image of her mother, which pleased Nate no end.

"You're welcome, Stalking Coyote," Evelyn said, calling Zach by his Shoshone name, as was her custom. Her Shoshone name was Blue Flower, which she favored over her Christian one, just as she was partial to Shoshone customs over those of her father.

Nate did not mind. He wasn't one of those who forced his outlook on life down the throats of his offspring. The way Nate saw it, children were a lot like flowers. They should be lovingly tended and nurtured but left pretty much free to grow as they saw fit.

Within bounds, of course. Nate would not tolerate disrespect. Sassing Winona or him was not permitted.

Nor could his children shirk their daily chores. They were required to perform them without complaint.

Indistinct movement in the woods brought Nate's musing to an abrupt end. He brought up the Hawken but had no definite target. Settling back, he craned his neck to take a gander at the heavens.

Judging by the position of the Big Dipper and the North Star, it was close to three in the morning. In another hour and a half the sky would begin to brighten, heralding a new day.

Minutes dragged by as if weighted by millstones. Nate kept expecting the war party to make a move, but nothing happened. Perhaps the warriors were waiting until daylight to make a concerted rush.

Over by the south wall, Winona did not let down her vigilance. Their enemies would need only a few moments to drive the horses off, so she must not let her attention stray.

Zach hoped that the warriors would act soon. The waiting ate at his nerves like a termite through wood. He was impatient to count coup.

In due course the eastern half of the firmament blushed pink. One by one the stars were swallowed by slowly spreading sunlight.

Across the lake birds erupted in throaty chorus, while on the north shore a small herd of elk slaked their thirst. In the vicinity of the cabin, located west of the lake, songbirds did not utter a peep. Deer, rabbits, and the like were conspicuous by their absence.

It led Nate to believe that the war party was still close by. As the shadows retreated under the onslaught of dawn, he sought some sign of the men who had shot at him.

Presently, a golden crown rimmed the eastern horizon. Under normal circumstances Nate would have been entranced by the spectacular vista of lofty peaks, forested slopes, and blazing solar arch.

17

"Where *are* they?" Zach wondered, craning his neck to see better.

"Keep your head down!" Nate exclaimed, giving his son a none-too-gentle shove. "Haven't I taught you better than that?" In the mountains, being impulsive was as bad as being careless. Either could get a body killed.

"Sorry, Pa," Zach said. He knew better. He was just tired of standing around twiddling his thumbs. "But shouldn't we do something?"

"I aim to, shortly," Nate informed him. They had enough food and water on hand to last for days, if need be. So it was not urgent that they break out. Being cooped up, though, rankled him. He would much rather take the fight to the enemy than sit there and wait for the war party to bring the fight to them.

Winona had overheard, and turned. "What do you plan to do, husband?" she inquired in her impeccable English.

"Go for my morning stroll," Nate replied with a grin.

"And be rubbed out? No." Winona gestured. "We have the advantage here. They cannot get at us except through the door, and they cannot get close to it without being spotted. It is best for all of us to stay inside."

"I don't fancy being hemmed in," Nate confessed.

"No."

If his marriage had taught Nate anything, it was that there was no arguing with a woman once she made up her mind. A man could talk himself hoarse. He could rant and rail. He could even pout and plead. But it went in one ear and out the other.

One tactic, and one alone, sometimes worked. As stubborn as a woman could be, she was usually willing to bow to irrefutable logic. "We've held our own so far, true," he said, "but what if more show up? I say we drive these off now, while we still can."

Winona gnawed her lower lip. She hated to admit it, but he had a point.

"The two of you can cover me," Nate proposed. "Once I'm in the trees, close the door and don't open it again unless I holler."

"I don't know . . ." Winona hedged.

Nate backed to the table to give himself a running start. "Time's wasting," he said.

Reluctantly, Winona switched positions, taking up his post by the door. As she passed him, she brazenly kissed her man full on the mouth. "Take care, Grizzly Killer."

"Always," Nate said, and hurtled on out.

Chapter Two

"I swear!" declared Shakespeare McNair. "I must not have been paying attention when the Almighty asked us to line up so he could pass out brains." His piercing blue eyes shifted to the lovely Flathead who rode beside him. When she offered no comment, he growled deep in his throat like a riled griz and said, "You're supposed to speak in my defense. Point out that everyone forgets things now and again."

Blue Water Woman bestowed an amused look on him. "I am? Sorry, husband. I did not see the need since everyone knows that you have been searching for your brains ever since."

"Wench!" Shakespeare huffed.

His wife's merry laughter tinkled on the wayward breeze. They were winding down a series of low hills bordering the high country valley that was home to the man Shakespeare regarded more as a son than a friend. "I just hope Nate finds it before Evelyn does," he said. "She's liable to use it to dig in the dirt or some such nonsense."

"It will wash clean," Blue Water Woman said, running a hand through her shoulder-length hair. In recent years more and more gray had speckled the black; her temples were completely silver.

"Easy for you to act so clam," Shakespeare carped. "It's not your favorite pipe."

"I do not smoke," Blue Water Woman reminded him matter-of-factly. "And as I have often begged you, I wish you would stop. It smells up the cabin."

Shakespeare adopted a pained expression and put a hand to his brow as if he were in torment. "How long shall I be patient?" he quoted from *King Richard II*. "Ah, how long shall tender duty make me suffer wrong?"

"I did not hear you complaining the last time we made love."

Acting shocked, Shakespeare said, "Hussy!" Then he launched into another quote. "O serpent heart, hid with a flowering face! Did ever dragon keep so fair a cave? Beautiful tyrant! Fiend Angelical! Dove-feathered raven! Wolfish-ravening—" Abruptly stopping, he rose in the saddle and scanned the valley.

"What is wrong?" Blue Water Woman inquired.

"Something ain't quite right," Shakespeare answered. He could not say exactly what, but the valley was . . . different . . . somehow.

East of them the sun was rising. Starkly revealed in the golden glare, the surface of the lake sparkled a rich blue. The pines were a striking green. It was hard to conceive of a more tranquil scene. Shakespeare pursed his lips, thinking he must be mistaken.

Then Blue Water Woman straightened. "There is no smoke," she said.

Shakespeare tensed. By this time of the morning

the King family would normally be up and about, and Winona would be fixing breakfast. It was a daily routine, never broken. He should be able to see the smoke that curled from their chimney, even if he couldn't see the cabin. Yet there was none. "I don't like it," he said, and jabbed his heels into his white mare.

At a brisk pace they descended to the valley floor, Shakespeare with his Hawken resting across his thighs, Blue Water Woman carrying hers in the crook of her left elbow.

McNair hated to think that harm might have come to the Kings. He'd never own up to it, but he loved all four of them as if they were his own flesh and blood. He was so much a part of their family, the kids had been calling him "Uncle Shakespeare" since they were knee-high to a grasshopper.

It was ironic how life worked out sometimes. Years back, when Nate's real uncle, Ezekiel King, had claimed the valley as his own, Shakespeare had been a mite irritated. He hadn't liked the notion of having a neighbor so close. Some might say he was making a mountain out of the proverbial molehill, since their cabins were twenty-five miles apart. But at the time, to Shakespeare's way of thinking, Zeke had been crowding him.

As it turned out, they had become fast friends. Shakespeare had taught Zeke everything he knew. Later, when Zeke lured Nate to the Rockies under false pretenses and then had the unmitigated gall to die on the boy, Shakespeare had taken Nate under his wing.

They shared a bond few easterners would understand, forged in adversity, tempered by hardship, seasoned by mutual affection. They had grown as close as two peas in a pod. If anything ever happened to

Nate or Winona or the kids, Shakespeare would take it mighty hard.

So he spurred the mare across the flats, winding among trees and vaulting logs with a skill few men half his age could boast. Blue Water Woman stayed right on the mare's heels, her long hair flying.

Shakespeare considered himself fortunate to be her mate. They'd first met and fallen in love shortly after his first trek to the mountains, way back in '98. Cruel circumstance had separated them, and it wasn't until many years later that they were reunited.

Sharing his life with her was literal heaven on earth. It never ceased to amaze him that now, in his waning years, when his joints ached half the time and his mane of hair and bristling beard were as white as driven snow, he had finally found supreme happiness.

The sight of someone moving along the north shore of the lake caused Shakespeare to raise his rifle. Slowing, he pointed, then said softly, "Go to the cabin. See if they're all right. Fire a shot if you need me."

Nodding, Blue Water Woman angled to the southwest. Shakespeare kept going until he was within a few hundred yards of the lake. Dismounting, he tied the reins to a low limb.

Due to the dense brush, Shakespeare had lost sight of the figure. His best guess was that he was due north of where he had last seen the man. So, making nary a sound, he snuck forward.

If someone were giving the Kings grief, Shakespeare would make damn sure the varmint lived to regret it. He'd die before he would let them come to harm.

It scared him to think about it. Which was strange, given that he had seen more than his share of massacres and rank butchery over the years. Why, once up in the Missouri River country, he had stumbled on a party of trappers, or what was left of them after the

23

Bloods got through. It had made him physically sick.

Then there was the time Shakespeare witnessed a clash between a band of about seventy Blackfeet and a village of Crows. He had been visiting the Crows when the alarm was given. Apparently, the Blackfeet had tried to make off with dozens of Crow horses and been caught in the act.

Outnumbered ten to one, the Blackfeet had retreated to the brow of a hill, fighting furiously the whole way. There, protected by a circle of boulders on three sides and a cliff to the west, they had dug in.

Again and again the Crows had tried to roust the Blackfeet from their refuge. Again and again the Crows were thrown back with great losses.

It had reached the point where the Crow leaders called a council. Many advocated giving up. That was when a black man, Edward Rose, who had lived among them for decades, stood and made an impassioned speech, saying that the Crows had small hearts, that if they abandoned the attack, other tribes would say Crow men were no more to be feared than old women. Rose fired the Crows to a fever pitch. And when he was done, those warriors streamed out of the village and up into the natural fort like a horde of rabid wolves.

The battle had been unforgettable. There was no describing the sheer ferocity, the brutal savagery.

Crammed into a space no bigger than an acre, the two sides had bashed, slashed, hacked, and rent one another with knives, tomahawks, eyedaggs, and war clubs until the grass ran scarlet and men slipped on slick puddles of warm blood.

From a vantage point on an adjoining hill, Shakespeare had observed the carnage in awed silence. At length the remaining Blackfeet had been forced to the crest of the low cliff. Some jumped. Some slid down.

At the bottom, twenty or so formed a compact square and tried to fight through to the north, but there were simply too many Crows. Side by side, the Blackfeet cut and smashed. Side by side, they died.

At length the last Blackfoot dropped. Shakespeare had thought that would be the end of it, but he was mistaken. For the Crows then proceeded to gather all the wounded Blackfeet and torment them.

Ears, noses, hands, and feet were all sliced off. Eyes were gouged out, tongues removed. But the worst had been when their bellies were slit wide and their intestines plucked out and strung on the ground like so many greasy, gory loops of rope.

To be fair to the Crows, they had suffered repeated degradations, losing many lives and horses to raiding Blackfeet. The two tribes were bitter, mortal enemies, and likely always would be.

Still, it had been a sobering lesson. From that day on, Shakespeare had always been ready and willing to take his own life rather than fall into the hands of hostile Indians. Better a quick, painless death than to suffer the unbearable torture of the damned.

A glimpse of buckskin dropped Shakespeare into a crouch. The scent of water was strong. Out on the lake, a fish splashed. Ducks quacked, geese honked.

Relying on all the stealth at his command, Shakespeare moved to a patch of high weeds rimming a bank that overlooked the shore. Parting the weeds with the barrel of his Hawken, he rose a trifle higher—and found himself staring into the muzzle of a cocked rifle.

"One of these days you're going to get yourself shot, acting the fool like you do," Nate King stated.

"You!" Shakespeare said, rendered numb by an equal mix of elation and embarrassment. Embarrassment prevailed. "What's gotten into you, you ornery young coon? Don't you know any better than to point guns at your best friends? And what in tarnation are you doing traipsing around half-naked? Where's your hunting shirt and your moccasins?"

"We were attacked last night."

Shakespeare promptly sobered and rose. "Anyone hurt?"

"No, thank God. We held them off until first light. I made a break for the trees, and when no one tried to part my hair with lead, I went looking for them. They're long gone, I'm afraid."

"Following their sign, are you?"

Nate indicated tracks close to the water's edge. "There were two of them. One wore boots, the other moccasins. Strangest footwear I ever did see."

"How so?"

"See for yourself."

The men who made the prints had been running. One wore peculiar high-heeled boots with spiked toes. The other wore moccasins with soles wider than any Shakespeare had ever seen. The stitching, too, clearly imprinted in a muddy spot, was new to him.

The toes of the boots were slanted outward; those of the moccasins were slanted inward.

"I'll be switched," Shakespeare said. "One of them was white, the other an Indian."

Nate rested the stock of his Hawken on the ground. "They left a couple of hours before dawn. By now they're miles from here."

"Are you cutting out after them?"

"What do you think?"

Shakespeare smirked. "Count me in, hoss. If you're going to get into a racket, I want to be there to cover your hind end."

Nate had no objection. He was glad his mentor had showed up. "Don't take this wrong, but what in the world are you doing back so soon, anyway? Next moon, you said before you left."

"I forgot my pipe."

"Oh. That's right," Nate said, leading the way to the west. "Evelyn came across it under the table. She took it outside and was digging in the dirt when Winona happened to notice."

"Wonderful."

"It's still in one piece. I cleaned it myself, and put it on the shelf above our bed."

A flurry of flapping wings announced the arrival of a flock of goldeneyes. A variety of ducks called the lake home, along with throngs of geese and a few gulls. High in the azure sky a majestic bald eagle soared, waiting for fish to rise near the surface. To the west, a red hawk circled over the pines.

"What I would like to know," Shakespeare said, "is who would be after your hide? Have you made some new enemies lately?"

The same question had been plaguing Nate. "Not that I'm aware of," he grimly responded. And to his knowledge, no one he had ever met wore shoes or moccasins like those of the mysterious pair who had invaded his mountain sanctuary. He couldn't wait to catch up to them.

"Fie! Fie!" Shakespeare quoted. "Unknit that threatening unkind brow. And dart not scornful glances from those eyes." He clapped the younger man on the back. "Brace up, son. Put a smile on your face."

"A smile?"

"For the sake of the womenfolk and the sprouts." Shakespeare started up the narrow trail that linked the lake to the homestead. "We'll get to the bottom of this, I swear. But it won't do to upset them any more than they already are."

Nate bowed to his mentor's wisdom and plastered a wan grin on his face. He pretended to be in jovial spirits as they strode within view of the cabin. It was well he did. Winona and the children were apprehensively awaiting his return. The children broke out in smiles and rushed down to greet their uncle.

"Carcajou! Carcajou!" Evelyn squealed. It was French for "wolverine," the name bestowed on McNair by fellow trappers more years ago than he cared to recollect.

"Little darling!" Shakespeare said, bracing himself. True to form, she threw herself into his arms like a pint-sized battering ram, nearly bowling him over. He hugged her, more glad than words could express that all of them were unhurt. He'd lost so many friends since the early days. So very, very many.

Winona walked to Nate and jabbed a thumb toward the corral. "Your stallion is saddled. I put pemmican and jerky in a parfleche."

Nate marveled at her uncanny knack for predicting what he would do. She seemed to know him better than he knew himself. "It shouldn't take long to overtake them if I leave right away," he said.

"Go, then. We will be fine."

Hastening indoors to don the rest of his clothes, Nate discovered Blue Water Woman preparing breakfast. Before he got a word out of his mouth, she asked, "Is my husband going with you?"

How did they *do* it? Nate wondered. "Yes," he said.

"Keep an eye on him. He is not as spry as he used to be. And I suspect his hearing is not what it once was, either. Two weeks ago he was out chopping wood and never heard a black bear walk up behind him."

Nate slid his hunting shirt over his head and smoothed it. His moccasins went on next. Ensuring both flintlocks were wedged securely under his belt, one on either side of the big buckle, he aligned a tomahawk on his right hip, a Green River knife in a

28

beaded sheath fashioned by Winona on his left hip. He angled the straps to his powder horn and ammo pouch across his chest so that they crisscrossed. That left his possibles bag, filled with his tinderbox and assorted other items no mountaineer could do without. Onto his head he jammed a beaver hat.

Zach had brought the black stallion around. "I want to go too, Pa," he declared as his father emerged. The prospect of adventure made him tingle with excitement.

"No."

Flooded by indignation at having his hopes dashed, Zach protested. "But, Pa—"

Nate swung onto the stallion. "What if they circle around and show up while we're gone? I want you here to help your ma, if need be."

Zach glanced at his mother for support. "You don't need me, do you, Ma? It's all right with you if I go, isn't it?"

"Do as your father tells you," Winona said. Among her people, it was unthinkable for a boy Zach's age to dispute his parents. Children did as they were told, when they were told. To disobey was to heap shame on one's shoulders.

Shakespeare looked around for his mare and suddenly remembered where it was. Slapping his forehead, he exclaimed, "I must be getting senile in my old age. I plumb forgot my horse."

Bending, Nate extended his arm. "Climb on behind me and we'll fetch it."

The women and children clustered and waved as the two mountain men trotted into the firs. Dappled by shadow, Nate threaded through the virgin woods, the stallion's hooves drumming dully on the thick carpet of pine needles. "Look in that parfleche by your right knee," he said. "Tell me what you make of it."

"Of what?" Shakespeare said, and drew out the

broken halves of an arrow. "Hmmmmm. What do we have here?"

"I dug it out of the cabin wall," Nate explained.

Just as no two tribes crafted their clothes or moccasins exactly alike, so, too, with their weapons. Some bows were made of wood, some from horns. One tribe was partial to ash arrows. Another favored arrows constructed of dogwood. Some tribes swore that bowstrings made from deer sinew were best; others would not use anything except buffalo tendon strings. And so on and so forth.

His far-flung travels had given Shakespeare more than a passing familiarity with the different tribes and their customs. At one time or another he had lived among the Flatheads, the Cheyenne, the Sioux, the Arapahos, the Crows, and others. If the truth were known, there wasn't a mountain man alive—not even Jim Bridger or Joe Walker—who knew more about Indians and their ways than he did.

So it came as quite a shock for Shakespeare to realize that he had never set eyes on a shaft quite like the broken one he held in his left hand. It appeared to be made of *mulberry,* but that was impossible. The only Indians who made bows and arrows from mulberry trees were those who dwelled in the arid regions west of the recently formed Republic of Texas. Pimas, Maricopas, Apaches, and the like.

Shakespeare recalled the strange moccasin tracks beside the lake, and gave a start. Now that he thought about it, the style had indeed been similar to those worn by tribes who lived in the arid wasteland far, far to the southwest. But how could that be? What would a desert country warrior be doing in the central Rockies? Not even the notorious Blackfeet roamed that far.

"Well?" Nate prompted. The arrow, the footprints, the attack itself, had him perplexed.

"There are more things in heaven and earth, Horatio, than are dreamt of in your philosophy."

"In other words, you have no idea which tribe it belongs to," Nate deduced.

"Did I say that?" Shakespeare countered, miffed. "Your bait of falsehood takes this carp of truth. And thus do we of wisdom and of reach, with windlasses and with assays of bias, by indiscretions find directions out. So, by my former lecture and advice, shall you, my son."

Nate failed to see what that had to do with anything. But then, half the time he never understood what the Bard meant. Secretly, he suspected that McNair didn't, either, but he would never say as much to his wrinkled face.

Among the closely knit brotherhood of trappers, McNair's passion for the Bard was legendary, as was his flair for quoting accurately from any of Shakespeare's plays and sonnets at the drop of a hat. Everyone knew that McNair never went anywhere without his rare volume of the complete works of the playwright, bundled in hides for protection from the elements.

Exactly why Shakespeare was so fond of the Englishman, no one had ever found out. Nate asked once. Shakespeare had looked up from a play he was reading, chuckled, and said, "Why? You might as well ask why the sun rises every morning, why the moon shines at night. Why do ocean tides go in and out? Why do buffalo migrate? Why are there so many stars? So few men of peace and goodwill? Why do birds have feathers, and we don't? Why do fish swim in water instead of walking on land? Why are we here? Why? Why? Why?"

Nate never asked again.

Ahead, a horse nickered. Nate reined to the left, saying over his shoulder, "Have you heard of anyone else being attacked? Old Hugh stopped by about six weeks ago and said things were quiet up in his neck of the woods. Too quiet.''

''Old Hugh's problem is that he thinks he's still thirty instead of seventy-four. Why, last spring that scrawny yak went into a bear den after a silver-tip that treated itself to some of his chickens. He fired at it and missed.''

''What happened?''

''What else? The grizzly ripped him to shreds. Shakespeare cackled at his joke, slapping his leg.

Another whinny by the mare guided Nate around a stand of saplings. The horse had its back to him and was prancing as if agitated. ''What's wrong with that contrary critter of yours?'' he said.

Both of them saw it at the same instant. Crouched ten yards from the mare was a huge tawny cat, its long tail flicking, its ears pinned back, tapered teeth exposed.

''A painter!'' Shakespeare bawled.

At the outcry, the mountain lion launched itself at the mare.

Chapter Three

Shakespeare McNair was especially fond of that mare. He had been riding her for a good many years. And while she was a feisty cuss given to nipping when his back was turned, she could outrun anything on four legs. To lose her would be a calamity. But he had one hand on Nate's shoulder and the other was between them, holding his rifle. He could not possibly get off a shot in time. "Nate!" he yelled.

The younger trapper was already in motion. There was no time to lift the Hawken resting across the pommel of his saddle, so Nate grabbed for one of his pistols. His right arm a blur, he jerked the flintlock out.

The cougar was already in midair. Nate fired from the hip, knowing he missed the second he squeezed the trigger. At the crash of the smoothbore, the black stallion shied.

The outcome seemed inevitable. But the white mare had resources of her own, namely a fighting spirit and sharp hooves. She bounded to the left as far as the reins would allow, and the cat alighted in the spot where she had been standing. Whinnying, she kicked, her forelegs lashing out with the force of heavy hammers, her hooves catching the mountain lion on the ribs and tumbling it into the brush.

Hissing and spitting, the frustrated painter heaved onto all fours and crouched to spring again. A glance at the onrushing stallion changed its mind. Venting a baffled snarl, it wheeled and fled, a tawny molten bolt of lightning that was gone before either trapper could resort to a rifle.

"Damn!" Shakespeare fumed, dropping off the stallion's hindquarters and running to his mount. "Mary, gal! Are you all right?" Snatching the reins, he stroked the quaking mare, soothing her. There were no claw marks that he could see, and he heaved a sigh of relief. "For a bit there, Mary, I was afeared you were a goner."

Nate rose in the saddle, scouring the terrain. The cougar seemed to be gone, but it was not wise to take anything for granted. Reloading the pistol, he arched an eyebrow at his mentor. "All these years, and I never knew you had a handle for that horse."

Shakespeare nodded, patting the mare's neck. "Mary," he said softly. "Named her after my sister."

"You never mentioned having one," Nate said. Truth to tell, McNair never talked about his past. Nate knew virtually nothing about his friend's personal history, but he would not think of prying. It was an unwritten rule that mountaineers mind their own business. Sticking one's nose into another's affairs was not only frowned on, it could result in an exchange of lead.

"She was the sweetest little gal ever born," Shakespeare recalled fondly. "Had her a doll she toted everywhere. We used to play in this big old maple tree out back of our house.'' His eyes misted. ''Those were fine days, Nate. Childhood is the best time of our lives, and we're too blamed young to realize it.''

Since McNair had broached the subject, Nate felt safe in asking, ''Is Mary still alive?''

Shakespeare blinked, and a tear stained his left cheek. ''I have no idea. Last I saw her was nigh on forty years ago. She'd married a weasel, a shiftless bastard who never did an honest day's work in his life. Swilled liquor like he was sucking his ma's teat.''

''Sorry to hear it,'' Nate said sincerely.

''That's not the worst. When he was in his cups, the scum would beat on her. On Mary! On a gentle soul who never hurt anybody!'' Shakespeare paused. ''Last I knew, they were living in New York City. I went back for a surprise visit. Walked in, and there was my sister, lying on the sofa, her face swelled up like a buffalo bladder, all black and blue and bleeding at the mouth.'' The white-maned mountain man fell silent.

''What did you do?'' Nate asked quietly.

''Went berserk. Sis told me he was at a local watering place, so I stomped on down, barged into the dive, and lit into him like the wrath of the Almighty. Beat him senseless, I did. His nose was bleeding, his mouth was bleeding, his left wrist was busted.'' Shakespeare shuddered. ''I damn near killed him. Had my hands around his throat and was choking the life out of the son of a bitch when Mary showed up. She pulled me off, begged me to let the buzzard live. Like a fool, I did.''

''He give you trouble later?''

''Did he!'' Shakespeare snorted. ''He was too much of a coward to trade blows, so he got back at me a better way. Through her.''

''He beat her again?''

35

"No. I cured him of that bad habit." Sorrowfully, Shakespeare climbed onto the mare and gazed into the distance. "She wrote me a letter. Sent it to Jacob Hawken, since she knew he was a friend of mine and I stopped by his shop once a year to stock up on powder and ammunition."

The memory was so bitter that Shakespeare had to cough to clear his throat. "She told me that she thought it best if I didn't go see them ever again. It would upset the polecat, and she didn't want to do anything to spoil things now that they were getting along fairly well."

"Did you do as she wanted?"

Shakespeare turned a pained expression on his protégé. "Wouldn't you have? She was my sister. I loved her with all my heart."

Nate said nothing. He could imagine how awful it must have been.

Shakespeare coughed again to dislodge the lump. Pressing a sleeve to his eyes, he commented, "Look at me! You'd think I just peeled a bucket of onions." Tossing his head, he clucked to the white mare and headed for the lake, saying, "As old William S. once phrased it, each of us must let our own discretion be our tutor. More's the pity, that."

For once Nate understood. He followed the mare to the shore, where the hunt began in earnest. Assuming the lead, he paralleled the footprints, which bore around the lake to trees fringing the east shore. Warily, he rode into the growth, and no sooner did so than he came on a small clearing. The odor of horse manure brought him to a halt.

Shakespeare dismounted to study two sets of hoofprints. "Here's where they tied their critters," he said, memorizing the tracks.

Nate thought of the beeline the pair had made along

the north shore directly to his cabin. "You know what this means, don't you?"

"Sure do. They knew right where to find your place." Rising, Shakespeare adjusted the foxskin hat Blue Water Woman had given to him on his last birthday. "Yet how could that be? I'd wager my poke that the varmints are new to these parts."

"We'll ask them when we catch them," Nate said, and forged into the undergrowth along a winding game trail the pair had taken.

"They sure lit out in a hurry," Shakespeare remarked, based on the loping gait indicated by the tracks. "Maybe they were afraid you were after them."

Nate doubted it. The two men had left long before daylight, when he was still in the cabin. Whatever motive they had for racing off was a mystery.

The game trail climbed to a broad opening between two sawtooth mountain ridges, an opening Nate had passed through countless times since it was the only way in and out of the valley on the east side. Below, rolling emerald foothills unfolded. Beyond the hills, for as far as the eye could see, rippled a sea of shimmering grass.

"Lookee there," Shakespeare said.

Nate had seen them. Strung out across the vast prairie was a long column of riders and pack animals. From that altitude they looked like ants.

Shakespeare clucked in disapproval. Only greenhorns would allow themselves to become that strung out in hostile country. A war party would make short shrift of them if they were caught in the open. "Shall we go see who they are?"

"We'd better," Nate said, kneeing the stallion. Whoever they were, he did not want them trespassing in his valley, and their line of march hinted they might just do that.

"Maybe they're pilgrims bound for the Oregon Country," Shakespeare suggested, although it was unlikely. Settlers always traveled in wagons. His second guess was that it might be an army patrol. But there had to be sixty riders, at least, and patrols rarely included more than forty soldiers.

Avoiding open areas, the mountain men wound steadily lower until they came to the crest of the last foothill. By then the sun was directly overhead. Hidden among pines, they spied on the newcomers, who were half a mile out.

"A mountanee man is leading them," Shakespeare said.

Nate leaned forward, squinting. For the life of him, he could not distinguish the features of the foremost figure. His mentor's hearing might not be as keen as it once was, but there was no denying McNair had the eyes of a hawk.

"Do you recognize him?" Shakespeare asked.

"Has the sun fried your brain? At this distance all I can make out are his buckskins and his beaver hat."

"What about the others?"

"I can't tell much," Nate said.

The column advanced until it was a quarter of a mile from the foothills. At that point the lead rider hoisted a rifle and barked a command. Noon camp was pitched. A fire was made. The pack animals were tethered but not stripped. Mounts were picketed. Amid the hustle and bustle sashayed three slender figures whose bearing and attire set them apart from the rest.

"Women," Nate said.

Shakespeare was more interested in the garb worn by the men. Most sported unusual pants that flared at the bottom. Wide-brimmed hats with high crowns were common, as were colorful sashes and capes. "I'll be dogged. Remember Santa Fe?"

Nate glanced around. How could he forget? A few years ago, he had let Shakespeare talk him into taking their families on a trek to Santa Fe. The excursion was supposed to be a grand holiday, a long-overdue break after several seasons of steady trapping. Instead, it had turned into an ordeal Nate would rather forget when Winona was taken captive by Apaches. "What about it?"

Shakespeare nodded at the camp. "I think they're Mexicans."

Nate scrutinized the party more closely. Yes, it appeared so. But what was a small army of Mexicans doing so far north of New Mexico, the nearest Mexican province?

"Let's ride on down and introduce ourselves," Shakespeare proposed, and clucked to Mary.

"Is that smart?" Nate said.

"Probably not. But if we only did things when we were sure of being right, nothing would ever get done."

McNair stuck to cover until they came to the tree line. Most of the Mexicans were resting. Sentries had been posted around the perimeter, and he figured one was bound to spot his white mare the moment he rode into the open. To his surprise, no shouts rang out. Holding the mare to a walk, keeping his hands where they could be seen, he smiled broadly to demonstrate his peaceable intentions.

Nate fingered his Hawken. "Why haven't they noticed us yet?"

"Either they're as blind as bats, or city-bred," Shakespeare said. It had been his experience that city dwellers were generally deaf and dumb. Oh, there were exceptions. But plop most of them in the wilderness and they were as helpless as newborn babes; they couldn't find water, they were pitiful hunters, and nary a one could track a bull buffalo through mud.

The cities were to blame, not the people, Shakespeare believed. City life was simply too easy. When people were hungry, all they had to do was walk across the street to a restaurant. When they required new clothes, there was the tailor. New boots? Off to the shoemaker.

Every need was met. They never had to fend for themselves, never had to shoot game for the supper pot or skin an animal for its hide so they would have something to wear, or learn how to find water so they wouldn't die of thirst.

It made them soft and flabby. It dulled their senses. Their eyes dimmed. Their sense of smell grew feeble. They clumped noisily about, oblivious to the world around them, ignorant of their fall from natural grace but as happy as clams.

Even worse, city life made people dependent on others, particularly on government. When that happened, they stood in dire risk of losing the cherished freedom their forefathers had sacrificed so much to preserve.

Shakespeare had had a bellyful of politicians well before he ever ventured west of the Mississippi. The groveling for votes, the lies and broken promises, the nepotism, had sickened him. He didn't want anyone telling him how he should live, and he could never comprehend how others were willing to abide it.

A hail brought an end to Shakespeare's reverie. He made a mental note to quit letting his thoughts wander as sentries converged and rifles were trained on him and Nate.

Butterflies fluttered in Nate's stomach. He hoped McNair knew what he was doing. None of the sentries acted friendly. Distrustful eyes marked their progress, fingers lightly touching triggers. If one of them should sneeze, all hell would break loose.

Unfazed, Shakespeare elevated his arms and showed all his front teeth. *"Buenos tardes, caballeros!"* he called out.

Other members of the party were drawn by the commotion, among them the three women.

A tall man in a black sombrero and a wide red sash pushed through the crowd to stand next to the sentry who had given the alarm. Inner flames burned in the depths of his brooding eyes. A thin mustache topped thin, almost cruel, lips. His left cheek bore a jagged scar. Snapping an arm at the frontiersmen, he barked in clipped English, "Halt where you are, *gringos,* or we will shoot!"

Shakespeare reined up. "Not very hospitable of you, friend," he said dryly. "Didn't your ma ever teach you any manners?"

The tall man's swarthy complexion grew darker. "State your business here, *senor. Pronto.*"

"Ignacio! That will be quite enough!"

A shorter man had appeared. Gray hair crowned a ruggedly handsome face lined by many years. His cape, jacket, and pants were immaculate, his boots polished to a shine, his white shirt unstained. Shoulders squared, he planted himself beside the man in the red sash. "What are you thinking, that you treat these men so? Remember where we are, and why we are here." Facing the trappers, he smiled and gave a gracious bow. "Greetings, gentlemen. Please forgive my son. He worries that we will come to harm, so he is a trifle overprotective."

"No harm done," Shakespeare said amiably. "I had me a pet bear cub like him once. It'd bite the hand that fed it."

The elderly man chuckled. "Permit me to make introductions. I am Don Manuel de Varga, at your

41

service." He pointed at Ignacio. "You have met my eldest son. Behind him is my middle son, Martin."

The man in question was short like his father, and stocky. He had a plain face, lacking mustache or beard. *"Senors,"* he said politely.

Don Varga beckoned. A youngster barely older than Zach sheepishly stepped from the group. "This is my pride and joy, Diego. He is not yet old enough to earn my consent to shave, but he is competent in many respects."

Nate happened to see the oldest brother, Ignacio, scowl, then quickly adopt a stony expression. What was that all about? he wondered.

"I am the head of this expedition," Don Varga continued. "We have been traveling for many weeks, and in all this time we have met few strangers. Your company is most welcome. Perhaps you would be so kind as to join us for coffee and cakes?"

"Don't mind if I do, sir," Shakespeare declared, sliding off. "Thank the heaven, Lord, thou art of sweet composure. Praise him that got thee, she that gave thee suck. Famed be thy tutor, and thy parts of nature thrice-famed beyond, beyond all erudition."

Blinking, Don Varga put a hand on McNair's wrist. "My English is not all it should be, *senor,* so perhaps I am in error. But is that not a quote from William Shakespeare?"

"Most assuredly," Shakespeare said, tickled that their host was versed in literature. "Not many would have guessed."

"I have been to London many times and attended some of his plays," Don Varga said.

"From Mexico to England. That's quite a sea voyage to make once, let alone many times," Shakespeare commented.

Don Varga was turning, and paused. "But you are mistaken, *senor*. My family is from Spain, not Mexico, although we hold extensive estates there.''

Shakespeare was intrigued. Spaniards had generally been unwelcome in Mexico since that country won its freedom from Spain twenty years ago. ''It doesn't make a bit of difference to me where you folks are from. Give us your paw,'' he said, holding out his hand. He introduced himself, then Nate.

At that juncture a lanky man in buckskins and a beaver hat walked up. ''Thought I heard you bellowin', McNair,'' he said coldly. ''It's been a while, hoss. I figured you'd been turned into worm food ages ago.''

''As I live and breathe, Jasper Flynt!'' Shakespeare said. ''You mean to tell me no one's hung you yet? As I recollect, the last time we met was in New Orleans, when you were about two hops and a skip ahead of the law.''

Don Manuel de Varga glanced from one to the other. ''What is this?'' he said uneasily. ''I was told that *Senor* Flynt is a reliable, trustworthy fellow.''

Shakespeare laughed. ''Who told you? Pards of his?''

Flynt bristled, taking a swift step and starting to level his Kentucky rifle. He froze when the muzzle of a Hawken blossomed in front of his nose.

''Don't do anything you'll regret,'' Nate King warned.

Flustered, Flynt snarled, ''Where do you get off buttin' into our spat, mister? It ain't healthy to get in a racket with me.'' Resentment spiked from his gray eyes. ''I didn't catch your name.''

Nate told him.

''King?'' Flynt repeated. ''Yeah, I've heard of you. Grizzly Killer, the Injuns call you. Word is that this old fart is your nursemaid—''

Once, Nate would have meekly stood for the insult. That was over a decade ago, back when he worked as an accountant for a crusty skinflint in New York City. Each and every day, the skinflint, his coworkers, and others had heaped verbal abuse on him, and each and every day he had taken it without batting an eye. At the time, he had flattered himself that he was turning the other cheek, that he was being noble.

It was amazing how a man's perspective changed.

In the wilderness, anyone who let another ride roughshod over him was asking for more of the same. Turn the other cheek to a Blackfoot on the warpath, and the Blackfoot would split it wide open with a knife or tomahawk. Try to act noble around cutthroats who would as soon stab someone they disliked as look at them, and those cutthroats would delight in making your life a living hell.

Putting on airs was a luxury only civilized sheep could afford.

So on being insulted by Jasper Flynt, Nate reacted without thinking. He swept the stock of his Hawken up and around and smashed it into Flynt's jaw.

The surly frontiersman dropped like a poled ox. Immediately, other expedition members flourished guns, pointed at Nate's head and chest.

"How dare you, *Americano*!" Ignacio stormed, his hand dropping to a pistol wedged under his bright red sash. "We invite you into our camp and you mistreat our guide."

Nate met the eldest son's withering gaze without flinching. For strained seconds no one else spoke or moved. Then Ignacio gripped his pistol more firmly and tensed his arm to draw it.

"*Con eso basta!*" Don Varga shouted, striding between them and gripping his son's arm. He launched into a string of Spanish incomprehensible to Nate, but the gist was self-evident. He was giving his son a tongue-lashing.

Vile spite was mirrored in Ignacio's eyes, yet he

bowed and addressed his father in a contrite tone.

Don Manuel de Varga faced the hulking young trapper. "My son apologizes for his outburst, *senor*. It has been a hard journey and our tempers are short. Please forgive him."

Nate was not disposed to do any such thing, but a nod by Shakespeare compelled him to say, "No hard feelings, then. Just keep a muzzle on your guide. I won't abide being treated with disrespect."

"We are a lot alike, I think," Don Varga said. He only had to snap his fingers for three men in broad-brimmed hats to collect the unconscious Flynt and haul him off. "Come, now," Varga said, smiling. "Let us start over. Be seated and we will talk."

"Our pleasure," Nate said, falling into step beside the Spaniard. He adopted a casual air, but as he crossed to the fire, he could feel Ignacio's eyes bore into his back.

Chapter Four

Nate King caught sight of other women as he fell into step beside the Spaniard. One was brewing coffee. Another was setting small round cakes on an ornate tray. A third was seated on a crate, stitching a shirt. A fourth was rummaging in a pack. All four wore simple homespun dresses and little jewelry.

In dazzling contrast, the three women Nate had noticed earlier were adorned in garments fit for queens. Colorful silken bodices flared into ankle-length, billowy skirts that swayed with every motion. Their earrings, necklaces, and bracelets were either gold or silver. Lace *mantillas* framed their slender shoulders. Two wore their rich, dark hair up in buns. The third, who was stunningly beautiful, had hair that fell clear to her waist.

Don Manuel de Varga stopped beside them. "These three lovely *senoritas* are my daughters," he revealed proudly, taking the hand of the beauty. "This is Maria, the oldest."

Maria coyly curtsied. "My pleasure, gentlemen," she said in sweetly accented English. "We did not think to come across other civilized souls in the middle of this vast wasteland."

"Wasteland?" Shakespeare repeated, and snorted. "Whatever gave you that notion, missy? All sorts of critters call the prairie home. There's more buffalo than you could count in a month of Sundays. Deer, elk, antelope, too. You name it, there's plenty. Not to mention all the Indian tribes that have staked out territories."

Maria stared out over the ocean of grass. "True, *senor*. But do not your own people call this the Great American Desert?"

Now it was Nate's turn to snort. "Only those who don't know any better, ma'am," he said. Some years ago the government had sent Major Stephen H. Long to explore the country west of the Mississippi. His official report had tarnished the plains as totally unfit for human habitation, and on the map he drew up and presented to Congress, he'd referred to the prairie as the "Great American Desert." The name had stuck.

Don Varga clasped the hands of his other daughters in turn. "This is Francisca," he said of one who wore a pretty red ribbon in her hair. "And my littlest is Luisa."

To call the youngest "little" did not do her ample bosom justice. Luisa curtsied, timidly studying the mountain men from under her hooded lids.

"Now be seated, if you please," Don Varga said. "I apologize for not offering more comfortable accommodations, but circumstances being what they are, I'm sure you will forgive us."

Crates had been arranged in a circle around the fire. Shakespeare sank onto one with a sigh. "Nothing to forgive, old hoss," he said, tapping the crate. "This is as good as a throne in these parts."

The Vargas took seats, the daughters primly smoothing their dresses. It was obvious the family bubbled with curiosity about the trappers. Except for Ignacio, who wore a perpetual frown.

Don Varga clapped his hands, and coffee was brought. The plump woman who carried the tray stood to one side and held out the tray for him to take his pick.

"I'm a mite surprised to see you've brought so many females along," Shakespeare mentioned. Given the many perils to be encountered in the wilderness, the Spaniards were flirting with calamity.

"Her?" Don Varga said, bobbing his chin at the plump woman. "Rosa is just a servant. I brought four up from our *hacienda* in Sonora. They do the best they can to meet our needs, but I should have brought along four more."

The comment, uttered so offhandedly, told Shakespeare a lot about their host. He smiled at Rosa, who shyly averted her face. "You folks sure are a long way from home," he said.

"That we are," Don Varga conceded, gazing thoughtfully at the towering ramparts to the west. Caps of snow shone on some. "And we have a lot farther to go before we reach our destination."

Frontier etiquette prevented Shakespeare from coming right out and asking where that might be. So he tried a roundabout tack. "Heading for Canada, are you?" he asked.

Don Varga pointed at a particular peak, the highest of them all, so starkly imposing, it dominated the entire range. "Do you know that mountain, *senors*?"

It was Nate who answered. "That's Long's Peak, named after an army officer who mistook it for Pike's Peak. No one has ever been to the top. They say it must be over fourteen thousand feet high." He did not add that the secluded valley in which his cabin lay was a short distance north of it.

"Montana grande," Don Varga breathed in awe. "Nearly three miles high, you say? These Rocky Mountains of yours are much more formidable than I was led to believe. They rival the Pyrenees, in my native land. Why, *Pico de Aneto*, the highest, would be lost among them."

"You're headed up there?" Nate said.

"Sí," Don Varga admitted. "Why? What is wrong? Your tone implies we should not."

Nate accepted a sterling silver cup from Rosa. "Thank you." Then, to the patriarch, he said, "What you do is your affair. You're the booshway of this expedition. But if you go dragging a bunch of women and greenhorns up into Ute country, you'll be lucky to make it back down alive."

The Vargas looked at one another. Ignacio reddened and declared, "Do you think we are cowards, *gringo*? Do you think we are unable to protect ourselves and the ladies?"

"It doesn't matter what I think," Nate said. "It's what the *Utes* will think that counts. And I can tell you right here and now that they won't take kindly to having their territory invaded by a small army."

"So?" Ignacio sneered. "We have fifty-five men under us, *vaqueros* and others from our Mexican *hacienda,* men who can shoot the eye out of a doe at a hundred paces. Each man has two rifles and two pistols. Let the savages come! We will send them running with their tails tucked between their legs."

Nate disliked the hothead more and more as time went on. "Fifty-five, huh?" he said. "Well, that's fine and dandy. But the Ute nation boasts over two *thousand* warriors. If all of them were to rise up against you, you wouldn't stand a prayer."

"Two thousand?" Don Varga said, troubled by the news. "Our guide did not tell us that."

Shakespeare had taken a sip of the coffee. It was thicker than he was accustomed to, but delightfully sweet. Sugar was a rare treat in the wild, and he smacked his lips in appreciation before saying, "That's just for starters, Don. To the north of here live the Sioux, who will steal every horse and mule you've got if they catch wind of them. And then there are the Blackfeet. Granted, they don't get down this way much, but if a war party stumbles across your trail, you'll lose a damn sight more than stock."

Rosa was about to hand a cup to Ignacio. He rudely pushed her away and jabbed a finger at McNair. "You seek to scare us with your tales, *Americano*. But we are not afraid. We have more than enough guns to hold off any heathens who dare risk our wrath."

Shakespeare could not resist. "Tell me. Do you spend a lot of time admiring yourself in the mirror?"

Ignacio snapped erect. "I take that as an insult."

"Sit down!" Don Varga ordered with an imperious gesture. After his son obeyed, he turned to Nate. "If these Utes are so dangerous, *senor,* how is it that they have not slain you? You and your family have lived on Ute land for quite some time, yet here you sit, unharmed."

About to raise the cup to his mouth, Nate glanced up sharply. "How do you know where I live?"

"Our guide, Jasper Flynt, told us," Don Varga said. "In fact, it is most fortunate that you came by when you did. We planned to pay you a visit tomorrow." He absently stretched his legs. "I hope you would not mind."

Nate's body grew as rigid as steel. The Spaniard's boots had uncommonly high heels and spiked toes, just like the pair of boots that made those tracks up by the lake. He swiveled. Practically all the men wore the same style. It could have been any one of them. Calming himself, Nate asked, "Why did you want to see me?"

Don Varga hesitated. "Now is hardly the right time. Perhaps you would do me the honor of accepting a formal invitation to be our guests this evening? Bring your family for supper. You, too, Mr. McNair."

"Don't mind if I do," Shakespeare said. "My missus loves to meet new folks."

Nate would rather have declined. Now that he knew one of their number had tried to kill him, he wanted nothing to do with the Vargas. But it would not do to have McNair enter the lion's den alone. "I'll be here," he promised.

"Excellent."

Their host and his offspring swapped smiles, with the notable exception of Ignacio, who opened his mouth to say something when a whipcord figure stalked in among them.

There was no warning, no outcry, no threats or lusty oaths. Nate glimpsed the figure out of the corner of his left eye and started to turn. A ringing blow landed on his jaw, knocking him to the ground. The cup tumbled as he tucked and rolled into a crouch, his right hand falling to the polished butt of a flintlock.

Jasper Flynt glowered down. His jaw was swollen and discolored, but he could still speak. "I'm going to gut you, bastard, for what you did to me." His Green River knife flashed from its sheath. "On your feet."

Don Varga leaped from his crate. Livid with outrage, he said, "How dare you, *Senor* Flynt! These men are my guests and will be treated accordingly."

Without looking around, Flynt rasped, "This is between King and me, mister. None of you butt in, or else.'' Wagging the blade, he circled like a cat about to pounce.

"Put down that weapon this instant!" Don Varga demanded.

"Go to hell, old man."

Indignation swept the Vargas. Francisca and Luisa gasped. Maria clenched her fists. Ignacio and Diego took steps toward the frontiersman, Ignacio placing a hand on the hilt of a dagger that jutted from under his sash. "No one speaks to my father like that, you cur! Turn and face me!"

Don Varga grabbed his son's arm and spoke in Spanish. Ignacio halted, but he shook with fury.

Shakespeare was the only person present who sat sipping his coffee, unflustered. To Flynt, he said, "Better lower your horns, Jasper. Better men than you have tried to carve him up."

"You can go to hell, too," Flynt said, not taking his feral eyes off the object of his hatred. "Maybe when I'm done with him, I'll cut off one of your ears for a keepsake."

"I tried," Shakespeare said with a shrug. To no one in particular, he remarked, "Some fools are so soured on life, they never get the acid out of their systems."

Don Varga was incredulous. "Are you just going to sit there and do nothing? Do you not care for your *amigo*?"

"In our neck of the woods, sir, a man has to stand on his own two feet or he's not rated much of a man."

While all this was going on, Nate had slowly risen. Bent at the waist, he held his knife low, close to his right thigh. Flynt suddenly thrust at his chest and Nate skipped backward. Countering, Nate nicked Flynt's sleeve.

The Vargas backed off to give them more room. *Vaqueros* and others were rushing from all directions to witness the clash. Even the sentries. Only Shakespeare McNair stayed where he was, contentedly sipping his coffee.

Jasper Flynt feinted, rotated, and slashed at Nate's leg. Nate parried, their blades ringing. Hooking a foot behind Flynt's ankle, Nate slammed his shoulder into his foe's. Down Flynt tumbled, but he regained his footing with pantherish swiftness.

Nate had met some hotheads in his time, but Flynt had them beat all hollow. The man had the disposition of a grizzly. He was one of those who seemed to think they had the God-given right to abuse others as they saw fit. No amount of talk or reasoning ever appealed to their better natures, because they had none. They were as dead inside as tombs, save for bitterness and spite that ate at them like a million gnawing termites.

A swipe of Flynt's glittering blade reminded Nate not to let his mind drift. Blocking, he pivoted on the balls of his feet and speared his knife at Flynt's neck. By a hair, Flynt evaded the blow.

Nate retreated, pretended to go left but went right. His hand flicked, drawing blood.

Jasper Flynt cursed, scarlet drops falling from the gash in his right wrist. "Damn it!" he said. "I'm through going easy on you!" Bellowing, he unleashed a flurry of cuts and swipes that drove Nate backward.

There was no denying Flynt was a skilled knife fighter. Nate was hard-pressed to stay out of his reach. The clang of their blades was like the ring of hail on tin. They stabbed, parried, hacked, and countered.

Nate held his own while slowly backing up. He aimed to make Flynt tire himself out, then finish it quickly. But he made a mistake that became apparent when Maria Varga cried out.

"Behind you, *senor*! The fire!"

At the same instant Nate felt searing heat on the backs of his legs. He tried to leap to the left, but Flynt anticipated the move. A foot caught him in the stomach, toppling him. Flames licked his back and shoulders as he crashed down on top of the burning logs.

One of the women screamed.

Shakespeare McNair's knuckles grew white where they gripped the cup. He was mightily tempted to step in, but by an iron effort of will he did not. Meddling was forbidden. Yet it tore at his innards to see the man he loved like a son suffer. He would rather chop off a hand or foot than have harm come to Nate King.

Jasper Flynt sensed victory. Agleam with triumph, he hiked his blade overhead, then brought it sweeping down.

Nate flipped to the right, gritting against the pain in his back and shoulders. He smelled burnt buckskin as he heaved up off the grass. Ducking under a swing that would have opened his neck to the bone, he lanced his long blade at Flynt's ribs.

Flynt twisted, but he was a shade slow. Breath hissed from between his teeth as the knife bit into his flesh. Clutching the wound, he propelled himself backward, into the ring of *vaqueros*. A burly man in a high-crowned brown hat gave him a shove. Flynt stumbled forward, tripping over his own two feet. Frantically, he sliced at Nate King to ward him off.

Nate met the blade with his own. Simultaneously, he levered his left fist up and in, throwing his entire weight into a punch that lifted Jasper Flynt off the ground and dumped him like a broken doll in a disjointed heap.

Flynt tried to rise. Eyelids fluttering, he gained his elbows but could go no higher. Drooling blood, he collapsed.

"Finish him, *senor*!" a man shouted.

Nate stood over the prostrate form, chest heaving, his knife poised. All it would take was a single stroke and the deed would be done.

"No," Shakespeare said simply.

Every sinew taut, Nate looked at his mentor. "He would do the same to me."

"More of him anon," Shakespeare quoted. "There is written in your brow, provost, honesty and constancy. If I read it not truly, my ancient skill beguiles me. But, the boldness of my cunning, I will lay myself in hazard." He paused. "To put it more plainly, you are not him."

"If I let Flynt live, what's to stop him from hunting me down later to get revenge?"

"Not a thing," Shakespeare admitted. " 'Tis called the evil." Taking a long sip, he smacked his lips. "But kill him now, son, in cold blood, and you won't be able to live with yourself the rest of your days. Like MacBeth, you'll be a haunted man, soiled by your own baser urges." McNair locked eyes with the younger man. "You're nobler than that, good Horatio."

Against his better judgment, Nate lowered his arms and sheathed his blade. "Sometimes you see more in me than I see myself."

"Well, I am not of that feather to shake off any friend when he must need me," Shakespeare said.

"You win." Leaning over, Nate plucked Flynt's knife from the man's limp fingers.

Ignacio Varga stepped forward. "That is all you are going to do, *Americano*? What manner of man are you that you allow his insult to pass unpunished? No Castilian worthy of the name ever would."

"Be quiet, son," Don Varga said quietly. "There are times when it takes more courage not to kill than to kill."

"My pardon, Father, but you speak in riddles," Ignacio said in disgust.

Nate sat on a crate and gratefully accepted another cup of coffee from Rosa, returning her friendly smile of encouragement. Some of Varga's many followers were whispering and pointing at him, their disappointment as keen as Ignacio's.

Don Varga barked words in Spanish. The burly man who had shoved Flynt came forward bearing a water skin, which he opened and tilted over Flynt. The man laughed when the frontiersman gurgled and sputtered and then sat up, panting.

"You have overstepped your bounds, *senor*," Don Varga said sternly. "I demand an immediate apology."

Gingerly touching his jaw, Flynt worked it from side to side.

"Did you hear me?"

Flynt nodded curtly. "My ears work just fine," he muttered. "Quit flappin' your gums, old man. I've had it with your uppity airs."

Don Varga's anger increased, his spine as straight as a broom handle. "What are you saying?"

"I quit this outfit," Flynt stated, standing and glaring at Nate. "I'm packin' my things and headin' back to St. Louis. From here on out, you're on your own."

Don Varga flung a hand out. "But you know we cannot find it without your help." He put a hand on the frontiersman's shoulder. "Remember, you gave your word to see this through. I even gave you some of the money in advance."

"Which I left for safekeepin' back in St. Louis," Flynt said smugly. Brusquely brushing Varga's hand off, he pointed at the Rockies. "The way I see it, I've brought you almost the whole way. So I've more than earned what you gave me."

"*Senor* McNair was right. You are a scoundrel."

A crafty gleam came into Flynt's eyes. "Don't be so quick to judge, mister. I might be persuaded to change my mind."

"For what? More money?"

Flynt hooked his thumbs under his belt. "No. The money ain't all that important." Lips quirking upward, he regarded Nate as a serpent might a mouse. "I want to stake this bastard out, skin him alive, and leave him for the coyotes and buzzards to finish off. If his partner McNair raises a fuss, we'll do the same to him."

Don Varga was genuinely shocked. "I would never stand for such an atrocity! You are insane."

"Not at all," Flynt said. "It's how we do things in these parts, Spaniard. But I guess you'll find that out the hard way." So saying, he ambled toward the horses.

Shakespeare finished the last of his coffee, his brow puckered. Jasper Flynt was as prickly as a cactus, but Flynt hadn't lived as long as he had by being stupid. And striking off by his lonesome to the Mississippi was just that. Something was not quite right here, but he could not figure out what.

Nate was glad to see the hothead leave. He felt no qualms, since Flynt had brought it on himself. As he raised the silver cup, Maria Varga materialized at his elbow.

"*Magnifico, senor.*"

"Ma'am?"

"Your fight with *Senor* Flynt. You are extremely adept with a blade."

"Seen a lot of knife fights, have you?" Nate asked, amused.

"*Sí, senor.* Castilian men are very hot-blooded. It does not take much to provoke them." Her gaze darted to her older brother. "Ignacio is widely regarded as one of the best in all of Spain. Knife, dagger, sword, rapier, he is a master of each."

"I'll be sure to remember that."

Swirling her hips, Maria rejoined her sisters. Over her slim shoulder she cast an impish, flirtatious grin, and winked. Nate was so startled that he gaped, forgetting his manners. She could not possibly be hinting at what he thought she was hinting at.

Ignacio and Martin were arguing with their father in Spanish, but they stopped when Nate set down his cup and stood. "If we're to make it back by evening," he said to McNair, "we'd better head out now."

"I reckon so," Shakespeare agreed, although he would not have minded another five or six cups of Rosa's delicious coffee. In his estimation sugar had to be the greatest invention since the wheel.

Don Varga walked them to their mounts. Warmly clasping Nate's hand, he said, "I am most sorry for what happened. Please do not hold it against us. We look forward to meeting your families."

"We'll be here." Nate swung onto the stallion and prodded it westward. He hoped to high heaven that he was not making a mistake. The Vargas seemed friendly enough. Why, then, was he reminded of the time his parents took him to Rickett's Circus in Philadelphia? Why, then, did he feel like the lion tamer about to stick his head into the fang-filled maw of the king of beasts?

Chapter Five

The mountain men were two miles up into the foot-hills when Shakespeare McNair spied four forms winding down toward them along the same trail. He was in the lead, rounding a bend. Reining instantly to the right, he rode in among a cluster of boulders and stopped.

Nate King had been deep in thought. Over and over he had reviewed the sequence of events since the mysterious attack on his cabin, trying to make sense of the whole situation. He knew too little, he concluded, to come up with any answers.

When his mentor angled off the trail, Nate mechanically did likewise. "What's the matter?" he asked, halting the stallion next to the mare.

"If you'd been paying attention, you'd know," Shakespeare scolded while dismounting. "Haven't I taught you that the only place you can let your guard down is in your own cabin?"

"I counted on you to keep watch for both of us,"

Nate quipped, which was a mistake in itself. In the wilderness, every man had to accept full responsibility for his own welfare. Others couldn't be expected to nursemaid him. Each man's hide was his own account.

Shakespeare did not make an issue of the lapse. Moving to a low boulder close to the bend, he hunkered to check his Hawken. The four men he had seen coming toward them might be members of the Varga expedition, but it did not pay to take anything for granted. Those who did usually did not live to enjoy a ripe old age.

Nate squatted and braced his back against the boulder. Higher on the slope an agitated jay squawked.

Jays, ravens, and squirrels were nature's sentries. When predators or humans intruded into their domain, they raised a fuss that alerted everyone and everything within earshot.

Shakespeare cocked his head at the approaching pad of soft footsteps. Deep voices droned softly in a tongue that he could not peg right off.

Nate sidled silently to the left so he would rise at the opposite end of the boulder from McNair. It was better to be spaced apart in case the owners of those voices proved unfriendly. He did not take his eyes off his mentor, and when McNair nodded, he shot erect, leveling his Hawken.

Shakespeare realized where he had heard that particular tongue before as he rose. It shouldn't be, yet there stood four Indians whose features and clothes marked them as dwellers of the desert country many leagues to the southwest.

The quartet drew up short, the man in the lead starting to lift his rifle but stopping when he saw they were covered. The middle pair carried a buck slung on a long pole balanced on their shoulders.

All four were bronzed and well muscled. They had

long trunks and arms, deep chests but narrow shoulders, and were bowlegged. Their big heads were framed by black hair clipped below the ears and across the forehead. Their nostrils were flat, wide and fleshy, their feet uncommonly large and splayed.

Other than long loincloths and high moccasins, they wore only short buckskin jackets. They were armed with rifles and knives, and the warrior at the rear also had a quiver containing a short bow and arrows slung over his shoulder.

They were Maricopas, Shakespeare realized. To find them here, in the Rockies, was as unsettling as it would be to run across an Apache in New York City.

So far as Shakespeare knew, the tribe was largely friendly to whites. The Maricopas, and their allies, the Pimas, had long helped the white man in their mutual relentless war against the Apaches. Hardy warriors in their own right, the Maricopas lived in villages and eked out a living by hunting and tilling the soil.

"We mean you no harm," Shakespeare said in the Pima tongue, which most Maricopas were familiar with. He did not know the Maricopa language itself. During the six months he had spent in Apache country years ago, he had lived with Pimas.

The foremost warrior seemed surprised. Smiling, he said, "I am Chivari. I did not think to hear a white man from this country use the tongue of our friends, the Pimas."

"You are far from home," Shakespeare said.

Chivari's eyes saddened. "Very far. I would rather be with my family and friends than here in this strange land. But we did not have a choice."

Shakespeare came around the boulder, lowering his rifle. "Every man has a choice," he said.

"Not when a great man with many guns comes into

your village and tells you to go with him or else your people will suffer,'' Chivari said.

They were made to come at gunpoint? Just as Shakespeare was going to ask, the fourth warrior grunted and said loudly, "Why do we delay? Don Varga sent us to bring meat for them to eat. He will be most displeased if we bring it late."

Chivari took offense. "Are we dogs, then, Azul, to scamper at their beck and call?" To Shakespeare, he said, "We are with the great man camped below on the plain."

"Manuel de Varga," Shakespeare said.

"And his sons."

McNair introduced himself and Nate. "We just came from your camp. *Senor* Varga did not tell us why he is in this country. Perhaps you could?"

"I cannot," Chivari said. "He has not told us."

"Why were you made to come?"

"To hunt, to track, to be on the lookout for unfriendly Indians. We were of much help when a band of Comanches tried to steal the horses."

"When will you see your home again?"

"I wish I knew, friend," Chivari said wistfully. Sighing, he stared toward the prairie. "We must go now."

"Be watchful," Shakespeare cautioned. "You are in Ute territory, and they are fierce fighters."

"More fierce than Apaches?" Chivari grinned. "I think not. Yet my people have been fighting Apaches for more summers than any man can remember, and we are still alive." He thumped his chest. "Maricopas fear no one. Let these Utes come. We will show them why the Apaches have never been able to defeat us."

Nate had been listening intently, but the parley was so much gibberish to him. As the four warriors filed off, he stepped to the trail. "Who were they?"

Shakespeare explained, ending with, "I have to

give Varga credit. It was damned clever to bring the Maricopas along. They're human bloodhounds. And they have twice the endurance of most Mexicans and whites.''

"But was it fair to Chivari and his friends?" Nate said. "You just told me that they don't want to be here."

"Chivari doesn't, that's for sure. I can't say about the rest. Maybe we'll get a chance to ask them tonight." Glancing down, Shakespeare stiffened. "Do you see what I see?"

Nate looked. A clear set of prints stared back up at him. Moccasin tracks left by the Maricopas. Exact duplicates of those he had found near the lake that morning. "One of them was in on it!"

"That'd be my guess," Shakespeare agreed.

"Let's catch up and question them."

Shakespeare snagged his friend's sleeve. "Hold on, hoss. Not so fast. We don't have any proof other than the tracks. Try prodding them and the culprit will clam up. And the Vargas might not take kindly to having their scouts roughed up."

"Are you saying I shouldn't do a thing?"

"For now."

Nate had never had cause to regret heeding his mentor's advice before. "Very well," he said, but he did not like it. Not one bit.

They mounted and resumed the climb, Nate in the lead this time, pushing hard to reach the valley. He did not slacken the pace once, not even when they came to the pass between the sawtooth ridges.

The setting was as peaceful as ever. Out on the lake ducks were feeding. Gulls wheeled and dipped.

Nate trotted along the south shore to the path his family used daily. He imagined that Winona and the children would be overjoyed to learn about the invitation. Winona adored having company and visiting others. On their annual treks to the Shoshone village, she spent every evening visiting kin and friends. As for Zach and Evelyn, they were as open and friendly as most kids their age.

Thinking of them brought a warm smile to Nate's lips. The smile died, though, when he noticed how quiet it was in the vicinity of the cabin. Zach and Evelyn were forever making noise, and the two women should be close by. But the cabin door was shut. A pall of silence hung over the clearing like a shroud.

"Winona!" Nate hollered. On receiving no reply, he jabbed his legs against the big black and galloped the rest of the way. He vaulted from the saddle, and was through the door before the stallion came to a stop. The interior was neat and orderly, as always. But no one was there.

"Zach! Evelyn!" Nate called out, rushing outside. The area nearest the door was a jumble of tracks, too many for anyone to make sense of.

Shakespeare had slanted to the corral. "Their horses are missing," he reported. "So is Blue Water Woman's."

"Where could they have gotten to?" Nate asked anxiously. Turning, he scoured the valley.

"They probably just went for a ride," Shakespeare said. Inwardly, he was more worried than he let on. Winona and his wife relied on their mounts only for long journeys. When they wanted to go most anywhere in the valley, they walked.

"Where would they have gone?" Nate responded. Not wasting another second, he climbed onto the stallion. "We'll split up. You take the south half, I'll go north. If you find anything, fire a shot into the air."

"Will do."

Nate cantered into the pines, moving in ever-widening circles, seeking fresh tracks. None were evident, so he swung in wider loops, growing more frantic the farther he went.

Ordinarily, Nate would have taken their absence in stride. But in light of the attack the previous night, he was deathly afraid the attackers had returned.

It was the one serious drawback to living in the wild, his constant dread that hostiles or rogue whites would make wolf meat of his loved ones while he was away. It was a fear every free trapper lived with. That is, every trapper who had a wife and sprouts.

The pines thinned. Nate bent low to better see the soil. There had to be tracks! There just had to be! Horses did not vanish into thin air. Coming to a knoll, he rode to the top and straightened in the stirrups. Still nothing. He prayed that McNair was having better luck.

Unknown to the young mountain man, Shakespeare was at that moment on one knee next to a line of hoofprints that pointed toward the slopes ringing the valley to the south. As he rose, he gazed at the mighty mountain beyond.

Longs Peak reared like a splintered crown, thrust high into the atmosphere, its double-peaked summit almost perpetually crowned by mantles of snow, for the weather at the top was always cold, often stormy. Blanketed by the purple gloom of pine forests, broken here and there by rocks upthrust by geologic upheavals ages past, it was a spectacle to stun the senses.

Shakespeare had never much liked the mountain, himself. Nate thought it was ''majestic'' and ''grand,'' but Shakespeare was more practical-minded. The peak was cold and stark and foreboding. No one had yet been to the top. Once, several drunken trappers had decided to try, but they only got about halfway up when it grew so cold, their feet went numb. The drunkest passed out, which gave the others the excuse they needed to give up in a manly fashion.

They carted him back down, loudly telling one and sundry that someday, *someday,* they would beat that mountain at its own coldhearted game.

Shakespeare had never understood the appeal of mountain climbing. It was popular in Europe, folks claimed. Rich people paid hundreds of dollars to be outfitted in special warm clothes and paid hundreds more for guides and helpers to tote their supplies and equipment. Using ropes and metal spikes, they scaled cliffs so sheer that mountain sheep avoided them. Undaunted, the climbers would forge to the summit, just for the honor of sticking a flag in the snow or leaving a personal article behind as a token of their triumph.

Scores died every year. Some fell to horrid ends. Some froze. Many others lost limbs or portions of limbs or had their lungs cave in. It was hardly worth the bother.

Shakespeare tore his gaze from the peak and mounted. Hastening on, he broke from the firs into a lush meadow, scaring a herd of deer. Bucks and does bolted in great vaulting bounds.

The tracks went straight across the meadow. It was not the meandering, easygoing gait the women usually adopted when out riding. It suggested they were trying to get somewhere in a hurry. But where? And why?

Shakespeare debated signaling Nate but decided against it. If the women and children had been taken captive, the shot would alert their captors. First, he would ensure they were safe.

The rugged terrain taxed man and beast. The mare had a facility for negotiating narrow trails that rivaled a mountain goat's, but even she balked when they came to a ribbon of a shelf winding below the rim of a gorge. A single misstep, and they would plunge to the jagged rocks below.

Had the women and children really gone this way?

No, for when Shakespeare surveyed the rim, he discovered where they had swung wide to go around the gorge instead of through it.

Shakespeare rode with his heavy Hawken at the ready. There were Utes to think of, and grizzlies, and painters. He also kept his eyes skinned for rattlesnakes that might be out sunning themselves. Watching a shadowy hollow at the base of a monolithic slab, he rounded a bend and heard a squeal of childish glee.

"Uncle Shakespeare!"

Evelyn and Zach pounded up, showing more teeth than a glutton at a bake sale.

"Is Pa with you?" the girl asked.

"What are you doing way up here, anyway?" Zach asked. "We didn't expect you back until dark, if then. Pa wasn't about to give up until he caught those skunks."

Shakespeare rested his rifle on his thighs. Just coming around a far bend were the love of his life and Winona King. They waved and smiled, plodding merrily along.

"Women," Shakespeare groused under his breath. Here he was, worried half out of his skin, and they acted for all the world as if they were on a Sunday gallivant in a town back east.

"What did you say?" Zach asked.

"Do yourself a favor, boy, and don't ever get hitched. You'll stay healthier." Shakespeare puffed loudly. "I swear, females are enough to make a man take to the bottle."

"Uncle!" Evelyn said in mock dismay. She knew how her white-maned uncle loved to tease.

Shakespeare playfully tousled her hair, then swung the mare around to await the women. Pretending to catch sight of something above them, he quoted, "But, soft! What light through yonder window breaks? It is the east, and Juliet is the sun! Arise, fair sun, and kill the envious moon, who is already sick and pale with grief, that thou her maid art far more fair than she.''

Evelyn giggled hysterically. ''Uncle Shakespeare, you're so silly!''

''Isn't he, though?'' Blue Water Woman said dryly.

Ignoring the barb, Shakespeare exclaimed, ''She speaks! Oh, speak again, bright angel! For thou art as glorious to this night, being over my head, as is a winged messenger of heaven unto the white-upturned wondering eyes of mortals that fall back to gaze on him, when he bestrides the lazy-pacing clouds and sails upon the bosom of the air.''

''More! More!'' Evelyn pealed, clapping.

Blue Water Woman shook her head. ''Do not encourage him, little one, or he will go on like this for hours.''

Deliberately, Shakespeare cried, ''Friends, Romans, countrymen, lend me your ears! I come to bury Caesar, not to praise him. The evil that men do lives after them. The good is oft interred with their bones.''

''Oh, please, husband,'' Blue Water Woman said in that special tone typical of long-suffering wives. To Winona, she remarked, as if in pain, ''See what I must put up with? Let us hope he does not get started on *Hamlet*—''

No sooner were the words out of her mouth than Shakespeare launched into, ''To be, or not to be, that is the question. Whether 'tis nobler in the mind to suffer the slings and arrows of outrageous fortune, or to take arms against a sea of troubles, and by opposing end them.''

Blue Water Woman brought her sorrel up next to the white mare, reached out, and gripped her husband's beard. ''Enough!'' she said, giving it a shake.

''Don't stop yet! More! Please!'' Evelyn begged.

Shakespeare pried his wife's fingers loose and

sniffed. "At least someone around here has a hankering for fine literature." Reining the mare around, he said, "Come, children. I know when I'm not wanted."

Winona had been chuckling the whole while. As her doting offspring trailed their uncle, she said to her friend, "I have been meaning to ask you. Has your man always been so fond of William S., as Carcajou calls him?"

"Not always," Blue Water Woman said. "We were not together at the time, but I have heard the story." She paused to verify her husband was not listening. "Did you know Carcajou had lived forty winters before he learned to read the white man's written tongue?"

"No!" Winona said in surprise. At Nate's request, she had mastered the strange squiggly marks the whites were so fond of, mastered them so well that she took turns reading to the children every night.

The task had been daunting. The tiny squiggles were so different from the symbols her people painted on hides and rocks that trying to make sense of them had been like trying to make it through a maze blindfolded.

Afterward, once she fully realized the wonderful gift her husband had shared, Winona came to marvel anew at the ingenuity of the whites.

In many respects the two peoples were much alike; they loved, hated, ate, played, worshiped, made war.

In as many respects, they were much different; the whites were like ants, always scurrying to and fro, always gathering things, always needing more, more, more. More money, more clothes, more land. As a people they were never content to sit still for very long. They were forever on the go, exploring where none had gone before, always seeking an elusive "something" that lay over the next horizon.

Her people were content to stay in one general area, to savor the quiet rhythms life offered, to admire the horizon rather than ride over it.

Oh, the women always wanted bigger lodges and the warriors always wanted more horses, but a woman who owned four garments was quite content with those four, while a warrior who had gone on ten or fifteen raids and acquired a sizable herd was content to stay in the village and let others risk life and limb to gain prestige.

Reading books had given Winona fresh insight into whites, and the differences between the two peoples. The Great Mystery had blessed Nate's people with a keen imagination and wanderlust, whereas her own kind were gifted with deep, abiding ties to Nature, ties so strong that many whites called it superstition.

Many whites felt that her people were wrong to be the way they were, just as many of her people believed the whites were terribly wrong in all they did. But was it a question of right or wrong? Or was it simply that they were *different*, and should learn to accept the fact?

"Winona? Did you hear me?"

Winona jerked her head up. Shakespeare was riding beside Blue Water Woman, both staring intently at her. "I am sorry. What did you say?"

"Zach told me that you heard shots? That you saw someone up on this ridge?"

"Yes," Winona confirmed. "I had gone to the lake for a bucket of water when there were two faint shots. When I looked up, I saw someone on a white horse."

"Thinking it was you, and that Nate and you might be in trouble," Blue Water Woman said, taking up the account, "we saddled our own horses and rode up."

"It wasn't me or Nate." Shakespeare was bothered by the risk they had taken, but he did not point it out.

They'd only scoff, or get angry at him for thinking they could not handle themselves. Women were funny that way. "Did you come across anyone?"

"No," Winona said. "A few tracks across the gorge. That was all we found."

"Curiouser and curiouser," Shakespeare said to himself.

In a clatter of hooves little Evelyn trotted back to them and indicated the slope below. "Ma! Uncle! There's Pa, waiting for us!"

"Why does he look mad?" Winona wondered.

"Oops," Shakespeare said, and elevating his Hawken, he fired a shot into the air.

Chapter Six

The Kings and the McNairs were two miles from the prairie when the sun relinquished the sky to gathering twilight. A cool breeze from the northwest fanned the trees and stirred Blue Water Woman's long hair as she shifted in the saddle to see the last rays of sunlight fade. "We will be late."

Shakespeare McNair shrugged. "Don't blame me," he said. His wife was a stickler for always getting places on time. It had to do with her upbringing. Flatheads prided themselves on being punctual, unlike, say, the Crows, who might show up half an hour or an hour late and think nothing of it. Shakespeare would never admit as much to Blue Water Woman, but there were times when he wished she were more Crow than Flathead.

"It is not polite to be late, husband. You told the Vargas we would be there by sunset, and we will not."

"I'm sure they'll save some food for us," Shakespeare said trying to make light of it.

"That is not the point." For years Blue Water Woman had tried to instill in her man a more mature sense of social obligation, to no avail. It was like trying to teach an old dog new tricks. He was too set in his ways, too cantankerous to much care what others thought.

"I'm sorry, wench," Shakespeare said. "But how were Nate and I to know that you gals had traipsed off to the mountains? If you'd been at the cabin when we showed up, we would have made it to Don Varga's camp on time."

Blue Water Woman looked at him. "Oh. So you blame us?"

Shakespeare wanted to kick himself. If there was one thing a female was touchy about, it was being accused of doing wrong. Women *never* did anything wrong. It was the first and most important lesson a married man learned. "Of course not, love of my life. It's just how things worked out. The Vargas will understand."

"I can hardly wait to get there," Evelyn chimed in. Her dun was in front of the white mare, and she had been chatting gaily with McNair the whole way down the high valley. "Are the ladies really pretty? And do they really have the prettiest dresses you ever saw?"

"Yep," Shakespeare said with a grin. Then he quickly added, "Of course, they're not nearly as pretty as Blue Water Woman. Or your ma."

"Why, thank you, sir," Winona called back, having overheard. She was in front of her daughter, Zach and Nate in front of her.

"This will be grand!" Evelyn declared. She loved going places. The annual rendezvous always dazzled her, with its many strange sights and smells, the air thick with excitement. She most loved to stroll among the traders' stalls with her mother and finger all the gorgeous Hudson's Bay blankets and jewelry and other trinkets the traders brought.

Winona was as excited as Evelyn. She had enjoyed the trek to Santa Fe years ago, enjoyed meeting Spanish people and learning their ways. They were so supremely friendly, so relaxed, so wonderfully carefree, so different from her people.

But Winona had to keep in mind what Nate had told her shortly before they left. He had taken her aside to voice his suspicion that two members of the Varga expedition were to blame for the attack on the cabin. She must stay alert, keep an eye on the children, and get them out of there at the first hint of treachery.

"Ma, do you reckon these folks know Francisco Gaona?" Zach asked, referring to a close friend of theirs with whom they had stayed when they were in New Mexico.

"It is possible, I suppose," she said.

Zach squirmed, eager to get there. His uncle's passing comments about the pretty *senoritas* had kindled his curiosity. From what his uncle had said, the sisters were older than he was, which was a shame. But they were pretty, and that was what counted. In the past year or so, much to Zach's surprise, he had grown fond of admiring attractive girls.

During their last summer trip to the Shoshones, Zach had spent most of his time in the company of a maiden named Morning Dove. She had been a playmate of his since he was old enough to walk. Many a time they had splashed in the river and caught butterflies and dashed laughing through high grass, chased by others.

This time it had been different. Morning Dove was

not the same girl. She was taller, wider, *fuller*. He had found himself staring at her when she was not aware, a peculiar tight sensation in his chest. He had liked how her skin shone, how her hair glistened, how she swayed when she walked. These were things he had never noticed before.

Nor was Morning Dove the only pretty girl to catch his eye. To Zach's amazement, he had discovered that the Shoshone village was chock *full* of pretty girls. Where they had all come from, he had no idea.

Now here was a chance to see three pretty Spanish girls, and Zach was champing at the bit. "Do you know much Spanish, Pa?" he inquired.

Nate had spotted several points of light on the prairie below. The Vargas had three fires going at once. He frowned. Advertising their presence was a grave mistake. Any Indians within five miles were bound to see the glow.

At his son's query, Nate turned. "Only a little," he admitted. "Shakespeare speaks it, though."

"He speaks *everything*," Zach said.

Sometimes it seemed that way. Nate knew of no one who had learned more tongues than McNair. Shakespeare liked to say that anyone could learn as many languages as he did if they lived in the mountains as long as he had. But it was more than that. McNair had a knack for picking up new tongues, a rare talent that had served him in good stead.

The trail wound into a wash between hills. Here the shadows were solid, the ground mired in pitch. Nate slowed, the clomp of hooves made louder by the close confines of the earthen walls. He stretched to relieve a kink in his back.

Something moved on the north rim. Nate tensed, prickling with apprehension. They were boxed in. Should a grizzly happen by, the bear would rip through them like a tornado through a grain field.

The shape moved again, rising slightly, enough for Nate to distinguish a head and two arms and a long slender object being pointed at his family.

Nate did not call out. He did not ask who it was, or what they were doing. He did not waste his breath, not when the lives of those who meant more to him than life itself were at stake. Whipping the Hawken to his shoulder, he hastily fixed a bead on the center of the figure, curled back the hammer, and fired. "Ambush! Ride! Ride!" he bawled, wrenching the stallion to one side so the others could flee past him.

Zach did not waste a moment asking what or who or where. He obeyed instantly, slapping his mount and galloping on down the wash, bending low to be a smaller target.

Winona pulled alongside her daughter, urging, "Go, child! Go!" As they pounded by her husband, shots rang out above. Lead spanged off rock. A horse whinnied, and she heard McNair roar like a wounded bear.

Shakespeare had been hit. He was raising his rifle when a gun blasted directly overhead. Pain seared his thigh as he snapped off a shot at the man who had shot him. The dark shape dropped, but whether Shakespeare had scored a hit or the figure had ducked was impossible to say.

Blue Water Woman brought her rifle to bear, aiming at a squat form that reared above her. At the crack, a man screeched. Putting her heels to the sorrel, she came abreast of her husband. "Let us go!" she urged.

"You first!" Shakespeare directed, unlimbering a pistol. "I'll bring up the rear!"

The sorrel flew along the wash, Blue Water Woman sliding onto the off side as her father had taught her to do when she was eight winters old. Guns boomed, balls zinged, but none came close to her or the sorrel. Reaching the mouth, she swung on top of her mount and sped off into heavy timber in the wake of the Kings. "Hurry, husband!" she cried, the crash of brush to her rear reassuring her that he was following.

Nate King swatted at limbs that tore at his face and neck. Shouts and curses testified to the frustrated fury of the ambushers. Fretting that the killers would give chase, he kept an eye cocked to their back trail. Thankfully, no pursuit materialized.

Winona was in the lead, flanked by her children. What did all this mean? she wondered. Now there had been two attempts to wipe out her family in just two days. Were the Spaniards to blame? If so, why? What did they hope to gain?

Hair flying, Winona jumped a low log, her body gracefully adjusting to the flow of her mount. She looked over a shoulder but could not see her mate. Worried, she reined up when a clearing broadened before them.

Little Evelyn's heart pumped madly. She had never been so scared, not even that time she had been out collecting wood for the fireplace and a rattlesnake had risen up a few feet away, its tail rattling furiously.

Zach drew rein and turned, half hoping their attackers were after them so he could count coup. It had all happened so fast that he had not thought to fight back.

Blue Water Woman galloped into the open. Breathless, she said, "Is everyone all right?" Assured they were, she swung her mount around as Nate King arrived. Peering beyond him, she sought her husband.

Nate began to reload, fingers flying, a drill he had practiced so many times, he could do it blindfolded if he had to. He sorely wished that he had gotten a good look at the figures on the rim.

"Where is Shakespeare?" Blue Water Woman asked.

"What?" Nate said. Scanning the clearing, he realized his mentor was missing.

"I thought he was behind me, but it was you," Blue Water Woman said. "Something must have happened to him." She lifted her reins.

"Hold on," Nate said. "I'll go take a look-see."

"Why you? He is my man."

Nate had to think fast. "My stallion is faster than your horse, and it blends into the dark better." He uncapped his powder horn.

Winona nudged her mare closer. "If you are going, we will all go."

"Evelyn too?" Nate used his trump card. "No, it's best if the four of you lay low. Once I find Shakespeare, we'll rejoin you."

"I am going," Blue Water Woman insisted.

Nate tilted the horn to pour powder into the palm of his hand. "What if they jump Winona? She'll need help protecting the kids."

"I'm no kid!" Zach objected.

Blue Water Woman bit her lower lip. She was torn between her love for her husband and her friendship for the Kings. What should she do?

"Besides, one person can move more quietly than two," Nate pointed out. Prudently, he did not mention that he did not want the added burden of having to watch her back as well as his own.

"Very well," Blue Water Woman said. But she did not like it. Not one bit.

"Wait for us where the plain begins," Nate said, yanking the ramrod out of its housing. "For all we know, the Vargas were in on this. We can't trust them until we learn the truth."

"Be careful," Winona cautioned.

With a nod, Nate was off. When he was within a hundred yards of the dry wash, he stopped to listen. The forest was unnaturally still. No voices. No drumming of hooves. As edgy as a critter in a slaughter-house, he ever so slowly advanced.

The dark mouth of the wash loomed like the maw of a gigantic creature. Overhead, stars sparkled. Twilight had been replaced by night, and the wind had increased, making it more difficult to hear faint noises.

Stopping again, Nate slid off and tied the big black. After stroking its neck to keep it from nickering, he crept toward the wash, placing each foot down as if he were treading on broken glass.

No sound broke the stillness. Nate pressed against the north wall and did not move for the longest while.

He did not like to dwell on his mentor's absence. Either Shakespeare had become separated and was somewhere off in the woods, which was highly unlikely, or one of the bushwhackers had done what certain tribes had been trying to do for more years than Nate had been alive.

McNair dead. The thought provoked a shiver. Shakespeare had always been there for him. As if it were yesterday, he vividly recollected when he first ventured to the Rockies. He had been as green as grass. Every day had been a trial, every week a test of endurance and resolve. And through it all, Shakespeare had always been there with a kind word or a pat on the back.

Nate could not imagine life without McNair. In many respects, Shakespeare was more of a father to him than his own father had been. He had never respected anyone more.

Creeping to the slope that led to the rim, Nate crouched and climbed. Suddenly dirt rattled out from under his right moccasin. He froze, braced for the crash of a gun or the yelp of an enemy.

His fears were unfounded. After a suitable interval, Nate went on. At the top, a gust of wind hit him full in the face. He flattened and crawled to the base of a pine. With it to shield him, he rose to his knees.

In the wash, the wind moaned. Or was it Shakespeare? Casting caution aside, Nate prowled the rim like a painter seeking prey.

Their attackers were gone. No bodies had been left behind. But twenty yards farther, Nate noticed a wide black spot that had a dull sheen to it. Bending, he touched his fingertips to the center. Sticky blood clung to them.

So at least one of the bastards had been made to suffer! Nate found no more blood, even though he hiked to the far end. Going over the side, he slid to the bottom and moved down the middle of the wash itself.

He had a vague recollection of where he had last seen Shakespeare. Nothing marked the spot, nor did he find any sign to indicate what might have occurred.

Nate hastened to the stallion. He didn't imagine their attackers would cart Shakespeare's body off if McNair had been slain, so there was hope he still lived.

Mounting, Nate commenced a search. Fifteen minutes of fruitless zigzagging convinced him that it would be best to return at first light. Despondent, he turned the stallion eastward.

What would Blue Water Woman say? What would she do? He had failed her. Worse, he had failed McNair.

It tore at his guts to ride off without knowing Shakespeare's fate. But what else could he do? He had the women and children to think of, as well.

Nate threaded through the woodland until he glimpsed the pale plain through the boles. Ahead, a horse whinnied lightly. Before he could prevent it, the stallion answered. As he leveled the Hawken, a whisper pierced the gloom.

"Pa, is that you?"

"You're lucky it is," Nate said. Guided by the sound to where his family and Blue Water Woman were huddled, he climbed down. "Haven't I taught you better than to call out like that when you don't know who might be out there?"

Zach bowed his head. It was a mistake unworthy of a Shoshone warrior. His only excuse was his worry over his father's welfare. And his uncle's. "Where's Shakespeare?" he said to change the subject.

Blue Water Woman pushed between Winona and Evelyn. "That is what I would like to know."

"I didn't find him," Nate said, then had to grab the Flathead so she wouldn't vault onto the sorrel and race off. "Hear me out! I hunted and hunted, but there's no sign of him. Our best bet is to wait for the sun to come up."

"I am not waiting!" Blue Water Woman said, tugging from his grasp.

Winona stepped in front of her friend. "Please, heed my husband," she pleaded. "What can you do in the dark?"

"Whatever I can," Blue Water Woman said. "Move aside." Her self-control had long been the envy of those who knew her best, but now tears of mingled outrage and frustration misted the corners of her eyes.

"No," Winona refused. "I will not let you go off and get yourself killed. There is strength in numbers. We must stick together."

Turmoil whirled Blue Water Woman in its petrifying grip. Logic warred with emotion. Love battled common sense. As she hung on the cusp of indecision, the matter was decided for her by the startling appearance of four spectral shapes that seemed to rise up out of the very ground.

Nate's instincts warned him a split second sooner.

Spinning, he pumped his rifle to his shoulder, but he did not shoot, for he saw who it was. "You!" he blurted.

"Pa!" Evelyn screamed.

Winona and Zach were beside her in a bound, guns cocked. A cold hand clutched at Winona's heart, inspired by the profiles of the swarthy men she faced. They were similar to Apaches, disturbingly so, reminding her of the terrible nightmare she had gone through in New Mexico when the Chiricahuas captured her during a raid on the Gaona *hacienda*.

The Maricopa called Chivari raised a hand and said in broken English, "Not enemy, white-eyes. We friends, remember?" He gazed at the others. "Where white-hair? Where one speak our tongue?"

"That's what we'd like to know," Nate said. Was it coincidence the Maricopas had shown up now, of all times? Or had the four been with those who ambushed them?

"Don Varga worry why you not come. Send us keep watch," Chivari said, as if he were privvy to Nate's thoughts. "We hear many shots. Find you."

One of the other warriors, the surly Maricopa named Azul, barked at Chivari in their own tongue. An argument ensued—over what, Nate could not guess. The upshot was that Chivari turned and said, "We take you Don Varga, yes?"

Nate balked. His family was safe enough where they were. At the camp, they would be hopelessly outnumbered. "Tell the Vargas that we cannot make it. We'll break bread with them another time."

"Eh?" Chivari said. "You not come, white-eyes?"

"No."

The Maricopas consulted. Presently, the tallest jogged off toward the distant glow. "Him bring big man," Chivari said. "You tell Varga no come. Not us."

They were afraid to do it themselves, Nate suspected. His opinion of Don Varga had dropped considerably after finding out that Varga forced the warriors to serve as scouts against their wishes. Now this. He regretted ever making the man's acquaintance.

Winona was also having regrets. Deciding to accept the Vargas' invitation had been a mistake. She pulled Nate aside to whisper, "I do not like this."

"You think I do?"

"We must leave while we still can."

Would the Maricopas let them? Nate mused. "Mount up, everyone," he directed. Slipping a foot into a stirrup, he gripped the saddle to pull himself up, but a bronzed form attached itself to his arm.

"You not go, white-eyes. Wait for big man."

So there it was, as plain as day. Nate glanced at the women. They were watching him, ready to back his play. So was Zach. One word, one gesture, and there would be a bloodbath. But the Maricopas might not be the only ones to go down. Chivari's brow was knit, as if he were suspicious, and the other two were uncomfortably close to Evelyn. Dared he give the signal?

"We'll wait for the Vargas," Nate announced. It pacified the Maricopas, who stepped to the edge of the clearing and hunkered.

Winona was far from pleased. "Why did you change your mind? On our account?" She held her chin high. "I am Shoshone, husband. I am not afraid to die."

"And how do you feel about maybe losing your daughter or son?" Nate said so only she could hear.

That quelled her protest. Winona would rather have burning coals placed on both eyes than sacrifice her children. "We will stay," she said, hanging her head.

Their wait was not as long as Nate figured it would

be. Hammering hooves heralded the arrival of Ignacio Varga and fifteen *vaqueros*. Rude as ever, without introducing himself, Ignacio snapped, ''King! Why have you not arrived at our camp yet? The food will burn if we delay much longer.''

''We were attacked,'' Nate explained. ''My friend, Shakespeare, has disappeared.''

''Attacked by who? Savages?''

''Your guess is as good as mine,'' Nate answered. Probably better. ''We prefer to stay here until dawn, then search for sign.''

''Nonsense. Remain here alone? With women and children?'' Ignacio motioned and the *vaqueros* parted, opening a path to the prairie. ''My father must hear of this. Come with us.'' Leaning on his saddle horn, he smirked. ''And I will not take no for an answer.''

Chapter Seven

There had once been a time when no one could take Shakespeare McNair by surprise. In his younger days, in his prime, he had tangled with the likes of Apaches, Comanches, Blackfeet, and Bloods, surviving more violent scrapes than he cared to count, and always with hardly a scratch.

How did he manage it? Friends claimed that he must live a charmed life, that his guardian angel was always watching out for him, that he had more luck than most ten men.

The truth of the matter was that Shakespeare had a finely honed sixth sense, intuition, if you will, that never let him down. When enemy eyes were on him, he could *feel* them. Even though there might be no outward evidence, he always *knew* they were there.

A typical instance occurred back in '06, when he had been leading a party through the northern Rockies. They had entered a wide canyon, a peaceful place where birds had been singing and chipmunks scampered about. There had been no sign of hostiles, none at all. Yet the moment Shakespeare rode into that canyon, he had known unseen eyes were watching.

The other members of the party had been flabbergasted when Shakespeare said they were to turn and take the long way around. They had argued. He was imagining things, they said. He was spooking himself. They insisted on going on.

Shakespeare practically begged them not to. He hung back as, one by one, they filed past, chuckling and grinning at his expense. He called out, warning them over and over, but they would not listen. "You're being childish, hoss," one man had said flatly.

Did those men still think he was childish when scores of Bloods rose up from hiding on top of the canyon walls? Did those men regret their stubbornness when arrows rained down as thick as hail? Did they curse their stupidity as they were transfixed again and again? What was on their minds as they toppled from their terror-stricken mounts, bristling with shafts like human pincushions?

Shakespeare was the only one to make it out of that canyon alive. He shot two of the Bloods, then fled before he joined his hapless companions in the Hereafter.

Time after time, his uncanny sixth sense warned him of impending danger. Even when he grew older and his sinews lost some of their steely strength and his senses began to dim, he could always count on his infallible intuition.

Until this night.

Shakespeare had no inkling that any enemies were within a hundred miles of the dry wash. When Nate fired and shouted, Shakespeare was as startled as the rest. Bedlam broke out. He was hit in the thigh, and he fired at the man who shot him.

Blue Water Woman came alongside. "Let us go!" she urged him.

"You first!" Shakespeare said, drawing a pistol. "I'll bring up the rear!"

His intent was to cover the others as they escaped into the woods. Galloping wildly down the wash on his wife's heels, he slowed when a target presented itself. His pistol belched smoke and lead, but at the very moment his trigger finger tightened, the mare swerved, throwing off his aim.

Shakespeare jammed the spent flintlock under his belt and produced the other one. The end of the wash was a dozen yards off. His wife rushed past it, Nate swinging the stallion in close behind her. Both were so intent on getting away that they did not look back.

Spiking his heels into the white mare, Shakespeare skirted a boulder. He was almost to the opening when five or six figures charged down the north slope and raised rifles to shoot at the unprotected backs of his wife and Nate King.

Shakespeare bellowed like a mad grizzly and cut on the reins. In a twinkling he was among them, the mare scattering half of them, his pistol clubbing two more. As he wheeled to plunge into the vegetation, a grasping hand closed on his ankle. He kicked, but the hand would not let go.

"Get him!" someone hollered.

"I've got the horse!" cried a man who caught hold of the mare's bridle.

Shakespeare bent to hit the polecat over the head, but as he did, two others leaped, seizing him around the waist and the shoulder. He swung, landed a glancing blow, and struggled to straighten. His right foot was yanked free of the stirrup. He smashed the pistol into a sneering upturned face, then had his gun arm gripped in an iron vise. His pistol was ripped from his fingers.

"Tear him off the nag, you jackasses!" someone raged.

Shakespeare felt himself being yanked from the saddle. Three men hurled him to the ground and sought to pin him. He punched, he kicked, he bit. Blows hammered him, but he was barely aware of them. His knuckles crunched against a nose. His left fist found a mouth.

"Damn it all!" shrieked the apparent leader. "He's just an old man! Hold him!"

Not for nothing had Shakespeare acquired the name Carcajou. Although puny in size compared to grizzlies and buffaloes, wolverines were renowned for their unbelievable savagery and utter lack of fear. They fought with a berserk fury that was awesome to behold. And they were Shakespeare's namesake.

He heaved up to his feet, throwing men right and left, his fists cracking heads and sinking wrist-deep into stomachs. His attackers were thrown into confusion by the unexpected resistance. They gave way. He saw the mare, ten feet off. If he could reach her, he might still live to see another dawn.

"Stop him!" the leader roared.

Shakespeare slammed into a man who tried, bowling him over. He bolted toward the mare, but another dusky form barred his path. Knuckles grazed his chin, the blow cushioned by his thick beard. His answering punch rocked the cutthroat on his heels. Barreling onward, Shakespeare was two strides from the mare and salvation when arms tackled him around the shins.

Down he crashed. Shakespeare twisted, thrashing mightily, but the arms were bands of stone. He flicked a right at the man's cheek and missed.

A shadow heaved over him. Shakespeare looked up into a pale profile that was vaguely familiar.

"You old buzzard!" the leader snarled. "If I want

something done right, I reckon I've got to do it myself!''

Shakespeare glimpsed a descending rifle stock. He tried to jerk aside and failed. His last thought before he was sucked into a swirling black well was that he hoped Blue Water Woman would find someone else to share her lodge and not end her days alone and heartsick.

"This is awful, *senor,* just awful!" Don Manuel de Varga declared. Smacking his palm with his fist, he said, "My men and I are at your disposal. As soon as it is light, we will scour the countryside for your friend."

The Spaniard was so earnest that Nate King found it hard to believe the man could be putting on an act.

"My Maricopas will find McNair," Don Varga said. "They can track anyone, anywhere."

Ignacio, Martin, and Diego were near at hand. The former stepped forward and pointed at a deer haunch being roasted on a spit. "What about the food, *mi padre*?" he asked. "We should not let it go to waste just because one of these *gringos* is missing."

Nate came close to slugging the cur. He balled his hand and shifted, but Don Varga beat him to it, backhanding Ignacio across the mouth, shocking son and onlookers alike.

"*Silencio!* How can you think of filling your belly at a time like this? Do you not see how upset these women are?" Don Varga said, gesturing at Winona and Blue Water Woman. "Do you not see the children?"

Ignacio had flushed scarlet, but he did not raise a finger against his father. Nodding at the wives, he said with blatant scorn, "But they are Indians and 'breeds, savages like those who attacked them. Why should we care?"

Don Varga stepped back as if stricken, his eyes wide in loathing. "Flesh of my flesh, yet you can talk so? Until this very moment, I did not realize . . ." His voice trailed off, and he turned to Winona and Blue Water Woman. "My heartfelt apologies, *senoras*," he said sorrowfully. "My son has no manners and less compassion."

Winona felt sorry for him. The shame of having a son like Ignacio was more than many fathers could bear. Among her people it rarely happened. When it did, often the father would sever all ties with his offspring in a formal ceremony, in effect washing his hands of his son for all time.

Blue Water Woman glared at Ignacio. Were she a warrior, she would challenge him and cut out his heart for his callous insult.

Don Vargo moved toward crates placed in a half-circle close to the spit. "Come. Please. Be seated. Have some coffee or tea, if you wish."

Neither the wives nor the children moved. All eyes turned to Nate. As strongly as he yearned to decline, as much as he wanted to climb back onto his mount and return to the foothills in search of Shakespeare, he had to be practical. Stepping to a crate, he sat, and the others followed suit.

Smiling wanly, Don Varga had two *vaqueros* drag another crate next to the one Nate had picked. Sighing as he sank down, he said ruefully, "Why does God afflict us so, *Senor* King? Why does he allow suffering and misery?"

"I know, sir!" Evelyn piped up, much to Nate's and Winona's surprise.

"You do, child?"

"Sure. Uncle Shakespeare told me. Bad things are like when you walk along a trail and trip."

Don Varga rested his elbows on his knees and

made a tepee of his fingers. "I am afraid I do not understand, little one," he said gently.

"Haven't you ever tripped and fallen?" Evelyn asked innocently.

"Well, yes, I have. Everyone has, I suppose."

"And what did you do?

"Pardon?"

"What did you do after you tripped? Did you just lie there?"

"No. I got back up and kept on going."

Everyone was listening. All activity had stopped.

"Well, life is just like that. We go along doing whatever it is we do, when all of a sudden something bad happens. We don't want it to. No one plans it that way. It just happens. And when it does, we have to get right back up and go on living our lives, just like we do when we trip."

Nate was shocked to see the elder Spaniard's eyes glisten. Just as perplexing was his daughter's boldness. Usually, she was shy around strangers. Evidently she had taken a shine to the Spaniard.

Don Varga cleared his throat. "You say that your uncle taught you that lesson? He is a very wise man, this McNair."

Evelyn nodded. "The wisest. He says that's how he got all those white hairs. Every one was a lesson he learned."

Touching his own gray streaks, Don Varga smiled. "His words are true, little one. I pray I get to talk to him myself before long." Turning to his daughters, who stood off to one side, he beckoned, and when they came, he rose and took hold of the oldest daughter's wrist.

"Papa, what—?" Maria said.

Don Varga unclasped a gleaming bejeweled bracelet and held it out to the light. It sparkled and shimmered in a blaze of brilliant hues. "This has been in my family for many generations," he said gravely. Then, abruptly turning to Evelyn, he dropped the bracelet in her lap. "Here, sweet child. This is yours."

The Varga sisters were stupefied. Maria opened her mouth as if to protest. Ignacio rose, flaring with anger. *Vaqueros* and servants gawked at one another.

Winona was as dazed as everyone else. Rising, she went over. "I am sorry," she said politely, "but we cannot accept so generous a gift."

"I insist," Don Vargo said, affectionately placing a hand on Evelyn's head. "Consider it a token of my gratitude."

"For what?" Winona asked.

Don Varga did not answer. Walking back to his crate, he said to Maria, "Close your mouth, daughter. What is one bracelet, more or less? You own more jewelry than you know what to do with. And since I gave you that bracelet to begin with, I can bestow it on the child if I so wish. The matter is ended."

Winona picked up the bracelet. She knew enough of civilized ways to know that it must be worth a small fortune. The wide band alone was solid gold.

"Can I keep it, Ma?" Evelyn asked naively. "The nice man said I can."

Winona looked at Don Varga, who stared at Evelyn with a haunted, wistful, melancholy expression that hinted at a tormented soul momentarily at peace. "You may keep it," she said.

Vaqueros brought crates for Maria, Francisca, and Luisa. Rosa and other servants brought trays bearing drinks and cheese and bread.

Nate had little appetite. He nibbled on a piece of cheese. A subdued air hung over the camp. Conversation was conducted in low tones. When people moved about, they did so as if on tiptoes. Meals were eaten quietly.

Maria Varga broke the icy grip by smiling broadly and turning to Winona and Blue Water Woman to ask about their respective tribes. She was so sincerely interested and friendly that the wives soon warmed to her, and the other sisters joined in.

Nate was glad. It would take their minds off Shakespeare for a while, maybe calm them enough so they could catch some sleep later on. He accepted a slender glass of wine from Rosa. "Mighty tasty," he said after sipping. "Goes down smooth, as the dandies back east might say."

Don Varga had a glass of his own. Swirling the dark red liquid, he said, "It comes from my own winery, *senor*. My grapes are the sweetest in all the land." After swallowing some, he sobered, then asked out of the blue, "What do you know of my country, if I might ask?"

"Spain? Not much," Nate admitted. "Most of what I hear has to do with Mexico."

"Ah, yes. Mexico," Don Varga said, somehow making the word sound as if it referred to a disease instead of a country. "Mexico is a nest of primitives. But Spain, *senor*! Spain is as grand as a nation can be! Once, we had an empire that spanned the world. Our fleets sailed the seven seas. Our *conquistadors* conquered whole continents. The life of the nobility was splendid beyond compare. Those were the days!"

"Times change," Nate commented.

"That they do," Don Varga said bitterly. "And what I most regret is that I lived to see them change so drastically in my own lifetime. As your sweet little one pointed out, adversity shows no favorites."

Nate did not see why Varga was so upset by the decline in Spain's fortunes. Many European countries had colonial empires once: England, France, and the Netherlands, to name just a few. Before them it had been the Romans and the Greeks. Empires rose and fell like the ocean tide. None lasted forever. They had their day and expired, to be replaced by yet another.

"The Varga family is an old family, *Senor* King. As old as Spain itself. Once we owned estates so vast, it took days to ride across. Now we have one small estate in Spain and a small *hacienda* in Mexico. Once we had hundreds of servants, today just a dozen. Once we lived like barons, *senor*. Now..." His voice trailed off.

Since his host was so intent on talking about it, Nate asked, "What happened?"

"Mexico happened," Don Varga spat. "My great-great-great-grandfather laid claim to thousands of acres in northern Mexico and set himself up in royal style. The tremendous amount of money it took to maintain lavish estates in both countries was of no consequence to him. Not with money pouring in from the Varga mine, the Varga winery, and the Varga shipping company."

"But something went wrong?" Nate guessed.

"The ore in our mine was depleted. Our shipping company failed. We owned three fine luxury ships at one time, but the first caught fire and sank, and the second was wrecked by peasant rabble during the Mexican Revolution to keep their rightful rulers from escaping."

"The third?"

"Ah, that was the cruelest cut of all. We lost it in a freak storm, with all hands and passengers." Don Varga slumped. "The stream of money that had swelled our coffers almost dried up. We cut back expenditures, but it was not enough. We had to rely on our savings. When they dwindled, we sold off sections of our property until we had no extra to sell."

"Why didn't you try new ventures?" Nate asked.

"Do you think we did not try?" Don Varga said. "But where before everything we touched turned to

94

gold, the new businesses my family started floundered and failed.''

"You still have the winery.''

Don Varga gazed at the wine in his glass. "That is *all* we have left, *Senor* King. I shudder to think what would happen if we were to have a bad year. A single spoiled crop and my family would be ruined. We would have to sell everything and live like common rabble. Us! The Vargas! It is unthinkable.''

"Maybe things will turn around,'' Nate offered.

The patriarch of the Varga family looked at him. "I am betting everything that they will.''

Loud laughter diverted Nate's attention to the women. Winona was saying something and patting her stomach. The Varga girls pealed with more mirth. So did Evelyn. Even Blue Water Woman smiled. He reckoned it had something to do with babies and turned back. Don Manuel de Varga was studying him oddly.

"Are you much of a gambler, *Senor* King?''

"Can't say that I am. Not unless you count pitching coins when I was a kid in New York City.''

"No, that is not the same. I am talking about bigger stakes, about putting all that you have on the table and wagering it on a single cut of the cards or a toss of the dice. A man can win big if luck favors him.''

"He can also lose his shirt.''

"There is an element of risk in all things. No risk, no gain.'' Don Varga peered into the crackling flames. "I have staked my family's future on this venture. If we succeed, we will be rich beyond our wildest dreams. Life will be like it was in the old days. Magnificent estates, servants galore, the finest clothes, a stable of Arabians, whatever our hearts desire will be ours. We will not be destitute.''

Nate could think of any number of people who would give their eyeteeth to be as "destitute'' as the

Vargas. The family still had an estate and a winery in Spain, and a *hacienda* in Mexico. Don Varga himself had mentioned that his daughters owned more fine jewelry than they knew what to do with. What the Vargas called poor, most folks would call rich.

Sure, the family had fallen on hard times. But they had a lot to be thankful for.

"Would you like to hear why I have traveled all this way from my own country? Why I nearly used up what little was left of my family's money to outfit this expedition? Why I have dragged my sons and daughters with me into the heart of this dark land?"

Nate did not respond. Varga was going to tell him whether he wanted to hear it or not.

The Spaniard bent forward, face taut, eyes gleaming. "Being American, you no doubt know that this whole region is now claimed by the United States."

"It was part of the Louisiana Purchase," Nate mentioned.

Don Varga did not seem to hear. "Once, though, this land was claimed by Spain. Three hundred years ago *conquistadors* explored the land a few hundred miles south of here. Later, missionaries tried to convert the savages. Later still, a few small settlements sprang up."

Nate wondered what the history lesson had to do with Varga's expedition.

"Rich veins of gold and silver were found deep in the mountains, and we mined them with the help of local Indians."

That was not entirely true, Nate reflected. In many cases, the Indian were compelled to work under the threat of being exterminated.

"Later, when the ungrateful savages rose up against us, we were forced to abandon the mines and were never able to return. But maps were drawn, showing their locations. Some were lost. Some were written so that only a few people could understand them, and those few people died without revealing the secret. A rare few are still in existence.''

Don Varga glanced both ways as if to verify no one was eavesdropping. ''I have one of those maps, *Senor* King. It shows where to find the richest gold mine in the world. And you are going to take me to it!''

Chapter Eight

Shakespeare McNair struggled up out of a clinging gray fog. He was lying on his right side. Pain lanced his head, his temples worst of all. He had a sour taste in his mouth, and his stomach was queasy.

A crackling noise was the first sound Shakespeare heard. Someone coughing was the second. He opened his eyes and blinked in the glare of a small fire less than twelve inches from his face. A low groan escaped his lips as he tried to roll onto his back. His wrists and ankles were bound, hampering him.

Hands fell onto his shoulder. He was roughly hauled onto his left side, so that he faced away from the flames. In front of him squatted a grungy character who, judging by the smell, had a lifelong aversion to water. "So you've finally come around, eh?" the man said. "Well, he said to wake him." Rising, the man walked toward sleeping figures scattered about a wide clearing.

Shakespeare's head began to clear. Overhead, stars

glittered. The position of the Big Dipper told him that it was the shank of the night. He had been unconscious for at least seven hours.

There was whispering. One of the prone shapes stood and approached, sleepily scratching his chin. Yawning, he squatted and smirked. "I'll say this for you, old man. You're as tough as rawhide."

"Jasper Flynt," Shakespeare said, wishing he could shove that smirk down Flynt's throat. "It was you who hit me with the rifle."

"Surprised you're still alive?"

"Somewhat," Shakespeare confessed. "What are you up to, you son of a bitch? Why did you try to make buzzard bait out of us?"

"All in good time, old-timer," Flynt said, stifling another yawn. "For now, the only thing you need to know is that you get to live for a while yet, unless you act up, in which case I'll slit your throat from ear to ear."

Shakespeare believed him. "Is all this just because Nate King beat the stuffing out of you?"

Flynt's features hardened. "I wouldn't remind me of that again, if I were you. Sooner than he expects, that bastard's going to get his due." A wicked smile creased his thin lips. "You just lie here and behave yourself. I'm going to catch some more sleep."

As his captor straightened, Shakespeare asked, "Was it you who attacked the King cabin the other night?"

"Me and a friend, yes." Flynt started to walk off.

"Why, Jasper? What did you hope to gain? You hadn't even met Nate then."

"No, but I knew roughly where his cabin was located, and I made the mistake of mentionin' it to that damn Spaniard. Varga decided he wanted to look King up. Just to pay a social call, he claimed. But I wasn't fooled. Varga was going to ask a lot of questions about Long's Peak and give the whole thing away. I couldn't let King get involved.''

"Give what away? Get involved with what?''

Flynt slid a hand under his arm and picked at his armpit. "Tomorrow, old man. We'll talk tomorrow.''

"But why go—'' Shakespeare began, and froze. In a blur of movement, the cutthroat had pressed a knife against his throat.

"You don't listen so well, do you, old-timer? Not another peep out of you, hear? I'm only keepin' you alive because you might be useful later on. But rile me again, and to hell with it.'' Flynt pressed on the hilt to accent his point. "If and when I feel the need, I'll tell you what this is all about. Until then, shut up. Savvy?''

Shakespeare dared not nod or speak. The cold steel might slice deeper.

Grunting, Jasper Flynt sheathed his long blade. "That's better.'' He walked off, remarking, "We've got a long day ahead of us tomorrow. I need to be rested up.''

Tittering drew Shakespeare's gaze to the grimy character standing guard.

"That Flynt sure is a card! Touchy as sin, ain't he, McNair?''

"Do I know you?''

"No, we ain't ever been introduced. But I know who you are. Hell, every coon who ever laid a beaver trap has heard of you.'' The man extended his right hand to shake. "I'm Jeb Calloway, from down Alabama way.''

Shakespeare just stared at him.

Realizing what he had done, Calloway blinked, then shamefacedly lowered his arm. "Sorry. I plumb forgot you was trussed up.''

"What's this all about, Jeb? What's Flynt up to?''

The Alabamian glanced toward the sleeping figures. "He'd gut me if I was to jabber."

"Whisper so he won't hear you."

Calloway licked his mouth and rubbed his palms on his pants. "Well, truth is, I don't know much. None of us do. Other than the fact we're all going to be filthy rich pretty soon."

"Did Flynt say how this miracle was going to come about?"

"Naw. He's too smart. He's playin' this real close to the vest, if you know what I mean."

"Where did you first meet him?"

"Oh, I've known Jasper for years. Most of the boys have. He only looked up those he felt he could trust. I was in a bar, half drunk, when he made me the offer."

"Where was this?" Any details Shakespeare could glean, however insignificant, might shed light on whatever Flynt was up to.

"St. Louis," Calloway said. "He rounded up all fourteen of us in St. Louis. We had to hustle some to get ready to leave in time. That crazy Spaniard didn't waste a minute once he hired Jasper."

"How does Varga fit into this?"

"I'm not too sure. Again, Jasper ain't been lavish with information. We've been doggin' the Spaniard's expedition for weeks now, and soon it'll pay off." The Alabamian sat down. A twig caught his notice. Picking it up, he pried at tobacco-stained teeth.

Shakespeare frowned and lay back. He had not learned much at all. His only hope now was that Nate track them down and rescue him. If not, well, he'd had a fine, long run, longer than most. He'd laughed and loved and never done harm except to those who asked for it. Maybe the Almighty would count that in his favor.

Beside him, the fire sizzled like a thing alive.

*   *   *

Nate King was awake before the first pale pink streak banded the eastern sky. Sentries patrolled the camp's perimeter, an extra man always near the horses since without their mounts and pack animals, the expedition must turn back to civilization.

Nate sat up and stretched. His family and Blue Water Woman were still asleep. He would let them rest a few more minutes yet. Standing, he turned, and was surprised to discover someone else already awake.

"I hope you will reconsider my offer, *Senor* King," Don Manuel de Varga said. He was seated on a crate, sipping coffee. "It means more to me than I can say."

Nate donned his ammo pouch and powder horn, stuck both pistols under his belt, and strolled over. Rosa was not far off, kneading dough. She looked up and smiled.

"What do you say, my friend?" Don Varga prompted.

Nate thought he had said it all the night before. He had made it clear that he would not serve as their guide. He wanted no part in the Spaniard's half-baked scheme. "I assumed we had settled this," he said as he helped himself to some of Rosa's delicious brew.

The Spaniard smiled thinly. "I am afraid that I am not a man who accepts defeat graciously. I need you, *Senor* King. I mean to have you help me, because without your aid, I could wander these mountains for years and not find the lost mine of Captain Pedro Valdez."

"Who?"

"A soldier in Spain's army. He and a small garrison were assigned to protect a tiny settlement built only forty miles south of here. Many people think that San Carlos, down on the Arkansas River, was our northernmost outpost, but they are mistaken."

Nate was one of them. Rumors had circulated for years, though, that the Spanish penetrated farther north than anyone ever suspected in search of the fabled Seven Cities of Gold. Here was proof.

"San Lupez, the settlement was called. Indians routinely came to trade with the settlers. One day, several showed up with some gold. Naturally, Captain Valdez was curious. He tried to persuade them to take him to where they found the ore, but they refused. Their people would not like it. The spot was taboo to outsiders."

Nate tried to think of all the tribes in the region who might have a secret source of the precious metal. There was only one he could think of, and if he was right, he most definitely wanted no part in the expedition. They would be going to their graves.

Varga continued the account. "Captain Valdez had to kill one before the other two would do as he wanted. He was taken to a cave high in the mountains, a cave lined thick with gold, so much gold that it made a man half mad to look at it."

"Valdez started to mine the ore?"

"Of course. But he had only scratched the surface when the Indians rose up in rebellion. The settlers were wiped out, every trace of the settlement destroyed. The good captain was lucky to escape with his life. Him, and a dozen soldiers. But he made a map, intending to come back one day. Unfortunately, circumstances prevented it."

"And now you have his map," Nate said. "So why do you need a guide?"

"Because the map is not as specific as I would like. Certain landmarks might be hard to locate." Don Varga stared at the emerald mountains. "I need someone who knows this area. *Senor* Flynt claimed he did. With him gone, you are the next logical choice."

Nate eased to the ground, his back to a crate. "Don

Varga, you've been open and honest with me. So I'll do you the same favor." He bobbed his chin at the formidable peaks. "Don't go up there. If your sons and daughter mean anything to you, you'll turn back while you still can."

"It is precisely because they mean everything to me that I am doing this, *senor*." Varga fondly regarded his slumbering brood. "They are my life, my joy. I must do what I can to restore our fortune, for their sake. I'll die a happy man if I know that they can go on living in the style to which they have become accustomed."

Nate drank more coffee, mulling how best to convince the Spaniard to change his mind. "Which tribe wiped out the settlement?"

"The Utes."

"I knew it," Nate said. The Utes were a proud, defiant people who had been holding their own against the Apaches and Comanches for generations.

Initially, the tribe had tried to drive Nate from the high valley. Over and over again, warriors were sent against him. Over and over, they failed. But the tribe was undeterred. For every warrior he slew, two more were ready to take their fallen friend's place.

His life had been a nightmare, one attack after another, for weeks and weeks on end. What made it worse was never knowing when the next attack would take place. Would it be when he went down to the lake for water? When he heeded nature's call? His nerves had frayed to the point where he jumped at shadows.

Ironically, the Utes ended the dispute by coming to him for help. As a worthy adversary, he had earned their respect. As an adopted Shoshone, he had been in an ideal position to parley a truce between the Utes and the Shoshones, who had clashed over which tribe could lay claim to a valley sacred to both.

Now the Utes left Nate pretty much alone. A prominent warrior had become his fast friend, and now and then stopped to visit. The rest avoided his valley, or watched his family from a distance.

Other whites were not so lucky. A couple of trappers had been killed the year before, stripped naked and scalped, after they had the gall to lay trap lines in Ute territory.

Nate scanned the camp. Was he looking at men and women already dead, who just did not know it yet? "Have you done much Indian-fighting?"

"*Sí*. The Apaches have plagued my *hacienda* for many years. They steal horses, kidnap women. But always we have driven them off. My *vaqueros* are a match for a number of red devils."

Where had Nate heard nonsense like that before? It was the sort of attitude that bred disaster. "I don't know what else I can say," he said frankly. "If you're bound and determined to be turned into worm food, it's your privilege. But I won't have any part in your suicide."

Don Varga pursed his lips. "I am most sorry to hear it, *senor*. My back is to the wall, as you Americans say. I must do what I must do."

"We all must," Nate said, figuring the matter was finally at an end.

Just about that time, Ignacio woke up and came over. "*Buenas días, padre,*" he greeted his father. To Nate, he merely nodded. Rosa brought him a cup of coffee, which he swilled in three gulps. "The sun will rise shortly," he said in English. "When do we leave, Father?"

"As soon as your brothers and the women wake up."

"They have slept enough," Ignacio said. Cupping both hands to his mouth, he hollered, "Wake up, everyone! Wake up!" He yelled the same in Spanish.

Don Varga winked at Nate. "With him for a son, who needs a rooster?"

The fires were rekindled. After a hurried, simple breakfast of *tortillas* and coffee, twenty *vaqueros* were picked to accompany Don Varga. As blankets and saddles were being thrown on horses, his three sons came over.

"Are we all going with you, Father?" Diego asked hopefully.

"You are, and Ignacio. Martin will stay."

The middle son had hardly spoken ten words to Nate since they met. The previous evening, Martin had stayed to himself, as quiet as a church mouse. Nate pegged him as a shy, dutiful son who never gave his father a hard time. So he was surprised when Martin objected.

"Why must I always be the one to stay behind? Let Ignacio do it for once."

Don Varga dismissed the request with a gesture. "You are more dependable. I leave you in charge. Do not fail me."

Martin was not appeased. "Why not Diego? Surely he is old enough to take the responsibility."

"Or why not Luisa?" Don Varga rejoined. "Or Francicsa? Or Rosa, perhaps?"

Ignacio found that hilarious. Slapping his side, he forked leather. "Cheer up, brother," he told Martin. "When you can shoot and ride as well as I can, Father will rely on you also when there is trouble."

Daggers shot from Martin's eyes, but he did not raise a fuss.

Winona, meanwhile, had saddled Evelyn's animal and was ready to climb on her own. She had slept fitfully, in part due to worry about Shakespeare, in part because she did not feel comfortable being with the Vargas.

Why that should be was a mystery. Most had been

pleasantly friendly, especially the three daughters. They were spirited, sweet girls, full of vitality and good humor.

Ignacio was another story. A number of times Winona caught him staring at her as if he wished she were dead. And she would never forget the stinging comments he made.

Winona had met his kind before. Bigots, Nate called them. Ignacio was one of those who hated her simply because she was an Indian. Such people built walls of hatred around them that no amount of kindness or friendliness could ever break down.

To be fair, Winona had known Shoshones and members of other tribes who were rabid haters of whites and Mexicans and anyone else not Indian.

Racial hatred was not limited to any one culture. All were afflicted equally. It amazed Winona that people could hold so much hate in their hearts, yet it was a sad fact of life.

The widespread bigotry among whites was one of the reasons Winona balked whenever Nate brought up the idea of traveling to New York to visit his brothers. Many whites loathed half-breeds, as the children of mixed marriages were called, even more than they hated full-blooded Indians. She feared for Zach and Evelyn if they were to make the journey.

"Are you ready, Winona?"

The question brought Winona back to the here and now. Blue Water Woman had already mounted and was waiting for her. She swung lithely up, her rifle under her arm. "I am ready."

Zach hovered nearby. He had appointed himself his mother's and sister's protector, and he never let them out of his sight. Whenever Ignacio came around, he would rest his thumb on the hammer of his Hawken, fully prepared to put a hole in the man if Ignacio gave him cause.

But now it was Diego who came toward them. Zach met the youngest Varga's smile with a tentative one of his own, and said, "Something I can do for you?"

Diego Varga's smile widened. "I just thought we could talk and get to know each other better. We did not have much of a chance last night."

"We're about ready to head out," Zach reminded him.

Diego was more interested in the Hawken. "That is a fine rifle you have. My father bought me this one in England." He held out an expensive long gun polished until it gleamed. "Perhaps one day we can have a shooting match. Your piece against mine."

"Shucks. It wouldn't hardly be fair," Zach said.

"Why not?"

"No gun made can outshoot a Hawken."

"You think so? But isn't it the shooter, not his weapon, that counts most?" Diego caressed the barrel of his rifle. "I am young, like you, but I practiced every day back home. Practiced until I can hit a small coin nailed to a wall at twenty paces."

"That's some shooting," Zach allowed. "When this is over with, we'll set up targets and go at it."

Nate was happy to see his son getting along with Varga's youngest. Don Varga and Ignacio were walking their mounts westward, giving everyone plenty of time to fall into step behind them. Nate caught up and said, "I can't thank you enough for doing this. Not many folks would go out of their way for a stranger."

"Nonsense," Don Varga replied. "You have shared my food, been company to my family. You are much more than a stranger. I consider you a friend."

"*Gracias,*" Nate used one of the few Spanish words he knew.

Don Varga shifted and raised an arm to give the

signal to head out. Instead, he gave a start and forked two fingers at Winona, Blue Water Woman, and Evelyn. "Why are they on horseback?"

It should have been obvious, Nate reasoned. "They're going along."

"Women and a child? What if we catch up to the savages who attacked you?" Don Varga clucked like an irate hen. "No, I will not have it. Tell them to stay behind. They will be perfectly safe. Martin will see to that."

Nate hid a grin. The old gentleman did not know Indian women very well. They did not take to being coddled. Why, most could ride as well as any man and wield a knife or bow with great skill. "I'm afraid not."

"How is that?"

"Where I go, my family goes. And a herd of horses couldn't hold Blue Water Woman back with her husband's life at stake."

Don Varga was none too pleased. He bent toward Ignacio, and father and son whispered back and forth. "Very well," Don Varga sighed at length. "If it cannot be helped, we must live with it."

"Don't fret yourself," Nate said. "My wife and McNair's can take care of themselves. And my children can hold their own better than most their age."

"Just to be sure, I will watch over them, Father," Ignacio volunteered. Hauling on his reins, he trotted back down the line and took up a position behind the two wives.

Winona did not like having him so close. He smiled at her, but it was a smile empty of warmth. She moved her mare so that Evelyn was between it and Blue Water Woman's sorrel.

The *vaqueros* and servants left behind nervously watched their departing comrades. Rosa waved, and a husky *vaquero* waved back.

Yellow and orange streaks painted the eastern sky. In a column of twos and threes the rescuers rode briskly, Don Varga's splendid Arabian prancing as if it were in a parade.

A figure on foot appeared in the distance, jogging toward them at a tireless pace. It was a Maricopa. Don Varga listened intently to the warrior's report, and grunted. "They have found the gully you told me about, *Senor* King. Chivari waits for us there."

"You sent them on earlier?" Nate asked, impressed by the Spaniard's efficiency.

"Before you woke up. Time is critical. More critical than you know."

"How so?"

"I can only spare one day to search. If we have not found your friend by late afternoon, I must turn back."

Nate was dumbfounded. With the rugged terrain and the head start the culprits had, overtaking them by nightfall was highly unlikely. "You can't!" he protested.

"On the contrary. I can, and I will."

Chapter Nine

The circulation in Shakespeare McNair's arms had been cut off for so long, they were numb. He tried wriggling his fingers to keep the blood flowing, and for a while that worked. But by the middle of the morning he could not feel his fingers or his wrists. By noon, he had lost all sensation clear up to his shoulders.

His legs fared better. Although his ankles were linked together under the belly of his white mare by a short length of stout cord, his thick moccasins protected them.

"How about untying my hands for a bit?" Shakespeare at last complained. "I give you my word that I won't act up."

Jeb Calloway was leading the mare by a rope. Glancing back, he said, "Sorry, old coon. But Jasper threatened to bust my noggin wide open if I let you get away." His left cheek bulged with chewing tobacco.

"Just for a short while," Shakespeare asked. "I won't do anything. Hell, I can't even move my arms."

Calloway spat brown juice, wiped the back of his mouth with a sleeve, and said, "If it were up to me, McNair, I'd take the gamble. I ain't about to rile Jasper, though. He's worse than a rabid wolf when his dander is up. Why, once I saw him chop the ear off a feller who wouldn't stop belchin'. It annoyed him so powerful bad, he went half-mad."

"A man with a temper like his can turn on anyone, at any time," Shakespeare said. "You'd do well to fight shy of this whole outfit as soon as you can."

Calloway tittered. "Nice try. Jasper warned me you could talk rings around a tree. But save your breath. I'm too slick to fall for any of your tricks."

As slick as molasses, Shakespeare thought. He attempted to swing his arms from side to side, to no avail. Chafing at his helplessness, he scanned the line of riders. They were as cold-blooded a bunch as he had ever come across. He could see it in their eyes.

They were cast from the same mold as Jasper Flynt. Outcasts, cutthroats, the dregs of human society, men who would murder their own mothers or sisters without hesitation if there was money to be made in it. Flynt had picked well.

A fluttering groan came from the last man in line, who rode slumped over, barely able to stay in the saddle. A dark stain marked the front of his buckskin shirt, and his lips were flecked with pink spittle.

"Poor Spence," Calloway commented. "He ain't long for this world. Took one in the lung."

In Shakespeare's opinion, the man got what he deserved. "Aren't we going to stop soon to rest?"

"When Jasper says," Calloway responded. "He's afeared them greasers are on our trail, so we might push on 'til nightfall. That man never tires like the rest of us. Sometimes I'd swear he ain't even human.''

Varga was after them? At Nate's request, Shakespeare bet. Shifting with difficulty, careful not to slide too far to either side, he studied their back trail. All morning they had been winding deeper and higher into the Rockies. Now they were on a narrow game trail hundreds of feet up, on a slope dotted with pines and boulders.

Not many miles to the southwest reared the snow-capped summit of Long's Peak. The massive, stark mountain towered to the sky, scowling down at the world like an earth and stone juggernaut out of mythology. Dark clouds floated across its jagged face; clefts scarred its pitted surface.

Shakespeare gave up looking for sign of the Spaniard's party. The dense woodland below could hide an entire army. As he faced forward, the slope leveled off, widening into a small plateau dominated by slabs of rock scores of feet high. In the shadow of a sheer monolith, Jasper Flynt drew rein.

"Ten minutes, boys. That's all we can spare."

The cutthroats ignored McNair. Dismounting, they stretched their legs or sprawled out, some treating themselves to jerky or pemmican, others taking swigs from water skins.

"How about me?" Shakespeare asked.

"What about you?" Jasper Flynt demanded, ambling over. "You'll get something to eat tonight, not before."

"Let me down."

"When buffaloes fly." Biting into a piece of jerked deer meat, Flynt slowly chewed while grinning sadistically.

Shakespeare was resigned to enduring more torment. "You still haven't told me what this is all about," he remarked. "There aren't enough of you to wipe out Varga's party, if that's what you're thinking. Sure, you could sell their jewelry and guns and horses for a tidy sum to the right buyer, but in a year or so you'd be broke again, right back where you started.''

Flynt snorted. ''Is that what you figure? That I went to all this bother just to rob that Spanish bastard?'' He wagged the jerky. ''Hell, McNair, you may hate my guts, but give me more credit than that. I ain't after no measly grubstake here. I'm out to make myself and all my boys as rich as King Midas.''

Shakespeare made a show of squinting at the azure sky. ''Methinks, Diomed, that you have been out in the sun too long.''

''Diomed?''

''That same Diomed's a false-hearted rogue, a most unjust knave. I will no more trust him when he leers than I will a serpent when he hisses. He will spend his mouth and promise, like Brabbler the hound.''

Flynt stopped chewing. ''Oh. I get it. You're quotin' that English feller. Heard you did that a lot.'' Jasper chuckled. ''You're one crazy son of a bitch, you old idiot. You know that?''

''Slanders, sir. For the satirical rogue says here that old men have gray beards, that their faces are wrinkled, their eyes purging thick amber and plum-tree gum, and that they have a plentiful lack of wit, together with most weak hams. All which, sir, though I most powerfully and potently believe, yet I hold it not honesty to have it thus set down. For yourself, sir, shall grow old as I am, if like a crab you could go backward.''

''I ain't no damn crab!'' Flynt growled. ''Stop jabberin' that nonsense.''

Shakespeare could not resist. ''For if the sun breed maggots in a dead dog, being a god kissing carrion—have you a daughter?''

''I'm warnin' you!'' Flynt said, lowering a hand to

one of the pistols under his belt. "You think I don't know that you're pokin' fun of me? Just 'cause I can't read nor write doesn't mean I'm stupid." Jerking the pistol out, he pointed it squarely at McNair's face. "I can shoot straight enough, remember."

"Too true," Shakespeare conceded, and did not press his luck any further. "So if it isn't robbery, then why? What do you reckon to gain by all this, Jasper?"

Flynt glowered a moment, then dipped his arm. "No, I can't kill you yet. Might need you to deal with King."

"What does Nate have to do with this?"

"Everything, now that I cut out on Varga. The greaser will need your pup to help him find the lost mine. I was hopin' to wipe both of you out and go back and beg Varga for a second chance, but King and his brood got away, thanks to you."

"Mine?" Shakespeare repeated, mystified.

Flynt took another bite. "You have no notion of what I'm talkin' about," he said smugly. "Ain't as smart as you like to pretend, what with those fancy quotes and all."

"Enlighten me. Rub my nose in my stupidity. There are no mines in these parts. Not unless . . ." Shakespeare paused, recollecting a vague tall tale bandied about years ago. "Can it be? The Spanish really found gold?"

"And Varga has a map showin' right where to find it," Flynt divulged. "You see, when he hired me, he was real secretive. Take me to Long's Peak, he says. Help me find a few landmarks, he says. He let it go at that, figurin' I was too stupid to catch on. Just like you."

"But you did," Shakespeare prompted.

"Bet your ass I did! I spied on the bastard. Went to the hotel where he was stayin' and climbed up a

115

spout to his window. Heard him and a couple of his sons jawin'."

"Pretty clever."

Flynt's chest swelled. "Damn right it was. My Spanish ain't near as good as my English, but I can get by in a pinch. I learned enough to piece together what he was up to."

"And you decided then and there that you wanted the gold for yourself."

"Why should that stinkin' Spaniard get it all?" Flynt's eyes lit with an inner glow. "I tell you, I went down that spout like it was greased with hog fat. It didn't take but a few hours to round up enough boys I could count on. Had 'em dog our trail, and every so often I'd slip off and double back."

"Enough?" Shakespeare said, gazing at the unkempt band. "Varga's *vaqueros* outnumber you four to one. And they're tough, Jasper. Real tough. When I was down to Santa Fe, I saw *vaqueros* go up against Apaches. Think about that. Think about what they'll do to you if you try to harm their *patrón*."

"I ain't scared of no greasers," Flynt declared hotly. "And numbers ain't everything." He paused, then added craftily, "There are ways of whittlin' Varga's bunch down to size. I got me a brainstorm that you wouldn't believe!"

Shakespeare would not put anything past his captor. Whatever Flynt had cooked up would be unspeakably vicious. He was worried for the Vargas, but even more concerned about those he loved the most. Would Nate help Varga locate the mine if Varga asked? Possibly. And what about Blue Water Woman, Winona, and the children? They were bound to go wherever Nate did.

Jasper Flynt began to pace and talk, more to himself than to the mountain man. "All I got to do now is lay low until your pup finds the mine for the Spaniard. After that, I'll play it by ear. Maybe let 'em dig out a few tons of ore before I make my move.'' Flynt rubbed his hands together in anticipation. "That's best. Why should we tire ourselves out when they can do the work for us?''

"You've got it all planned.''

Nodding, Flynt tore into the jerky. "My whole stinkin' life I've been grubbin' to make ends meet. Most of the time, I barely have enough in my poke to make it jingle. Soon it'll all be different! Six months from now I'll be livin' in a mansion in New Orleans. Servants will wait on me hand and foot. I'll have the best clothes, the finest carriages. And women! Pretty ones that bathe regular and smell nice. A new female every night.'' Dazzled by his dream, Flynt stopped. "Folks will treat me like a gentleman. Call me 'sir.' I'll *be* somebody, McNair.''

"A wolf in sheep's clothing is still a wolf.''

Flynt spun, his lips curling back from his teeth. "Even wolves can grow fat and lazy. When I'm lyin' in a plush bed with a naked beauty at my side, I'll think of you, McNair. I'll think of your fancy quotes and your high-and-mighty airs, and I'll drink a toast to your bleached bones.''

"We're going too slow,'' Nate King said.

Don Manuel de Varga reined up. Taking a silk handkerchief from a jacket pocket, he mopped his sweating brow. "Would that we had wings on our feet, *senor,* so we could fly to your friend's aid. We do the best we can.''

Nate knew that. Since leaving the gully where the ambush occurred, Varga had spurred his men as fast as was prudent. Blaze marks left by three of the Maricopas had guided them ever higher into the mountains. Overhead, the sun gleamed like a gem in a diadem. On all sides the wilderness pulsed with life;

birds, squirrels, chipmunks, and deer romped through a verdant paradise.

"I can make better time myself," Nate said. "You stick with your *vaqueros* and I'll ride on ahead."

Don Varga pushed his *sombrero* back on his head. "I do not think that best, *Senor* King. I do not want anything to happen to you."

While flattered by the man's consideration, Nate had McNair to think of. "At this rate, we'll never catch up by nightfall. I'm going on."

The Spaniard pondered, his dark eyes inscrutable. "Very well. But I insist you take Chivari along."

The bronzed Maricopa stood a few yards away, patiently waiting to lead them on. Hours of constant climbing had not tired him one whit. Nate had the impression that Chivari could run all day and all night and be as fresh as a daisy the next morning.

"Fair enough," Nate said to forestall an argument. "I'll be right back." Bringing the stallion around, he rode down the line to where his family and Blue Water Woman were spaced close together.

"We are going with you," Winona said before her mate could get a word out of his mouth.

Nate had to grin. "One of these days you'll tell me how you do that trick. But I'd rather you stayed." Giving a barely noticeable bob of his head toward Evelyn, he said, "You'd only slow me down."

Zach was quick to put two and two together. "I wouldn't, Pa," he protested. "I can keep up, easy."

"So can I," Blue Water Woman said. She had held back long enough. Half the day had been wasted, and they were no closer to her man than they had been when the sun rose.

Nate was naturally inclined to refuse. But what right did he have to deny her, when it was Blue Water Woman's husband whose life hung in the balance?

As for his son, he said, "Zach, it's better if you stay with your ma and sister."

"Ahhhh, geez."

"No arguments, boy," Nate said. "Watch your mother's back, you hear? Trust no one."

"Does that include me, *senor*?"

Unnoticed, Ignacio Varga had ridden up. Nate looked him right in the eyes and replied, "It includes *everyone,* mister. If anything happens to my family while I'm gone, I'll hold you and your father personally responsible."

"What could happen?" Ignacio said, irritated. "What kind of men do you take my father and me for?"

Nate did not answer. Placing his hand on Winona's, he tenderly squeezed. "I wish there was another way. Take care."

"Go," Winona urged, a knot of raw anxiety forming in her breast when he did so. Blue Water Woman gave her a smile of encouragement and she returned the favor, but she did not feel as self-assured as she pretended. Moving her mare closer to Evelyn, she waved when Nate glanced around.

Leaving his loved ones was a trial in itself. Nate waved, then blew a kiss to Evelyn. One of the *vaqueros* snickered, never knowing how close he came to losing his teeth. Nate faced around and saw Don Varga and Chivari shoulder to shoulder, whispering. The Maricopa spotted him and said something. Immediately Varga straightened in the saddle.

"Chivari is ready, *senor*. I told him to catch up with the other Maricopas as swiftly as he can."

"Just so he keeps up with us," Nate said, and prodded the stallion into a trot.

Blue Water Woman lashed her sorrel with the reins. She was opposed to having the Maricopa along, but since Nate had accepted it, she did not protest.

Nate had had all morning to reflect on the attack. That it had been white men had been obvious, confirmed by the tracks of more than a dozen shod horses found in the vicinity of the gully.

But who had been behind it?

Nate would be the first to admit that he'd made a few too many enemies. The personal code by which he lived was partly to blame. He would not abide being insulted, or laid a hand on, or being threatened. Since he did not do any of those things to others, he required that others treat him with the same degree of respect.

It was inevitable that Nate would clash with others who did not share his outlook. The wilderness bred hard men. Living in the mountains took a special breed who were tempered by the ordeals they daily endured until they were as hard as the land itself.

Back in the States, such men were lions among sheep. They did as they pleased, when they pleased. They never backed down, never turned the other cheek. Like the prow of a great ship plowing through the sea, they plowed through life. Anyone who got in their way was trampled under or pushed aside.

Nate was one of these men, but his hard exterior hid a soul more sensitive than he would ever confess. He was gentle to the core, as gentle as a kitten to everyone who treated him as he treated them. But let a ruffian challenge him, let a rowdy try to run roughshod over him, and the kitten became a raging mountain lion.

That was why Nate had gone up against more than a few unscrupulous characters. Thieves, killers, roughnecks, even cannibals, you name it, he had taught them the error of their ways.

The logical question for him to ask, then, was whether one of his old enemies was to blame for the ambush and the attack at his cabin. He could think of no one, mainly because ninety-nine percent of them were dead, and the few who weren't had quit that part of the country long ago.

That left a recent enemy. And Nate had made only one in many months: Jasper Flynt.

Yet blaming Flynt raised more questions than it answered. The attack at the cabin had taken place *before* they met, so what possible reason could Flynt have had for seeking him out and trying to blow his head off? And if Flynt was indeed to blame, who were the men riding with him? It was not as if Flynt could pluck an entire band of cutthroats out of an empty beaver hat.

The only way to answer the question was to overtake the gang of killers. To that end, Nate held to a trot where the lay of the land permitted. By two o'clock he had covered almost as much ground as Don Varga had all morning.

The Maricopa kept up the whole way. At a tireless dogtrot, he trailed them, and when Nate finally stopped to give their mounts a breather, the horses were breathing harder than Chivari.

"Another two hours," Blue Water Woman guessed, judging by the hoofprints. She took it as a good omen that they had not found Shakespeare's body. Whoever was to blame wanted her husband alive. For how long, though?

"Don Varga plans to turn back by sunset, but we're not about to," Nate said. "If we have to, we'll light torches and track at night. I'm not stopping until Shakespeare is safe."

Blue Water Woman was jolted by the news. "Why is he turning back so soon?"

"He's gold hungry," Nate disclosed. "He's hunting for a lost Spanish mine, and he's not about to delay any longer than he has to."

"I wish I had known this last night," Blue Water

Woman said. "I would not have stayed in their camp." She had only done so because she counted on Varga's help in tracking Shakespeare down.

Nate felt a twinge of guilt for not sharing the information sooner. "He didn't tell me until we were about ready to ride out," he explained.

"I should have seen this coming," Blue Water Woman said. "I do not trust Varga, or his eldest son." The sorrel fidgeted, so she stroked its neck. "I do not trust any man who treats women as they do."

"How's that?"

"Varga's daughters told us that they cannot marry until their father says. That they must do as he wants at all times or he punishes them severely. And that if they were to so much as kiss a young man of their choice, Varga would have him cut to pieces."

Among most Indian tribes, Nate had learned, parents were nowhere near as strict as their white counterparts. Hitting a child was unheard of. Even raising the voice was frowned on. So by Flathead standards, Don Varga was a tyrant.

But a person should never judge someone else's bushel by their own peck. In Europe, where suitors flocked to pretty maidens like bears to honey, parents had to be stricter or risk having their daughters socially shamed, or worse.

Young single women who lost their virtue before wedlock were branded as wanton, a stigma they carried with them the rest of their days. No upstanding man would marry them. They were left to fend for themselves, their prospects dim, often making ends meet by doing what had brought about the stigma in the first place.

It was unfair. Nate did not deny that. Someday, maybe it would change. Until then, men like Varga would be overly protective of their daughters for their own good.

"Where is the Maricopa?" Blue Water Woman suddenly asked.

Nate glanced up in alarm. Chivari was gone. While they talked, the warrior had slipped away. "Come on!" he said, and hurried to the southwest. Blaze marks were spaced at regular intervals. Here and there he came on moccasin tracks that proved the Maricopa was not far ahead.

Try as he might, Nate could not narrow the gap. He did not spot Chivari again until he climbed to the rim of a plateau dotted by enormous slabs of rock. To his surprise, all four Maricopas were waiting.

"Trail gone," Chivari said in chopped English. "We not go on."

Nate rode past them, scouring the barren earth. Where there should have been plenty of tracks, there were none. Someone had erased every last one. Swish marks betrayed how the deed was done. The dusty loincloths of the four Maricopas added proof. He roved the far edge. Finding nothing, he covered the opposite slope, which was so rocky his stallion did not leave prints. It was the same. The Maricopas had done their job well. His mentor's abductors had seemingly vanished into thin air.

Furious, Nate climbed back up to the plateau. His intent was to make the Maricopas say why they had wiped out the sign, and reveal which direction the cutthroats had taken. Again, however, he was foiled.

Chivari and the others were gone.

Chapter Ten

Winona King was uneasy from the moment Nate left. She was distrustful of the Spaniards and their Mexican *vaqueros,* many of whom made no attempt to hide the spite in their eyes when they looked at her. They despised her simply because she was an Indian.

Her uneasiness was proven justified by what Don Varga did half an hour after Nate and Blue Water Woman departed. On coming to a meadow, Don Varga halted his men. At first she assumed it was to let the horses rest awhile. Then she saw the *vaqueros* stripping saddles and settling down for an extended stay.

Bewildered, Winona marched over to where Don Varga and Ignacio roosted on a low mound. She held Evelyn's hand; Zach was at her elbow.

Varga and his eldest son were chatting in Spanish. They saw her but did not stop their conversation. Taking another step, Winona interrupted. ''Pardon me,

Don Varga. But you seem to have no intention of going any farther.''

"True, *Senora* King," the Spaniard said suavely.

"But my husband will need our help if he overtakes the men who ambushed us," Winona said. "We must ride on right away."

Don Varga glanced at Ignacio, who grinned like a fox that had outwitted hounds. "I have decided to wait here for your husband to return."

"You cannot!" Winona objected. "The men who took McNair will be on their guard. My husband cannot save Shakespeare with only Blue Water Woman to help him."

The Spaniard's jaw muscles twitched. "I can do whatever I want, *senora*," he said in an icy tone. "Rest assured that I have everything well in hand. Nate will be back by dark, or shortly after. He will come to no harm. You have my word."

Winona could scarcely credit what she was hearing. "Were you not listening earlier? He is not going to quit until he catches up to Shakespeare. How can you abandon him this way? He is relying on you to be there when he will need you the most. And what about your scouts, the Maricopas? Will you desert them, as well?"

Ignacio laughed. "Chivari and the others know what to do. They will be here soon enough. Wait and see."

Winona did not see the sense in any of this. "I must insist," she said. "Please, Don Varga, we must go on before it is too late."

"No."

"Very well," Winona said stiffly. "My children and I will take our leave of you, then. We will tell my husband that you are not going to help, as you said you would."

Don Varga sighed. "Two things, *senora*. First, I told your husband before we ever left camp that I could only devote one day to the search. Second, it would be unwise of you to ride off unescorted. These mountains teem with hostile heathens and wild beasts. You should stay with us."

"I am sorry. We cannot." Winona turned to go.

"Hold on, *Senora* King," Don Varga said. "Evidently I did not make myself sufficiently clear. I am not *asking* you to stay. I am *telling* you that you will." Smiling, he gestured past them.

Winona looked, and her blood ran cold. *Vaqueros* were unsaddling the Kings' horses, unbidden. "What are they doing?" she demanded. "Order them to stop!"

"I am afraid I cannot," Don Varga said. "I have only your best interests at heart, believe me. Make yourselves as comfortable as you can. We will be here for several hours, at least."

Releasing Evelyn, Winona gripped her Hawken with both hands. Something was dreadfully, terribly wrong. She had to get her children out of there right away.

Zach shared his mother's sentiments. He had never liked Ignacio, and trusted him even less. The father he had taken for a bossy but basically kindly old man. Now that Don Varga had turned against them, Zach was bound and determined to leave and help his pa. He started to raise his rifle.

Don Varga, surprisingly, still smiled. "I would not be so hasty, were I you." He nodded to their left.

Six *vaqueros* had them covered.

"A word from me," Don Varga said, "and they will shoot. To maim, of course, since a Varga does not kill women or children. But it will be most unpleasant for all of us. So do yourselves a favor and place your guns on the ground at your feet. *Por favor.*"

Winona was in a quandary. Her man needed her, and a Shoshone woman never let her mate down. But Varga had the upper hand. Indeed, she gathered that he had planned this all along, that they were no more than pawns to him, to be played with as he saw fit. So mad she saw red, she lowered the Hawken and placed both pistols beside it.

Zach hesitated. *If* he could snap his rifle up fast enough, and *if* he could cover Don Varga before the *vaqueros* fired, he could force Varga to do as they wanted. He tensed.

"No!" Winona said softly but urgently. "Do not sacrifice yourself. Your sister and I need you alive, my son. Together, we can find a way out of this."

Zach still hesitated. A jerk on his rifle was all it would take. Just a quick jerk.

"Please, Zach," Evelyn said. "I don't want you hurt."

Ignacio stood. "Really, boy. Are you as stupid as most 'breeds? Our father would be upset if I or my brothers were to shoot you, so we won't, but our *vaqueros* will riddle you with holes. Go ahead. Shoot. I will dance on your grave."

Zach had never hated anyone before as much as he hated Ignacio Varga at that moment. He wished that he was older and bigger so he could tear into that mocking countenance with his fists flying. As it was, every nerve quivering with indignation, he deposited his guns on the grass.

"Excellent!" Don Varga said. "That was not so hard, was it? Now sit and rest. You are welcome to share our coffee when it is done."

"I want nothing more from you, ever," Winona said. "Except an explanation."

"All in good time, woman," Don Varga responded. "Everything will be clear as soon as your husband shows up." Leaning back, he nodded at a shaded spot at the meadow's edge. "There is an ideal spot to spread out your blanket."

Winona deliberately began to walk farther into the meadow so she would spot Nate that much sooner. Varga's upraised hand stopped her.

"Again you misunderstand. I did not leave it up to you. You *will* sit under those trees, out of the way, and you will not cry out when your husband arrives." Don Varga snapped his fingers. "Pedro, if you please."

The six *vaqueros* surrounded the Kings. A short man who wore a yellow sash and jingling spurs motioned, saying, "After you, *senora*."

To be thwarted at every turn was humbling. Winona draped an arm protectively over Evelyn's slim shoulders and walked to where their belongings had been piled. Collecting a blanket and a parfleche filled with pemmican, she walked to the spot Don Varga had selected and gave the blanket to Zach to spread out.

Zach watched the *vaqueros* out of the corner of his eye. If only one would step close enough and let down his guard! But they were too savvy. They sat ten feet away, at ease, their rifles across their legs.

Pedro looked elsewhere when Winona glared at him. "I am most sorry, *senora*," he said, "but we must obey our *patrón*."

Evelyn leaned against her mother, distraught. "What do we do, Ma?" she asked. "What do we do?"

Hugging her daughter, Winona had to face the truth. "There is nothing we can do, little one. We are at their mercy."

* * *

Nate King was not conscious of the passage of time. Simmering with resentment, he retraced their route, anxious to confront Manuel de Varga. He tried not to think of Shakespeare, alone and helpless, or what might happen to his friend because of Varga's treachery.

Blue Water Woman was also somber. Her hopes of rescuing her husband had been dashed, and she blamed the Maricopas. The four warriors must pay for what they had done.

As the minutes became hours and the afternoon waned, it dawned on Nate that they should have met up with Don Varga's party by then. Had Varga gone back already? His question was answered by tendrils of smoke to the northeast. Based on the location, he deduced that Varga had stopped shortly after they separated. His anger mounted.

Nate covered the last mile at a gallop. Bursting into a meadow, he spied Varga and Ignacio at their ease on a low mound and angled toward them. Close by squatted the Maricopas. In his angry state, he did not bother to survey the rest of the meadow. It was a mistake.

"What the hell are you trying to pull, mister?" Nate bellowed as he brought the black stallion to a halt. Vaulting from the saddle, he stormed up the mound.

Unruffled, Don Varga savored a sip of coffee. "Calm yourself, *amigo*," he said. "Why are you so disturbed?"

"You know damn well why," Nate said, and slapped the tin cup from the Spaniard's hand. Varga flushed but did not lift a finger to defend himself. "What are you up to?"

Ignacio sprang erect, fists clenched. "Beware, *gringo*! No one mistreats my *padre*. Ever!"

"Hush, son," Don Varga said. "We will hear

Senor King out. He has a grievance he would like to air."

The man's calm demeanor agitated Nate even more. "Grievance!" he exploded. "That's a fine word for what you did. *Why?*" He grabbed the front of Varga's jacket. "Why did you have the Maricopas erase the sign?"

Ignacio Varga coiled, his hand on the hilt of his dagger. "Take your hands off him, *Americano!*" he warned.

Nate was aware of *vaqueros* rushing from every direction, but he paid them no heed. Only the truth would satisfy him, even if he had to wring Manuel Varga's neck to get it. "Why?" he repeated.

Don Varga might as well have been carved from granite for all the emotion he showed. "I told you, my friend. I made it plain that I could not spend more than a day searching for McNair. When it grew apparent that you were not willing to give up no matter how long you had to hunt, I took steps to stop you."

"You did *what?*" Nate said, rankled by the man's gall.

"I instructed Chivari to catch up to the other Maricopas before you could. I told him to make sure that you could not track the *bandidos*—"

Nate lost his temper. He shook Varga as a panther might shake a buck. "What gave you the right? Do you have any notion of what you've done?"

A hint of movement gave Nate a split second to react. He let go of Varga and pivoted, bringing his rifle up in time to block the downward sweep of Ignacio's dagger. The hothead slammed into him and they both crashed to the ground, tumbling down the mound to the bottom. Nate had to release the Hawken to clasp Ignacio's wrist as the keen steel sought his throat.

Locked together, they grappled, Ignacio livid, nostrils flared. Nate twisted, slammed his fist into Ignacio's stomach, and heaved his legs upward. It enabled him to spring into a crouch, but that was as far as he got. Hands seized both arms.

"Hold him!" Don Varga commanded.

Nate glanced at the two *vaqueros*. Others were moving in to encircle him. Still others had rifles trained on Blue Water Woman. He relaxed as if in defeat, and when the two *vaqueros* let their grips slacken, he erupted like a volcano, driving a foot into the groin of the man on the right even as he hauled on his left arm and flung the other *vaquero* as if the man were a flea.

"Damn you!" Nate roared, and threw himself up the mound at Manuel Varga. *Vaqueros* swarmed over him, four, five, six of them, their combined weight bearing him to the ground where brute strength failed. He swung lustily, punching faces, jabbing throats, kicking and thrashing.

"Do not hurt him!" Don Varga cried. "The man who does will be shot!" Catching himself, he repeated it in Spanish.

Nate fought with the silent ferocity of his breed. A frontiersman never succumbed, not while life animated his limbs. Nate knocked one of the *vaqueros* off him, upended another with a well-placed kick. Knuckles scraped his cheek, pounded his iron jaw. A boot caught him in the stomach.

"Hold him!" someone thundered.

More *vaqueros* piled on. Nate felt his arms pinned. Someone grasped his left ankle and was treated to a brutal swing of his right foot. Then his legs were held flat under irresistible pressure.

Panting from the exertion, stinging from bruises and scrapes, trembling with the intensity of his rage, Nate glowered at Don Varga. "So help me—!"

Wearing patience as if it were armor, the Spaniard

walked down and sank to one knee. "Do not be hasty, my friend. What I have done, I have done because I had to."

"*Why?*" Nate said again. "What can you gain?"

"Your cooperation," Don Varga said, and folded his hands. "I have been honest with you from the beginning, my friend. I told you that I needed your assistance in finding the mine."

"Is that was this is all about?"

"What else? Nothing matters to me except restoring my family's wealth and prestige." Don Varga mustered a smile that had no effect on Nate. "Tomorrow I move my people into the mountains on the last leg of our journey. To succeed, I require your services. Now that you can no longer track your friend, you have no excuse not to help me."

"You son of a bitch," Nate said. "You'd sacrifice a man who never did you any wrong just so you can get your hands on the gold that much sooner."

"Have I ever pretended otherwise?" Don Varga answered. "Do not blame me for doing exactly as I said I would do. Blame Jasper Flynt, if you must fault anyone. If he had not run out on us, I would have been content to question you about Long's Peak and whether you knew about the legend, and gone my way."

Nate burned with white-hot wrath. "So now you expect me to behave and do all I can to locate the mine? You must be *loco,* mister."

"Oh, I think you can be persuaded." Don Varga grinned and spoke in Spanish to two of his men, who rushed off and were back in no time, prodding Winona, Zach, and Evelyn at gunpoint.

Sickly giddiness churned Nate's insides. "You wouldn't," he declared.

Winona ached to go to him, but when she took a step, a *vaquero* jabbed her with a rifle. "Refuse him, husband!'' she called out. "We will stand by you!"

Nate's mouth had gone desert dry. He had been licked, and licked as neatly as you please. "What happens after you locate the mine?"

Don Varga rose. "I am not a callous killer, *senor*. Once I have mined all the ore we need and we are ready to leave for Santa Fe, you and your family will be released unharmed. On this, you have the solemn word of Manuel de Varga."

Blue Water Woman had been a furious onlooker to the sequence of events. She did not resist when a *vaquero* pulled her off the sorrel and another snatched her rifle and pistols. Now she tried to brush past them to get at Don Varga. "And my husband, Spaniard? What of him, and of me?"

"Whether you see your *esposo* again, *senora,* is in the hands of God. I would very much like for you to keep *Senora* King company until we have finished our mining operation."

"That could take months!"

"*Sí*. I regret the imposition," Don Varga said, "but if I were to let you go, you might take it into your head to sneak up on me some night and shoot me."

Given half the chance, Blue Water Woman would have done just that. But she was desperate to go after Shakespeare, desperate to the point of sacrificing her outrage to her love. "What if I give you my word that I will not try to harm you or any of your people?"

Don Varga stroked his mustache. "Would that I could believe you."

Blue Water Woman grew frantic. "What if you keep my rifles and pistols? My ammo pouch and powder horn, as well? Would you feel safer?"

"And leave you with nothing but a knife? How would you rescue your husband?" Don Varga shook his head. "No, you would ride to your death."

"It is my life to do with as I want," Blue Water Woman stated. She would gladly brave any danger, tackle any risk, to save her husband.

Ignacio stopped glaring at Nate long enough to say, "Don't listen to her, Father. Her kind are not to be trusted. Keep her with us."

At the annual rendezvous, it was not uncommon for lurid language to be bandied about as freely as the rarefied mountain air was breathed. Cusswords flew thick and fast once the mountaineers had scorched their throats with enough whiskey. Blue Water Woman could not help but pick up additions to her vocabulary. Never before this day, though, had she resorted to them.

Generally, Flatheads did not swear. When a warrior was angry, he vented it by growling or roaring, much like the wild beasts with whom he shared his domain. Women might mutter or smack something. But hellacious cursing, as Shakespeare called it, was rarely done.

Blue Water Woman had never done so before this day. Now she launched into a string of oaths that would have turned the head of any mountaineer alive. She insulted Ignacio. She insulted Ignacio's mother. She insulted his intelligence. And last, but not least, she insulted his manhood.

Ignacio, true to character, bristled and moved toward her. "I will teach you to hold your tongue, bitch."

"No!" Don Varga said. "Enough of this. Release the woman, but keep her guns, her bullets, and her powder. She has my blessing to leave in search of her *esposo.*"

Her heart soaring, Blue Water Woman stripped off her pouch and powder horn for them. Willingly, she handed them over, then rotated toward the sorrel. Her eyes caught Nate's. "I must do it. You can see that, can you not?"

"Go," Nate said.

Blue Water Woman entwined her fingers in the sorrel's mane and swung up. She gazed at Winona, at the children, and froze, stricken in her soul by self-torment.

Winona divined her friend's turmoil. They were more like sisters than friends, the bond they shared second only to the bond they had with their husbands. To soothe her, Winona smiled and said, "We all do what we have to. Do not look back."

Whipping the reins, Blue Water Woman rode off before the Spaniard changed his mind. She did as Winona advised, and it made the heartache bearable. Once trees shrouded her, she vowed aloud, "I will be back, my friends."

In the meadow, a lump in her throat, Winona watched the vegetation close around the sorrel's rump. *She will save us,* Winona thought. *Blue Water Woman will free Shakespeare and they will return.* She refused to admit the overwhelming odds against it.

Don Varga clapped his hands to get everyone's attention. "Let King up," he commanded. "Tie his hands in front of him so he can ride, and keep them tied until I am convinced he will not give us trouble. We leave for the prairie in ten minutes."

The *vaqueros* had acquired a healthy respect for the power in the mountain man's blows. Four held him while two others bound his wrists.

Winona, Zach, and Evelyn rushed to his side as soon as the *vaqueros* walked off. Winona and Evelyn embraced Nate, Evelyn sniffling quietly, Winona with her eyes shut tight.

Zach expressed his relief in a different fashion. "If they had made wolf meat of you, Pa, I wouldn't rest until every one of them was crawling with maggots."

Nate smiled, which was all he could do with his hands tied. He did not let on how disturbed he was by the pledge. Was that what it would come to? Would Zach waste the rest of his life tracking down each and every *vaquero* involved?

Don Varga carried a water skin toward them. "A peace offering, *senor*. To prove I am not the cruel fiend you undoubtedly think I am."

Zach could not keep silent. "You could have fooled us, mister. Holding us against our will. Beating my pa. You have a heap to answer for."

"Your youth betrays you, boy," Don Varga said. "When you have children of your own, come to me and we will see if you feel the same."

"There is no excuse for keeping us prisoner," Winona said stiffly. "You have no right. This land is claimed by my husband's people, not yours." The whole concept of claiming land as one's own was silly to her, but since other whites liked to do so, she reasoned the Spanish would as well.

Nate caught something in the Spaniard's expression, a crinkling of the eyes and lips that suggested Winona had found a weak spot. But what did Varga care who owned the land?

"Bear with me," said their captor. "In a few short months it will be done with. You can go your way, I will go mine, and our paths will never cross again."

"You're forgetting a few things," Nate said. "The Utes, for one. Whoever ambushed us, for another." He indicated the lofty peaks to the west. "These mountains might be your final resting place."

Vargo gave the water skin to Winona. "Pray that is not the case. For if it is, these mountains could be yours, as well."

Chapter Eleven

Twilight claimed the high country when Blue Water Woman was still miles from the plateau where they had lost the trail. She was tempted to keep going. But soon the big predators would be abroad. With the sorrel to think of, and her own safety, she must find a safe haven to spend the night.

The only weapon the *vaqueros* had left her was her knife, a Green River blade given to her by Shakespeare. It would not help much against a hungry grizzly or a roving mountain lion.

She was passing through a belt of pines, the sorrel's hoofs thudding dully on the thick carpet of needles. A cluster of boulders appeared. Investigating, she found they were arranged in a horseshoe shape, the narrow open end pointing south.

There was not much for the sorrel to eat, but they would be protected from the brisk wind that invariably sprang up once the sun went down. Even better, the boulders afforded some protection from the wild beasts and would make it hard for anything passing by to pick up their scent.

Dismounting, the Flathead led the sorrel into the middle. From one of her parfleches she took a short length of rope, which she used to hobble the sorrel's front legs.

To lose the animal now would be a disaster. Stranded afoot, virtually unarmed, her prospects of saving her husband would be slim to none.

Blue Water Woman was not going to bother with a fire, so she did not gather wood. She did go off among the trees, hunting until a fallen limb caught her eye. It was as long as she was tall, as thick as her upper arm, and had not lain on the ground long enough to begin to rot away.

Blue Water Woman spent the next half hour whittling the narrow end, sharpening it into a long point. Until she could construct a better weapon, the spear would have to do.

Collecting other limbs, she intertwined them into a barrier across the open portion of the horseshoe. It was too flimsy to keep out a bear or a big cat if they were determined to get in, but it might slow them down long enough for her to use the spear.

Supper consisted of a single piece of pemmican. Lying on her side on her blanket, listening to the woodland come alive with howls, snarls, and growls, she slowly munched and pondered.

Fate had dealt them a cruel blow. Whoever had abducted Shakespeare would not keep him alive forever. And despite Don Varga's assurance that he would not harm the Kings, she could not shake the feeling that they were in as much danger as her husband.

Her own situation was not much better. She was up against more than a dozen men, and they had a full day-and-a-half head start.

Not that she would ever give up. Blue Water Woman loved McNair too much to even entertain the thought. Having lost him once, she was not about to do so again.

A smile lit her face as she recalled those early days when they first met, when they were young and head-strong and in the prime of their lives. She had loved him the moment she set eyes on him. Later, she was to learn that he had felt the same way about her.

Uncaring circumstance had separated them. She had wound up the wife of a warrior who treated her decently enough, while Shakespeare acquired a number of wives over the years. But in their heart of hearts, neither forgot the other.

Later in life, with their mates dead, they met again, and it was as if the decades spent apart never happened. Their love blossomed anew.

Shakespeare's hair had grown white and he was not as spry as he once had been, but Blue Water Woman loved him with just as much passion as she had when the two of them had been as green as grass, as Shakespeare might put it.

The first time he kissed her, a tingle had shot down her spine to her toes. It had caused her heart to drum madly, her breath to catch in her throat. Never, in all the years she was Spotted Owl's woman, in all the times he had kissed her, had she ever felt like that. It was both astounding and frightening that a man could provoke such deep feeling.

Twenty years they had been separated. Twenty years! Sometimes when she dwelled on it, tears damp-ened her eyes. To have wasted so much of their lives apart! When she thought of the joy that could have been theirs, the many wonderful experiences they would never know, the children they would never have, her soul ached.

Tearing off more pemmican, Blue Water Woman

rolled onto her back and stared at the myriad stars. How tragic life could be. And yet how glorious. She would not trade the years Shakespeare and she had been together for all the yellow rocks or beaver plews in the world.

True love. That was how the young trapper Nate had once described his life with Winona, and Blue Water Woman felt it fit her life with McNair perfectly.

True love. When a man and a woman meant to be together found each other.

As a young maiden, she had laughed at the idea. When friends lavished praise on warriors they admired and raved about the wonderful feelings their love inspired, she had chuckled and said that they were being hopelessly romantic.

Now she knew they had been right. True love was the greatest of gifts. Precious beyond words. What made it more so was the distressing fact that many people lived their entire lives without ever having experienced it. These blighted unfortunates never felt the thrills, the joys, the unrivaled ecstasy.

What amazed her the most was that Shakespeare came from an entirely different culture. They had been born thousands of miles apart, yet they wound up side by side. Their peoples were as different as night from day, yet their affection blazed like the rosy glow of a new dawn.

How strange, how incredible, that they should be drawn to each other over so vast a gulf! McNair was eleven years her senior; she had not even been born yet when he was old enough to help his father work the family farm. She had been in a cradleboard when he held his first job.

Yet they met and fell in love. Despite the gulf of cultures and years and distance, they were meant to be together.

Shakespeare liked to say that their guardian angels were responsible. He claimed the angels often led lovers to each other.

Blue Water Woman scoured the heavens, thinking about the many invisible spirit beings Shakespeare believed gamboled about in the ether. Were angels real, or figments of white imagination? Did guardian angels truly exist?

She would like to think they did. Her own people believed in many spirit beings, some of whom could be called on to safeguard those in need. Maybe angels and the spirits of her people were one and the same, only with different names. After all, the Great Mystery of the Flatheads and the Lord God Almighty of the whites had much in common, although the God of the whites was much more stern and took a more personal hand in the course of human affairs than the Great Mystery.

Blue Water Woman yawned. It had been a tiring day. She shifted onto her left side, folded her hands under her cheek for a pillow, and drifted off. She slept fitfully. The least little noise awakened her. Toward midnight she finally slipped into a heavy slumber.

She dreamed that she was in a fragrant field of flowers and clover, Shakespeare lying by her side. Whites horses frolicked nearby. When one pranced close and nickered, she smiled at it. The horse nickered again, louder, so she sat up and reached out to rub its nose. Shying, the animal nickered a third time, insistently, as if trying to tell her something.

Blue Water Woman opened her eyes with a fourth nicker sounding in her ears. Befuddled by sleep, her mind as sluggish as a snail, she sat up and blinked.

The sorrel had moved nearer and towered above her, ears pricked. It was staring at the barrier.

Then she heard loud sniffing. Something was out there! Clutching the spear, Blue Water Woman pushed onto her knees and extended her weapon.

The sniffing grew louder. Whatever it was, it was big. Through gaps in the branches she distinguished a gigantic bulk rendered black by the gloom, a bulk so immense that it could only be one creature.

Grizzly! Blue Water Woman crouched, her scalp prickling. The brute could smash through her feeble breastwork as if it were made of twigs.

Her sorrel bobbed its head and started to whinny again. Quickly, Blue Water Woman straightened and covered its muzzle with her hand.

A rumbling snort was the bear's response. Branches crackled and snapped as it applied an enormous paw. A hole mushroomed.

Blue Water Woman braced the spear against her hip. She would be ripped to shreds, but she would not go down without a fight. The grizzly grunted and stopped pawing at the limbs.

She remembered Nate telling her that bears were the most unpredictable creatures alive. Grizzlies, in particular, were as temperamental as four-year-olds. No two ever acted alike. Where one might flee at the mere sight of a human, another would roar and charge.

Among the trapping fraternity, Nate King was considered the most knowledgeable about grizzlies. He had slain more of the great bears than any ten trappers. His Indian name, Grizzly Killer, was a tribute to his prowess.

Blue Water Woman recalled a talk she had with him once. Several years before he had been working a trap line when he blundered onto a grizzly seeking to get at a beaver caught in one of his traps. The bear bristled and snarled. Nate took aim, cocked his Hawken, and squeezed the trigger. But the gun did not go off. Unwittingly, he had gotten it wet resetting the previous trap.

Out of the water shuffled the bear. Nate had stood his ground, since to run was to invite attack. When the bear growled, Nate did the same. Suddenly elevating both arms, Nate roared and took a few swift steps forward.

It was an insane bluff, yet it worked. The grizzly had *whoofed,* spun, and lit out of there as if its hind end was on fire.

Nate loved to tell that tale. Maybe, just maybe, what had worked for him would work for her.

Blue Water Woman stomped her feet and roared as best she was able. With bated breath she waited for the grizzly to react. The next moment it did, but not in the manner she anticipated.

Growling, the monster reared onto its hind legs. It was so tall, half its body was above the barrier. Eyes tinged red by a trick of the pale starlight fixed on her.

As still as a stump, Blue Water Woman matched the bear's unblinking stare. It sniffed loudly. Paws that could crush the sorrel's skull with a casual swipe rested on the top of her frail barrier. Claws the length of her fingers shone dully.

Snuffling hungrily, the grizzly took a shambling stride. On two legs it was as awkward as a drunk. But once it lowered onto all fours, not a living thing anywhere could withstand its onslaught.

Blue Water Woman took a gamble. Suddenly bounding toward it, she hollered in her own tongue, "Go away, bear! Find something else to eat!"

For frozen seconds the grizzly stood stock-still. Then it grunted, lowered itself, rotated ponderously, and plodded into the woods without a backward glance.

Blue Water Woman did not twitch until the crunching of brush and twigs had faded in the distance. Her legs grew weak and she sank down, astonished she was still alive. "I did it," she said in awe.

Or had she? For after she settled onto her blanket and was gazing at the sky, she thought again about Shakespeare's guardian angels. Could it be that one was up there now, watching over her? Had her voice scared the giant bear off? Or did she have help from an unseen source?

Who could say?

Another day. Another ten hours or so of hard riding spent trussed up like a turkey for slaughter. Shakespeare McNair glumly checked the position of the sun. It was close to nine A.M., by his reckoning. Flynt's band of renegades had been wending their way toward Long's Peak since daylight.

Jeb Calloway led the white mare, as usual. And as usual, he hummed to himself, the same tune over and over and over. Evidently, it was his all-time favorite.

A cry from the rear of the line brought the band to a halt. Shakespeare heard a thud and a groan. Jasper Flynt galloped past.

Calloway had turned his mount partway around. "It's Spence," he reported. "He's down again."

Shakespeare had guessed as much. The wounded man had fallen three times the day before, and twice since dawn. Blood stained his clothes from his neck to his knees, and he was as pale as a sheet. How he had lasted this long, Shakespeare would never know.

Soon Flynt came clattering forward, drawing rein when he was abreast of the white mare. "That's one we owe you and your friends, McNair."

"He's dead?" Jeb Calloway asked.

Flynt curtly nodded. "We'll ride on until we find a likely place and bury him."

"That's awful decent, Jasper," Calloway said.

Flynt rolled his eyes. "The only reason I even bother is I don't want the Utes or anyone else to find the body. If I had my druthers, I'd let the coyotes and buzzards fill their bellies. They deserve to eat like everyone else.''

Shakespeare observed the deceased being draped over the dead man's mount. ''When Fortune in her shift and change of mood spurns down her late beloved, all his dependents which labour'd after him to the mountain's top even on their knees and hands, let him slip down. Not one accompanying his declining foot.''

''I told you to stop jabberin' that nonsense,'' Flynt reminded him.

''You can't read, can you, Jasper?''

''What the hell does that got to do with anything?''

''Figured as much,'' Shakespeare said. ''If thou didst put this sour-cold habit on to castigate thy pride,'twere well. But thou does it enforcedly.''

Flynt balled a fist and shook it. ''One more fancy word out of you, damn your bones, and you'll eat teeth!''

''Sorry,'' Shakespeare said. ''I didn't mean to rub your nose in your own ignorance.''

Thunder and lightning danced on Flynt's thick brows. He leaned toward McNair as if to strike, then swore and trotted to the head of the line. Soon they were on the move again.

Jeb Calloway clucked at the mountain man. ''Keep that up, old-timer, and you're askin' for an early grave. Jasper don't take that kind of guff off of anyone. I'm surprised he ain't slit you yet.''

To be honest, so was Shakespeare. Flynt had hinted that he was being kept alive for a definite purpose. What could it be? Knowing Flynt, it had to be something devious, something Shakespeare would regret being part of.

Another hour drifted by. Mountains flanked them, majestic ramparts thrust heavenward. Most impressive of all was Long's Peak, rising thousands of feet higher than its nearest neighbor and wearing a mantle of snow.

The game trail brought them to a narrow valley bisected by a gurgling stream. Jasper Flynt drew rein, pointed at four of his men, and announced, "You do the buryin'. And do it deep enough that no coyote's going to come along and dig Spence up."

Three of the four climbed dutifully down. The fourth, a heavyset man whose florid cheeks quivered when he spoke, complained, "Why do I have to help? You're always giving me chores to do. I must do twice as much as everybody else."

Flynt's rifle was across his pommel. A deft twist, and the muzzle pointed straight at the malcontent. "Are my ears playin' tricks on me, Galt? Or did you just sass me?"

Galt's jowls quivered. "I'd never do that, Jasper. Honest. I was just saying that it only seems fair for some of the others to do a little more work."

"*I* decide who does what, and when," Flynt said, a honed edge to his tone. "*I* say what's fair and what ain't. Anyone who doesn't like it had better light a shuck while he still can."

Galt joined the other three over by a spruce. Shovels were produced and a suitable hole was dug. No words were spoken over the grave. No one doffed a hat or showed any sorrow whatsoever.

"Oh, hell," Shakespeare said. A little while before, Calloway had untied his ankles so he could dismount, and he had promptly knelt at the stream's edge and plunged both hands into the cold water. Cupping some, he had drunk slowly, aware that to drink too fast invited cramps.

Now, standing, Shakespeare strode to the foot of the grave. "Even this worthless sac of pus deserves a eulogy of sorts."

"A what?" Galt asked.

"Bow your heads, you miserable husks," Shakespeare said, doing just that, his bound hands folded in front of him. "Pretend you're in church."

Cracking his eyelids, Shakespeare saw that most of them had complied. Of those who had not, two were thirty feet away, another was on his rump chewing jerky, and the last, Jasper Flynt, had turned away in disgust. None of them was anywhere near the horses.

"Oh, Almighty One," Shakespeare began, and quoted from *Proverbs*. "For the ways of man are before the eyes of the Lord, and He pondereth all his goings. His own iniquities shall take the wicked himself, and he shall be holden with the cords of his sins. He shall die without instruction, and in the greatness of his folly he shall go astray."

The pair thirty feet away had finally joined in, lowering their heads in respect. As callous as they were, as bloodthirsty as they might be, the words had struck a responsive chord in their raw natures.

"A naughty person, a wicked man, walketh with a froward mouth," Shakespeare continued, surreptitiously watching Jasper Flynt. "He winketh with his eyes, he speaketh with his feet, he teacheth with his fingers. Frowardness is in his heart, he deviseth mischief continually. He soweth discord."

Jasper Flynt walked farther away, kicking at weeds and dirt clods.

Shakespeare scanned the assemblage. No one was between him and the mare. "These six things doth the Lord hate. Yea, seven are an abomination unto him. A proud look, a lying tongue, and hands that shed innocent blood, a heart that deviseth wicked imaginations, feet that be swift in running to mischief, a false witness that speaketh lies, and he that soweth discord among brethren."

The moment was ripe. Shakespeare started to shift

toward the animals, but a question from Calloway thwarted him.

"When did you learn the Bible so good, McNair? I thought you liked that English stuff better."

"I read them both," Shakespeare said brusquely. "Now, don't interrupt. I'm almost done."

Some of the rowdies had looked up. To get them to bow their heads again, Shakespeare said, "Humbly we bow to your greatness, O Lord." The majority took the hint. "My son," he quoted, "Keep my words, and lay up my commandments with thee. Keep my commandments and live, and my law as the apple of your eyes."

Shakespeare peeked from under his eyebrows. No one was paying any attention to him. It was now or never. "It is as sport to a fool to do mischief, but a man of understanding hath wisdom. The fear of the wicked, it shall come upon him. But the desire of the righteous shall be granted."

Sidling toward his white mare, Shakespeare solemnly intoned, "The wicked flee when no man pursueth, but the righteous are bold as a lion." He passed several ruffians without being challenged. "Whoso keepeth the law is a wise son. But he that is a companion of riotous men shameth his father."

Shakespeare was only a few yards from the mare. None of them had caught on yet. Jasper Flynt was staring at Long's Peak, and the glutton stuffing his mouth with jerked venison was picking at a tear in his pants.

Raising his voice, Shakespeare took a final step. "And so we ask, O Lord, that you accept this cur's soul into Hell where it belongs, and that you see fit to punish the rest of these sons of bitches for ambushing innocent women and children."

Whirling, Shakespeare was on the mare before the first outcry. Although bound, he could hold the reins.

Raking his heels, he goaded the mare into motion. Like a white bolt of lightning, she streaked on up the valley.

Shouts and profanity were thrown at him. Laughing, Shakespeare looked over his shoulder. The dimwits were darting to their animals to give chase. But there wasn't a horse alive that could catch his mare once he gave her her head.

Then Shakespeare saw Jasper Flynt. The killer was sighting down his Kentucky rifle. *He wouldn't!* Shakespeare told himself. Flynt needed him alive.

But he was mistaken! With a start, Shakespeare saw that Flynt was aiming at the *mare,* not at him. Instantly, he brought her to a lurching halt.

Jasper Flynt lifted his cheek from the stock of his rifle. "Nice try, old man!" he yelled. "Now, turn that nag around before I put a ball into her just for the hell of it."

What else could Shakespeare do?

Chapter Twelve

The Varga expedition trekked into the foothills the next day. Don Varga sent the Maricopas ahead to scout the route indicated by the map. As a precaution against surprise attack by unfriendly Indians, he always had six heavily armed *vaqueros* follow a short distance behind the main column. Outriders were also posted on both sides.

The King family was always under guard. Four watchful *vaqueros* were constantly close by, even when they slept. Varga was taking no chances.

The expedition angled to the northwest, to a river that sliced through the foothills toward their destination, Long's Peak. Each noon the column halted for half an hour. At the end of every day, Varga selected a campsite that could be readily defended.

Nate's main worry was the Utes. Sooner or later, the tribe would learn of the incursion and there would be hell to pay. As yet, he had seen no sign of warriors on the ridges, which was surprising given the racket made by the riders and the pack animals as they clattered, clanked, and rattled ever higher.

It took them three days to traverse the foothills. Another two were spent reaching a verdant spot south of the Twin Sisters Peaks.

Nate gazed longingly at them. Just beyond lay the valley his family called home. So close, yet so far!

Ahead reared the jumbled cluster of peaks dominated by Long's. More than a dozen stretched in a ragged row from northwest to southeast. Most did not have names of their own.

The closer the column came, the more often Don Varga consulted an aged yellow parchment. Afterward, he always folded it and stuck it inside his shirt. No one else, not even his sons and daughters, was permitted a peek.

Not once had Varga asked Nate for help in locating landmarks. Nate was beginning to think that Varga had made a mistake and brought them along unnecessarily, when that very night, as he sat sharing coffee with Winona, the Spaniard approached their fire.

"Greetings. I trust all of your are faring well?"

"As well as can be expected for captives," Winona answered. She had developed a profound dislike for the man and his suave but sinister character. He was one of those people who would do anything to get what they wanted, which made him doubly dangerous.

"Please, sarcasm ill becomes you," Don Varga said. Smiling at Evelyn, he went to pat her on the head.

Evelyn scooted aside. Exhibiting the natural bluntness of children her age, she said, "Stay away from me. You're a bad man. A very bad man. I want nothing to do with you."

"I feel the same," Zach announced. His blood boiled whenever any of the Vargas were nearby.

151

Well, almost any. He had grown fond of the daughters, who made it a point to ride with the Kings for several hours each day, chattering gaily, like merry chipmunks. Luisa, in particular, was special.

Sometimes the two of them would ride side by side and talk quietly so the *vaqueros* could not overhear. Luisa and her sisters were very sorry for what their father had done. Were it up to her, she would let them go. But in her family the women had no say in important affairs. Her father ruled with an iron fist.

Don Varga turned to Nate. "We must talk. Come with me, *Senor* King."

"And if I don't?" Nate responded testily.

"Do not be childish, *senor*. Or would you rather I have my men tie your hands again, and your feet, as well, and keep you separated from your loved ones until you decide to cooperate?"

Boiling with resentment, Nate set his tin cup down. "Lead the way."

Varga walked to another fire shared by his sons and daughters. "Away with you," he said, gesturing. "Go somewhere else for five minutes."

Maria, Francisca, and Luisa obeyed without a word of protest. So did young Diego. Martin, frowning, trailed, but Ignacio did not rise. He began addressing his father in Spanish. Manuel cut him off with a wave of a hand and said, "In English, son, for the benefit of *Senor* King."

"What do we care what he thinks?" Ignacio asked in English. "Our private affairs are none of his concern."

Don Varga put his hands on his hips. "How long, son? How long before you use your head for something other than to fill a hat? Always think before you speak. Tact is a sign of maturity, of which, unfortunately, you have a mere trifle."

"I only wanted to know when the rest of us can

see the map,'' Ignacio said defensively. Spearing a finger at the darkling mountains, he snapped, "We are almost there, yet we have no idea where the mine is. What if something happens to you before we find it? What if the map is lost?"

"Your concern is touching."

Ignacio shoved himself erect. "Do not twist my meaning, Father. I would die for you. You know that."

"True," Don Varga conceded. "Whatever faults you may have, however much you argue with me, I know that in your heart you are my most loyal son."

Nate did not believe that for a moment. Martin was the most obedient, therefore the most loyal. Not once had Nate ever heard the middle son dispute his father, as Ignacio routinely did.

"Well, then?" Ignacio said. "Do I see the map, or not?"

"No," Don Varga replied. "Soon, though. Very soon." Smiling tenderly, he rested a hand on his eldest's shoulder. "Trust me, my son. Have I ever let you down?"

"No," Ignacio grumbled. "Very well. I will be patient a while longer." He pivoted on a boot heel and sulked off into the night.

"He has always been his own person," Don Varga said softly, as if thinking aloud. "Of them all, he is the proudest, his blood the hottest. Another twenty years and he will be fit to take my place."

"Provided you live that long," Nate commented.

Varga sat and motioned for the trapper to do likewise. "Spare me your fear of the Utes, *senor*. My Maricopas have seen no evidence of them. And Jasper Flynt happened to tell me that while the Utes claim this area, it is on the fringe of their territory." He paused. "Their villages are many miles to the southwest, are they not?"

"Yes," Nate admitted. "But hunting parties pass through here all the time on their way to the prairie for buffalo, and war parties go through on raids against tribes to the north."

"That is a risk I am willing to take," Don Varga said. "Now, let us attend to the matter at hand." Glancing both ways, he unbuttoned his shirt and slid a hand underneath. "We have reached a point where I require your assistance."

Curiosity got the better of Nate. Sitting, he leaned over the faded parchment as Varga carefully unfolded it and spread it flat on his lap.

The handwriting, of course, was in Spanish, the ink faded in spots but still legible. Whoever sketched it had done an adequate job of noting all the major peaks and ridges. Long's Peak was marked by a large black X. Tiny dots represented the route to the mine, and at various points landmarks had been scribbled in.

"Captain Valdez was in a hurry when he drew this," Don Varga said. "He was fleeing south with his men, hotly pursued by the Utes. So all the landmarks were drawn from memory. He was not able to go back and verify he had gotten them right."

"If he didn't, you've gone through all this for nothing," Nate said.

"I will have tried my best for the sake of my family," Don Varga stated. "No more can be expected of any man." He gazed after his offspring. "I daresay you would do the same for your wife and children, *senor.*"

"I wouldn't go as far as you have."

"You only say that because you have never been in the same position I am. But you would talk differently, I think, if it were your family that was threatened with the loss of everything they owned. You would do whatever it took to secure their future happiness.''

''There are lines no man should ever cross. Not if he wants to go on holding his head high.''

Don Varga reflected a moment. ''Ah, you imply that I have shamed myself by holding you against your will, and not trying harder to save McNair? I will agree that what I have done is not entirely honorable. But even you must admit that I have not stepped over the thin line that separates a decent man from killers and thieves and other trash.''

''Not yet,'' Nate said.

''And I will not, ever,'' Varga declared. ''If I were truly the ogre you make me out to be, I would be making your life utterly miserable instead of doing all in my power to make your stay with us be pleasant and bearable.''

''Don't expect any thanks.''

Anger flared, and Varga pounded his leg with a fist. ''How dare you, *Americano!* How dare you set yourself up as my judge. That is for God alone.'' He took a deep breath to calm himself. ''No one treats me with disrespect. Not my servants, not my own sons, and certainly not you.''

Several *vaqueros* had come closer on hearing their *patrón*'s outburst. Varga said a few words in Spanish and waved them off. ''Now, then, where was I? Oh, yes.'' Bending over the map, he said, ''Tomorrow we will reach a river that runs from north to south, yes?''

Nate nodded.

''Will it be difficult to cross?''

''Not if we're careful.'' The current was swift, the channel narrow. Nate knew of two fords, one well to the north, the other to the south where the river flowed into a broad basin.

Don Varga read a note on the map. ''Once on the other side, there is a sandy creek?''

"It's fed by a lake higher up," Nate recalled. "I trapped beaver there a few winters ago."

"Then the map is accurate," Varga said confidently, folding it. "That is all I need for now. Once we reach the lake, I will require your services again. You are dismissed."

But Nate did not stand. A question had been nagging at him ever since the Spaniard informed them that they would be released once sufficient ore had been mined. "How long, exactly, are we going to be your prisoners?"

Don Varga was replacing the map. "Prisoner is such a harsh word, *senor*. I prefer to regard you as my guests." He plucked at a button. "How long exactly? I cannot say. It depends on factors over which I have no control."

"Give me some idea. Two weeks? Four? Six?"

Varga pointed to where the animals were tethered. "I intend to load every pack animal I can spare with as much gold as they can carry. Twenty-five animals, at least. Possibly thirty. With my men working in shifts around the clock, I estimate that it will take a month and a half."

"And what will my family and I be doing the whole time? Twiddling our thumbs?"

The Spaniard laughed. "What a quaint American expression. You may do whatever you want, *Senor* King. Hike. Fish, if you like. Go for rides. Always under guard, of course."

"Of course," Nate said dryly.

"Why do you ask?"

Nate picked what he said next with exquisite care. "A minute ago you claimed that you are a man of honor. I'd like you to prove it by letting my wife and children leave."

"You know I cannot do so. They are my leverage,

senor. Without them, what is to keep you from turning against me?''

"My oath not to," Nate said. "What if I promise to do whatever you want for as long as you want, provided you let my family go?"

"I would like to, but—"

"All I'm asking is that you give it some thought. Our cabin is just over that range, there," Nate said with a poke of a finger at the Twin Sisters. "Not more than two days' ride. I'd feel better if they were there instead of with us."

Don Varga scratched his chin. "That close, eh?"

Sensing that the Spaniard was wavering, Nate said, "If you're really the gentleman you make yourself out to be, you'll agree."

It was a full minute before Varga spoke. "You tempt me, *senor*. I am not cruel, despite what you might feel." He scrutinized Nate closely. "But the question I must ask myself is this: 'Is the *Americano* to be trusted?' Before I can give my permission, I must decide whether *you* are a man of honor."

Nate hid his disappointment. Antagonizing Varga would not help his cause. "Fair enough. If that's how it has to be, I can wait for you to make up your mind. After all," he said with a smirk, "I'm not going anywhere, am I?"

"No, *senor*. You most definitely are not."

"Why the hell haven't they shown up yet?" Jasper Flynt rasped. Pacing back and forth, he raked the slopes below for sign of movement. "It's been a week, hasn't it? Where the hell can they be?"

The cutthroats in his band swapped looks but did not speak. They knew his moods all too well, and none wanted to earn his wrath.

Shakespeare McNair, though, had no such qualms. "Long's Peak is a big mountain," he commented.

"The mine could be anywhere on it or near it. That's a heap of territory."

"You reckon I don't know that?" Flynt snapped. "Why do you think I've been sendin' my boys out in pairs to scour the countryside?"

"For exercise?" Shakespeare cracked.

Flynt was not amused. Striding to where McNair sat on a flat boulder, he kicked the mountaineer in the shin. "I'm tired of you rubbin' my nose in how stupid you think I am. One more time, old man, just *one,* and I'll slit your wrists and tie you to a tree for a griz to sniff out."

Wincing from the pain, Shakespeare rubbed his leg. He would be damned if he was going to shut up. Being struck was a small price to pay for the satisfaction of making Flynt's life miserable. "Don't blame me if you haven't planned this out very well," he said.

"Like hell," Flynt said. "What would you do that I haven't, you old fart?"

Shakespeare pretended to be interested in something on the ground so they would not see the gleam of triumph that came into his eyes. Flynt had played right into his hands. "I'd wait until nightfall, then send riders out in all directions. An outfit the size of Varga's is bound to have three or four fires going. They should be easy to spot in the dark."

Jeb Calloway forgot that Flynt was in a foul frame of mind. "The old geezer has a point, Jasper. You've had us do all our huntin' in the daytime."

"Who asked you?"

The Alabamian realized his error and timidly grinned. "Sorry, Jasper. No offense."

Flynt walked to the edge of the shelf on which they were camped. Situated five thousand feet up on the east side of Long's Peak, it afforded a magnificent vista of the foothills to the east and the sprawling expanse of upthrust peaks on either side.

Shakespeare hobbled to a spring partially hidden in a cleft. They had discovered it by accident, when they stopped on the shelf to rest briefly and a horse strayed over to take a drink.

As punishment for his escape attempt the other day, Shakespeare's ankles were linked by a two-foot length of rope when he was off the mare as well as on. It was to prevent him from getting any more "bright stupid ideas," as Flynt had phrased it.

Kneeling, Shakespeare dipped his lips to the cool, refreshing water. This was his second drink in less than half an hour. None of the cutthroats noticed how thirsty he had become, which was fine by him.

Earlier, Shakespeare had spied a jagged piece of quartz more than six inches long. It was ideal, but it was also lying on the narrow rim toward the rear of the spring, well out of reach. He could not get to it without wading in, and the renegades were bound to notice.

Reluctantly, Shakespeare walked back in time to overhear Jasper Flynt.

". . . like the idea. When the sun goes down, eight of you will ride out in pairs and search around. The rest of us will stay put and keep a small fire going so you can find your way back."

"What if something happened to the Spaniard?" asked a man whose salt-and-pepper beard was as curly as the hairs on his head. "What if the Utes got him? They could get us next."

"You worry too damn much, Jansen," Flynt said. "We ain't seen hide nor hair of those red devils this whole time."

Shakespeare shuffled to the flat boulder. If eight of them left later, that would leave five to contend with. Too many. Somehow he had to whittle the odds even more.

Cards were broken out, and some of the men hunkered to play. Another cleaned his rifle. Two others rolled dice. One man slept.

Jasper Flynt continued to pace the rim. A restless bundle of energy, he could not sit still for more than five minutes at a time. His restlessness fit his surly, quixotic disposition. From one moment to the next his moods fluctuated. Small wonder his own men lived in fear of him.

Shakespeare massaged his thigh. It was still sore from the bullet wound. Scar tissue had formed and the gash was healing nicely, but he would bear a reminder of the ambush for the rest of his days.

A shadow fell across him. Shakespeare was startled and looked up. "What do you want, Flynt?" he demanded, flustered that his nerves had turned traitor.

"How highly does Nate King think of you?"

"We're friends."

Flynt squatted so they were eye-to-eye. "That's not what I meant, damn it. Everyone has heard tell that the pup is right fond of you. I need to know *how* fond."

The query was so strange that Shakespeare grew wary. "What is it to you, mister?"

Like a striking sidewinder, Flynt's hand lashed out and closed on the mountain man's windpipe. His fingers tightened, but not enough to choke off Shakespeare's breath. "I swear, old man. You must have a secret hankerin' to push up weeds. Just answer my questions, you old goat."

"We're *close* friends."

"Would he die for you?"

Shakespeare hesitated. Undoubtedly Nate would, but dare he reveal as much? Of what use was the information to Flynt? "Ask him," he hedged.

Flynt's steely hand clamped fast, his fingers gouging deep. When Shakespeare grasped his wrist, his other hand materialized holding a pistol, which he cocked and pressed against the trapper's temple. "Lordy, you're dumb! I could blow a hole in you and not bat an eye."

Shakespeare was unable to respond. His throat was on fire, his lungs heaved for air. Flynt relaxed the hand, chuckling, and Shakespeare sucked in deep breaths. *If only I was thirty years younger!* he thought. No one had ever roughed him up when he was at his peak.

"Ready to behave?" Flynt mocked him.

"I've told you what you wanted to know. We're friends, for God's sake."

Flynt tapped the pistol against Shakespeare's head. "There are friends, and there are friends. Take Calloway, for instance. He's a pard, but he ain't about to sacrifice himself for my sake."

"In what manner?" Shakespeare asked, stalling.

The renegade chewed on his lower lip a bit. "Say, for example, we were jumped by Utes, and I was knocked out of the saddle. If Calloway had a choice between ridin' back to save me or hightailin' it to save his own hide, he'd head for the hills and leave me to bleed."

"The quality of a man's friends mirrors his own character," Shakespeare said.

Flynt chortled. "Where do you come up with this stuff, McNair? Is it more of that English feller?"

"Truth is truth."

Standing, Jasper Flynt let down the hammer on his flintlock. "How anyone could stand to live with you for more than two days is beyond me. I'd go *loco*. That squaw of yours either can't speak English, or she's stupider than spit." He found his own humor hilarious.

Shakespeare rubbed his neck, imagining how sweet

it would be to have his fingers on Flynt's. "Is that all you wanted?"

"You've told me enough, yes."

"I didn't tell you a thing."

"That's just it," Flynt gloated. "By hedging like you did, you showed me that you were afraid to fess up with the truth. King does care for you, McNair. Enough to die for you, if need be. And that'll be his undoing."

Shakespeare stared at the cutthroat's retreating back, then at the sky. In another four hours the sun would set and he could put his plan into effect. The last time, he had let Flynt buffalo him by threatening to shoot the mare. This time, he wasn't going to back down no matter what. He would escape, or he would die trying.

It was as simple as that.

Chapter Thirteen

A quarter of a mile lower down the mountain grew a wide belt of aspens. Their slender trunks were spaced close together, superb cover for the tall woman who gazed longingly at the shelf.

Blue Water Woman had been shadowing the cutthroats for quite some time. On the day after her encounter with the grizzly, she had found their tracks and nearly ridden the sorrel into the ground to catch up.

Staying close without being observed had taxed her wilderness skills. She was not as versed in stealth and warfare as a Flathead warrior would be, but she proved to be up to the challenge. The whites rarely made any effort to hide their tracks, and not once had they sent a rider to check their back trail as a Flathead war party would have frequently done.

Many times Blue Water Woman had glimpsed her mate, his white mane setting him apart from his captors. On each occasion her heart fluttered with joy to find him still alive and apparently well, although twice he had seemed to be limping slightly.

For all their blunders, though, the whites were smart enough to pitch their camps in easily defended spots that gave them an unobstructed view of the surrounding countryside. She could never get close enough to spirit Shakespeare away.

Since it appeared the men were not planning to move on, and would probably spend the night on the shelf, Blue Water Woman devoted her attention to another problem.

Food.

She had almost finished the pemmican. It had not occurred to her to take more than a few days' supply when they left the King cabin. They were only going to the base of the foothills, after all, and she had anticipated being back at the cabin by the next afternoon.

How was she to foresee the nightmare that befell them?

In order to stay close to her husband's abductors, she needed to refill her parfleche. Jerky was the logical choice. But that meant she must go off in search of game, leaving Shakespeare alone with them.

She balked at the idea. It was comforting to stay close, reassuring to know that she could fly to his aid if it became apparent he was in imminent danger. Although of what help she could be, armed with only a knife and crude spear, was an issue she chose not to dwell on.

Forlornly, Blue Water Woman tore her gaze from the shelf and glided through the aspens to where the sorrel had been tied. She mounted and rode northward, avoiding open places, never exposing herself to view.

After a mile Blue Water Woman felt safe enough to leave the aspens and cross a meadow into dense pines. For one of the whites to spot her at that distance, he would need the eyes of a hawk.

She hefted her spear. At that elevation game was not quite as plentiful as down in the valleys. Elk were abundant, but they were so big that a single cast might not bring one down. Black-tailed deer were also common, but they were extremely alert and fleet of foot.

Blue Water Woman would gladly settle for a whistler, as her people called the small brown animals that lived in burrows and whistled shrilly to warn their fellows when predators were abroad. Woodchucks, Shakespeare said they were, although they differed slightly from the kind he had seen as a boy back in Pennsylvania. Some whites called them marmots.

In any event, one of the animals would provide her with enough meat to last four or five days if rationed.

Whistlers lived in rocky, elevated areas, often along the crest of ridges. A ridge to the northwest seemed as likely an area as any, so Blue Water Woman bent the sorrel's steps toward it.

Presently, she came to the end of the trees. Beyond, a gradual grassy slope climbed to the bony crest. She slowly moved into the open, scouring the boulders that dotted the heights, seeking telltale furtive movements.

The sorrel had gone only a few yards when Blue Water Woman detected motion. But it was to her right, not above her. A large black-tailed buck stood forty feet away, regarding her nervously, ears high. She drew rein, and the buck turned as if to run off. But instead of bounding into the pines, it shied from them, prancing uncertainly, glancing from the undergrowth to her and back again.

Puzzled, Blue Water Woman did not try to kill it. She could not hurl her spear that far, and the buck would vanish in a heartbeat if she were to rush closer.

Again the animal started toward the vegetation.

Again it stopped and stamped a hoof. Suddenly snorting, it spun and fled northward along the edge of the pines rather than into them.

Blue Water Woman did not know what to make of its peculiar antics. It was almost as if the buck was afraid of something that lurked in the undergrowth.

She was right.

The next second, a thicket parted and out rode a muscular, broad-shouldered warrior on a fine bay. He had an arrow notched to a bow. His black braided hair, the style of his buckskins and moccasins, his rugged features, all identified him as an Ute.

Blue Water Woman stiffened. The man had been after the buck, but now he was more interested in her! Where there was one, there must be more. Either they would kill her for being an enemy, or they would capture her and take her back to their village.

Slapping the sorrel, Blue Water Woman bolted up the slope. The Ute yipped like a coyote and gave chase. She bent low to present a smaller target.

An arrow buzzed past her shoulder. Had it been a warning to stop, or intended to slay her? Glancing back, Blue Water Woman saw him reach over his shoulder to snatch another shaft from his quiver.

The sorrel's legs pumped, its hooves digging into the soil, raining clods in its wake. Blue Water Woman goaded it with the blunt end of the spear.

Once she gained the ridge, she would make a stand. But she was merely delaying the inevitable. Her puny weapon was no match for a bow. The warrior could stay out of throwing range and keep her pinned down. Should she try to flee, he might drop the sorrel. Once other Utes arrived, her fate would be sealed.

Frustration choked her. To be so close to Shakespeare, and have this happen! She smacked the sorrel again. She had to get away! She just had to!

Abruptly, the spear was wrenched from her grasp

and fell. Bewildered, Blue Water Woman looked back and saw an arrow jutting from it. The Ute had shot the spear from her hand! Such a feat spoke highly of great skill and daring.

He was smiling now, following hard but not too hard, confident he had her. Instead of nocking another arrow, he slung the bow over his left shoulder.

No! Blue Water Woman would not let him take her captive. Somehow, some way, she must foil him. The sorrel churned higher. She spotted a gap in the boulders and slanted toward it. Twisting, she surveyed the tree line. As yet, additional Utes had not appeared. But it was only a matter of time.

The gap was narrower than it had seemed. Blue Water Woman had to spur the sorrel through, scraping her legs in the process. Vaulting off, she scooped up a rock the size of a melon and stepped to the gap.

The Ute was fifteen feet below. His bay had slipped on a patch of slick bare earth and was down on its front legs. He was struggling to get the animal to stand. Glancing up, the Ute saw Blue Water Woman and the rock she held. He laughed.

Whipping her arm, Blue Water Woman hurled it. She hoped to knock him off and send him tumbling down the slope, which would give her time to remount and escape. But just then the bay heaved upward, straightening, and the rock meant for the Ute's chest struck the bay in the head.

The animal whinnied in pain and scrambled backward, losing its balance completely. Legs flailing, it toppled. The rider tried to regain control, but gravity took over. The Ute shifted to spring clear, but as he did, the bay gave a sharp lurch that threw the warrior off balance. He cried out as he was pitched from the saddle—*under* the falling animal.

Blue Water Woman heard an awful crunch and rending of bone. The bay kept kicking and nickering as it slid lower, right over the prone warrior. In a spray of dust and dirt, the horse eventually came to a stop and rose unsteadily.

The Ute did not move. Blue Water Woman suspected it might be a trick to lure her near. She picked up another rock and ventured down. A spreading scarlet puddle was the first sign that it was not a ruse. She stepped closer, and tasted bile.

Pale, gleaming bone had ripped through the warrior's hunting shirt. Shattered bone also jutted from the left thigh. Red froth rimmed his lips and dribbled from his nostrils. His eyes were locked wide in the amazement he must have felt at the moment of his passing.

Blue Water Woman was no less amazed. She had not meant to slay him, although she would have if he had persisted. Swallowing the bile, she knelt beside the bloody ruin. His body had been crushed, his chest flattened like a board. Gingerly, she pried at his shoulder, lifting him high enough to see the bow and quiver. The bow was broken, the arrows useless.

Easing the body down, Blue Water Woman rose. It was too bad. The bow would have come in handy.

She had no remorse over the mishap. These things happened routinely in the wild. Her people lived daily with the knowledge that they might not be alive to greet the next day. Enemies, beasts, accidents, all claimed a fierce toll.

Knowing how frail existence was, her people had a keen zest for life. From childhood, Blue Water Woman had been reared to regard each and every day as a priceless gift. She never took life for granted, as many of her husband's acquaintances seemed to do.

Violence. Bloodshed. They were part and parcel of existence. Why that should be, she could not say. The ways of the Great Mystery were beyond human understanding.

Shakespeare had told her that his people believed humankind once lived in peace and harmony. Then two brothers disputed, and one killed the other. Cain, one was called. She couldn't remember the name of the other. But from that day on, violence had plagued the human race, a lingering legacy of their fall from grace—

The sorrel whinnied. Blue Water Woman turned and saw that it was staring past her, at the forest below. She did the same, and her breath caught in her throat.

Three more Utes had emerged from the trees.

Fully half of the renegades were dozing. Others were involved in cards, a favorite pastime. Flynt was off by himself, brooding, as was his custom.

Two hours remained before nightfall. Shakespeare found it difficult to curb his impatience. He went to the spring again to eye the piece of quartz that promised to be his salvation. As he cupped water to his mouth, boots scuffed the ground behind him.

"What's the matter with you, old-timer? Are you sickly?"

Jeb Calloway had his rifle in the crook of an elbow. He bit off the end of a plug of tobacco and offered some to McNair. "Want a chaw?"

"Thank you kindly, but no," Shakespeare said. "I had the habit once and I grew out of it. Having yellow teeth never appealed to me."

"Why not?" Calloway said, touching his own. "I always thought yellow was a pretty color."

Shakespeare stood, his sore leg twinging. "Never lived with a woman, have you?"

"Just whores," Calloway said. "Had me a fat one down to New Orleans, once. Lordy, how she jiggled! And her lips! When she kissed a feller, it was like sinkin' into a pillow. I sure did like her."

"Why did you split up?"

"I ran out of money."

Shakespeare limped on by to return to his boulder. Ordinarily the cutthroats left him to his own devices, but now the Alabamian was in a talkative mood and dogged his steps.

"What's it like, McNair, havin' an Injun wife?"

The mountain man stopped dead. "Why do you want to know, Calloway?"

"Lower your horns, old man. I ain't out to insult you. I've just been thinkin' of gettin' me a woman of my own one of these days, and I've heard tell that Injun gals are easy to live with."

"Who fed you that yarn?" Shakespeare said, sitting. "Females are the most contrary critters on God's green earth. Compared to them, mules are downright levelheaded. You've never seen stubborn until you try to get a woman to change her mind."

Jeb Calloway chuckled. "Hell, if they're that bad, why do menfolk take up with 'em?"

"We're gluttons for punishment, I reckon," Shakespeare bantered. Of all the renegades, only Calloway had treated him halfway friendly. The Alabamian had no business riding with a rogue like Jasper Flynt. Calloway was a none-too-bright coon hound who had taken up with a pack of ravening wolves. He was in way over his head.

"You're joshin' me, old-timer. You must like females, or you wouldn't have a missus."

"I've had several," Shakespeare disclosed. And he had outlived every one. "They have their good qualities."

"Such as?"

"Where to begin?" Shakespeare said. "Trying to tell a man who's never had a wife how great it can be is like trying to tell a man who's never eaten painter how delicious the meat tastes."

"I've ate panther."

"You're missing the point." Leaning back, Shakespeare let his mind drift over the many years he had lived, recollecting the high points of his dealings with the opposite gender. "Women can be soft and tender and loving. They make us laugh, mend us when we're hurt, comfort us when we're troubled." He paused. "They bear our children. And if you've never seen a woman give birth, you have no idea of the hurt they put themselves through. I could never do it."

"Do what?"

"Have babies."

Calloway cackled. "That's a silly notion. Men ain't got the right parts."

"Thank God," Shakespeare said. "I'd make a terrible woman. I could never put up with the shenanigans men pull. All that drinking and cussing and complaining about everything under the sun. And the liberties they take."

"You've done lost me, friend."

"Ever hit a woman?"

"Just once. A whore tried to steal my poke. If she hadn't tripped over her cat, I'd never have caught her."

"Ever forced yourself on one who didn't want your attentions?"

"No, sir. My ma taught me better than that. She used to take a dagger to Pa whenever he got too frisky and she wasn't in the mood. Taught me not to get stuck, it did." Calloway's forehead creased. "What's all this got to do with what we were talkin' about?"

"I was trying to show you how hard it is for women to put up with us men."

Jeb snickered, then said, "You must be gettin' addlepated, old feller. I want to know why a man should take up with 'em, not why they shouldn't take up with us. What's the reason?"

"Because they're there."

"Huh?"

"It beats kissing a tree all hollow."

"You're pokin' fun again." Calloway had a bulge in his cheek big enough to choke a bear. Tobacco juice commenced to dribble from the left corner of his mouth. "The way I see it, a woman is good for cookin' and sewin' and cleanin' and such. And the other thing, naturally."

"Other thing?"

"You know," Calloway said, his cheeks tinged red.

It was Shakespeare's turn to laugh, and he did so uproariously, drawing mixed stares from the other renegades. "Oh, she doth teach the torches to burn bright! It seems she hangs upon the cheek of night like a rich jewel in an Ethiop's ear. Beauty too rich for use, for earth too dear!"

Calloway blinked. "Who does all that?"

"Women, friend. Women."

The Alabamian spat. "You're a mighty peculiar bird, McNair. One minute you act like one of us, the next you're spoutin' that flowery talk like those fellers who prance around on stages in dresses." He spat again, hitting a beetle. "My ma drug me to one of them affairs when I was a kid. I couldn't help laughin', which riled her so bad, she walloped me on my ear and split it." Pulling his long hair aside, he showed the scar. "See there?"

"Incredible," Shakespeare said.

"If'n you ask me, they ought to warn folks about them plays in advance. Hell, how was I to know it was—what did my ma call it—a tragedy?" Calloway shook his head. "I thought those fellers was jumpin' around like they had ants in their britches to be funny."

Coins clinked in the quiet when Jeb stopped talking. One of the sleepers snored lightly. And faintly, from the north, the breeze brought with it the distinct sound of war whoops.

Shakespeare pushed to his feet. So did all the cutthroats who were awake, their hands falling to pistols or grabbing rifles. Jasper Flynt came running, leading a general rush to the far end of the shelf.

"We'd better give a listen," Calloway said, jogging to join his companions.

Shakespeare began to follow, then halted. No one was watching him. Why wait for nightfall, when here was a perfect opportunity? Hustling to the cleft, he paused to confirm that the band was riveted on the slopes to the north. In two more paces he was at the pool. Another took him into it, the cold water rising as high as his waist as he waded across.

The bottom of the pool was slippery stone. Footing was treacherous, made more so by the rope that hobbled him as if he were a horse. Stepping carefully, he reached the middle. A few more feet would do it.

Out on the shelf someone shouted. Had they discovered he was missing? Fearing that was the case, Shakespeare lunged toward the quartz. In his eagerness, he overextended himself. His right foot was tugged up short by the rope. His leg slid out from under him. He desperately grasped at the edge for support, but he was not close enough.

Shakespeare went under. Since the pool was only three and a half feet deep, he was not alarmed. He would plant both feet, stand, and everything would be all right.

But when he tried to steady himself, his moccasins kept slipping. Matters were made worse by the fact that he could not use his arms for added balance, not with his hands bound in front of him. He tried again to break the surface and nearly succeeded, when he was spilled onto his backside.

From being laughable, the situation had grown deadly serious. Shakespeare could feel water in his ears, in his nose. His lungs were in need of air. Placing both hands flat, he shoved upward, thrusting with his knees to gain momentum. It worked. His head surged clear, and he greedily sucked in a breath.

It was a momentary reprieve. Shakespeare attempted to straighten, but the soles of his moccasins were like liquid glass. Down he sprawled, inadvertently swallowing water as it closed over him. His hat was swept off.

How could this be happening? Shakespeare asked himself in disbelief as he propped both knees under him. He'd had strings of bad luck before, but nothing to rival this latest.

Thrusting his arms upward, Shakespeare knifed toward the rear rim. Air replaced the water. Undulating like an eel, he cleaved the pool. He had to grit his teeth against searing pain when he accidentally smacked his hands against the jagged edge.

Clinging for dear life, Shakespeare calmed himself. Ever so slowly, he lowered his legs and uncoiled. The piece of quartz was inches away. Palming the slender rock, he examined the serrated edge. It wasn't as sharp as a knife, but it would do nicely.

Resisting an urge to hurry, Shakespeare waded toward the cleft opening. He retrieved his beaver hat, which had begun to sink. Climbing out was an exercise in concentration.

At last, dripping wet, McNair straightened. After wringing the hat out, he plopped it on his head. Then he bent and slid the quartz under the top of his knee-high moccasin. Wriggling his leg so it would slide even lower, he hobbled into the open.

The renegades were returning. Jasper Flynt's eyes narrowed and he asked suspiciously, "What in the hell happened to you?"

174

"I fell in," Shakespeare lied. Wagging his tied wrists at the hobble around his ankles, he groused, "It's these damn ropes! How do you expect me to get around trussed up like this?"

Jeb Calloway burst into throaty mirth. "Fell in!" he repeated. Others rated it just as humorous, and soon practically every last cutthroat was braying lustily.

Shakespeare meekly grinned. Let them enjoy their moment. His was about to come. He had the quartz. Now all he needed was for the sun to set.

Chapter Fourteen

The three Utes took one look at their fallen friend, glanced up at Blue Water Woman, and were transformed into vengeful demons. Uttering piercing war whoops, they raced up the slope after her.

Blue Water Woman did not wait a second before wheeling and bounding to the sorrel. Swinging astride its back, she flew northward, her long hair streaming in her wake. She had no weapon other than her Green River knife, but she had a substantial lead on the Utes and a horse that Shakespeare had selected for its speed and stamina. She was confident she could shake the warriors, then return to help her husband.

The three Utes gained the ridge. The first man through the gap slowed, swinging his bow to the left and the right. When he spotted her, he gave chase, yipping in fierce abandon.

Through the gap filed the other two. The second man rode a small, wiry horse with an odd speckled coat and a shaggy mane. Its body was too low to the ground, its legs too short, its tail skimpy. In short, it was everything a horse should not be, the sort of animal that no seasoned horseman would ever want, a scraggly mustang that did not seem fit enough to go fast or far. But that animal could fly!

Blue Water Woman glanced over a shoulder and was filled with consternation on seeing the horse flash toward her like a four-legged dragonfly.

The Ute riding it wore a wolfish grin. He knew what his mount was capable of. He knew that he would overtake her, that there was no getting away.

Using her reins and legs to full advantage, Blue Water Woman pushed the sorrel to its limit, and slightly beyond. They streaked past boulders, trees, and shrubs. They jumped logs, skirted deadfalls, tore through brush that clawed at them and drew blood.

Howling and screeching, the Utes came on. The man on the speckled animal did not exert himself all that much, yet his horse narrowed the distance with astounding rapidity. His grin widened as her lead shrank.

Hope presented itself in the form of a pine-covered slope. Blue Water Woman shot in among the trees at a reckless speed. Weaving and winding, she fled deeper and deeper into the woodland. If only she could find a spot to hide until the Utes had gone by!

A boulder the size of Nate King's cabin offered her the chance she needed. Reining around to the rear, Blue Water Woman stopped and leaned forward to keep the sorrel from nickering. Within moments the Utes pounded on by, still whooping and hollering. They had been following her by sight instead of by her tracks, so they did not catch on to the deception right away.

Tingling with elation, Blue Water Woman waited until the cries tapered before she kneed the sorrel back around the boulder and turned to the south to cement her escape. She faced front, and froze.

Fifteen yards away stood the speckled horse, its rider smirking smugly. He had guessed her ruse and outfoxed her.

Instantly, Blue Water Woman cut the sorrel to the right and hurtled into the densely packed trees. Limbs gouged her, buffeted her, nearly blinded her. She swatted at them, receiving a gash on her forearm.

Suddenly, hooves drummed beside the sorrel. The Ute was right there, reaching for her arm. Blue Water Woman jerked away, then kicked at him. She hit his leg, but all it did was enlarge his smirk.

Their horses burst into the open. Blue Water Woman veered to the right again, but the speckled horse was superbly trained; it stayed alongside the sorrel, never missing a stride. Again the Ute lunged, his hand locking on her wrist. She tried to pull free, but he was too strong.

Slowing, Blue Water Woman swung her knife at the warrior's chest. He let go of his reins to snatch her wrist, and twisted sharply. The blade slipped from her pain-racked fingers. As their horses came to a stop, she struggled with all her might to slip from his grasp.

With a lusty yell, the Ute threw himself at her. Blue Water Woman was borne from the small Flathead-style saddle. She tried to turn so that he would land on the bottom, but he was too heavy. They fell on their sides, the warrior scrambling to his knees before she could and pinning her shoulders.

A wildcat gone berserk, Blue Water Woman fought ferociously. She clawed. She punched. She sought to knee the Ute in the groin. He planted his knee on her left arm, rendering it useless, and nearly succeeded in the doing the same to her right. Wrenching loose, she glimpsed the knife lying close by and grabbed for it, but her fingertips fell a whisker's width short.

The Ute let out with a series of yells. Blue Water Woman did not need to speak the Ute tongue to know what he was doing. Soon his fellow warriors would arrive.

Redoubling her efforts, Blue Water Woman bucked upward and almost dislodged him. He clung to her like a tenacious vine, even when her knee drove into his ribs hard enough to elicit a grunt.

Underbrush crackled not far off. Blue Water Woman had only moments in which to act. She heaved upward and to the left, both knees ramming into the Ute's torso. His grip slipped. Capitalizing on her opportunity, she shoved him and was on her feet quicker than a startled antelope. Three long bounds brought her to the sorrel. She flung her arms onto its neck and started to pull herself up.

Arms corded thickly with sinew closed on her waist. She was roughly hauled off and thrown bodily to the earth. Dazed, Blue Water Woman saw the undergrowth part. The other two Utes angled toward her.

Desperately, she catapulted to her feet. She aimed a kick at the man who barred her way, but he sidestepped, seized her leg, and dumped her flat on her back. She put her hands flat under her, refusing to give up, even now, when she was surrounded, when the other two warriors were almost on top of her, when continued resistance would prove futile.

She made it to her knees. Diving figures slammed into her from behind and from the left. It was akin to being butted by two buffaloes at once. She crumpled like a piece of rotted bark.

Breathing heavily, Blue Water Woman went limp. Maybe, if they believed all the fight had gone out of her, they would relax their grips. Maybe they would also relax their guard and let her get up on her own.

All it would take was a couple of steps to reach the sorrel.

The Ute who owned the swift horse reared over her. He held a coiled rawhide rope. At sight of it, Blue Water Woman resisted more fiercely than ever, but they were too many. She was rolled onto her stomach, her wrists tied securely. A loop was then made around her neck and she was roughly pulled erect.

The man with the rope regarded her from head to toe. He addressed her in his tongue, and when she did not react fast enough to suit him, he slapped her.

Blue Water Woman held her head high, her shoulders squared. She could expect no mercy from any of them. They undoubtedly believed she had slain their comrade deliberately, and they would treat her accordingly.

A heated parley broke out. The stoutest of the Utes argued with the man who had caught her and the third warrior, who had a hooked nose. Stout, as she thought of him, made his intentions perfectly plain by tapping his knife hilt and gesturing as if he were slitting a throat.

Evidently, Rope and Hook Nose did not want her killed immediately. Rope, especially, appeared to want to take her back to their village. Finally Stout turned away, his expression proof he had lost the dispute.

Blue Water Woman was half-carried, half-dragged to the sorrel. Rope and Hook Nose each grasped an arm and propelled her upward, but the sorrel, spooked by the unfamiliar scents and guttural growling of Rope, shied. Instead of being draped across the sorrel's broad back, Blue Water Woman plummeted, striking her forehead hard enough to stun her.

Hook Nose ran after the sorrel, which would have vanished in the trees if not for Stout. With remarkable alacrity, he intercepted the horse and snagged the reins.

Again the warriors carted her over. Again she was treated like a sack of grain. Stout held onto the sorrel's neck, so even though it nickered and pulled back, Blue Water Woman wound up on her belly on top.

Rope forked the speckled horse. Holding the other end of the rope, he set off at a brisk walk. Whenever the sorrel slowed, he would tug on it, and she would goad the sorrel with her legs.

It made more sense to loop the rope around the sorrel's neck, not hers. Blue Water Woman suspected that the Ute wanted her to suffer in retribution for the death of the warrior who had been crushed. Whatever the case, her neck soon grew sore and raw.

Her spirits fell. To have been so close to Shakespeare, and now this! Once they reached the Ute village, the likelihood of escape was slim. They would have her under constant guard. Should, by some miracle, they spare her, misery would be her lot, either as an unwilling mate to a warrior or perhaps as a slave to one of the older women, a practice of the Sioux and other tribes.

Crestfallen, Blue Water Woman slumped as limply as a wet rag. She hardly gave any consideration to the lengthening shadows, or the fact that the Utes were backtracking to the ridge where their companion lay. All she could think of was Shakespeare.

What would happen to him now?

Evening fell. The renegades ate an early meal. There was a lot of talk about the war whoops they had heard. Everyone was of the opinion that it had to be Utes, and several wanted to investigate. They changed their minds after Jasper Flynt insulted their intelligence and their mothers, concluding with,

"Only a jackass goes askin' for trouble. Maybe the Utes were after the greaser. They sure as hell don't know that we're here, and we're not about to advertise it."

Twilight cast the Rockies in pervading gloom. Flynt paired off six of his men and gave them instructions. They were to fan out and look high and low for distant campfires. Should they spot any, one man was to stay put while the other hurried back to the shelf.

Shakespeare McNair stayed apart from the renegades. Out of sight, out of mind, he hoped. Only Jeb Calloway bothered to talk to him. The Alabamian waxed nostalgic about his childhood, telling of memorable bear hunts he had been on as a boy. "One fall, my pa and me killed twenty-eight black bears," he bragged. "Lost a good hound to one of the brutes we cornered, but when we were done, we had us enough meat to last our family pretty near two years. Poor Ma about worked herself into an early grave skinnin' and dryin' those rascals."

"That's a lot," Shakespeare said.

"Shucks, it ain't hardly half as many as Davy Crockett brought down in a single season. My pa used to say that ornery Tennessean was the best damn bear-killer who ever lived." Jeb sobered. "Too bad them Mexicans had to do him in like they done."

The story of the Alamo had been on everyone's lips a few years back. Even mountaineers living in the remotest stretches of the Rockies heard about the glorious battle and its aftermath.

"Do you reckon there's any truth to the rumor that Crockett was taken alive and executed?" Calloway asked.

It was widely known that a handful of defenders were brought before Santa Anna after the battle and were summarily bayoneted. Some claimed that Davy Crockett had been one of them.

"I wasn't there," Shakespeare said, "but I recollect hearing that Crockett had some kind of illness. They say he collapsed a couple of times when he overtaxed himself. Maybe that's what happened in San Antonio. He fought until he dropped, then they finished him off. Either way, he died game."

"Maybe," Jeb said without conviction. "But if'n you ask me, Davy went down shootin' and clubbin'. That's how a real hero ought to die, ain't it?"

Shakespeare did not point out that brave men seldom had a choice as to how they met their Maker. Happenstance dictated the manner of one's passing, just as it did one's life.

Jasper Flynt strolled over. "Jeb, you'd best throw a saddle on that scrawny nag of yours. I want you and Fletcher to ride to the southeast."

"Me?" Calloway said. "But I thought I was to guard McNair, here?"

"Galt is going to watch over him while you're gone."

"But why him and not me?" Calloway complained. "I'd rather stay put."

"I'm sure you would, you lazy southerner," Flynt responded. "Fact is, you're gettin' too damn friendly with this old bastard to suit me. Did you think I wouldn't notice how the two of you are always jawin' and laughin' like the best of pards?"

Jeb did not know when to leave well enough alone. "What are you sayin', Jasper? That I'd turn against you? That I'd help him get away?"

"Not even *you* would be that stupid," Flynt declared. "No, what bothers me is that you'll turn your back to him one time too many and we'll have to plant you."

"McNair would never hurt me," Calloway said,

and nudged Shakespeare's leg. "Would you, hoss? Tell him."

Flynt slapped the Alabamian on the shoulder. "See? That's exactly what I was afraid of. You're too damn trustin'. Sometimes I wonder if you ever grew up." He poked Calloway in the chest. "Galt stays. You go. And that's the end of it."

"Whatever you say, Jasper. Don't I always listen good?"

Shakespeare was glad that Jeb would be gone when he made his move. No one, absolutely *no one,* would be allowed to stand in his way. That included the Alabamian.

A couple of stars glimmered overhead when the eight cutthroats trotted from the shelf. Their comrades lined up to watch, a few waving. A pall of silence gripped those left behind. Untold wealth would be theirs if Varga's expedition was found, but they were too worried about roving Utes to relish the prospect.

Shakespeare plucked a blade of grass and stuck it between his teeth. Galt waddled toward him, hitching at a wide belt that barely contained his ample girth.

"Well, looks like it's you and me, old man. Behave yourself and we'll get along just fine. Don't behave, and I'll split your skull." To emphasize his warning, Galt pantomimed busting the trapper's head with the butt of his rifle.

"I get the hint," Shakespeare said.

From then on, it was just a question of waiting for the ideal moment. Three of the renegades huddled to play cards. Galt honed a knife. Flynt roamed the rim, restless energy oozing from every pore like lava from a volcano.

Standing, Shakespeare inquired, "Mind if I go for some water?"

"Be my guest," Galt said, stroking the blade across the whetstone. "Just don't fall in again. I can't

184

swim, and I'm not about to jump in that pool to help you. You can drown, for all I care.''

"Don't fret yourself on that score," Shakespeare said. "Once was enough." Ambling to the cleft, he went sideways through the opening and sat next to the spring. No one had followed him. None of the renegades was the least bit interested in what he was doing. That included Flynt, who was too concerned about the scouts out crisscrossing the countryside.

In the cleft it was darker than on the shelf, dark enough for Shakespeare to pry the quartz from under his moccasin without fear of being caught. Palming it, he reversed his grip and sliced at the rope binding his wrists, a painstaking chore if ever there was one.

The sawtooth edge cut exceedingly slowly. Applying steady pressure for minutes on end in that awkward position used muscles he had not resorted to in ages. Twice Shakespeare had to stop to ease the agony in his wrists and fingers.

Slowly, inevitably, the rawhide rope parted. He was almost done when a shadowy shape filled the cleft and Galt barked, "What the hell is keeping you so long, McNair? You could've drank the spring dry by now."

"I was just enjoying a few moments of peace and quiet," Shakespeare said. "It's why I came back over here so often earlier."

"I was afraid you'd found a way out the back," Galt said, moving to one side. "Get your carcass out of there. From now on, you have two minutes to do whatever needs doing. Two minutes, and not a second longer. Savyy?"

"I understand," Shakespeare said. As he began to stand, he tucked his right leg to his chest so he could slip the quartz down his moccasin.

"Move it."

The mountain man walked to where his saddle and

parfleches had been placed, not far from the horse string. By holding his wrists close together, he concealed the cut he had made in the rawhide. After spreading out his blanket and covering himself from the waist down, he lay on his side.

Galt was scratching his armpit. "Turning in a bit early, aren't you?"

"When you're my age, you'll turn in early too," Shakespeare said.

"It stinks to grow old, doesn't it?"

"It beats the alternative."

The heavyset cutthroat had to ponder a bit before he caught on, and laughed. "Oh. I see your point. Even so, I reckon I'd rather be blasted by a lead ball or be stuck with a quiver full of arrows than to die of old age."

"A shallow philosophy," Shakespeare commented, "born of ignorance. White hairs have a lot to be said for them."

Galt snickered. "Name one thing."

"You get to look back over your life and see all the mistakes you made. You grow to appreciate what's really important, and what's so much cow manure. Every dawn becomes a natural masterpiece, every night you're grateful for the gift of another day. You look ahead to the unknown, and you thrill to the new adventure you'll face on the other side of the veil."

"Spare me, old man," Galt said. "When a body dies, they die. That's it. Nothing else. No heaven. No hell. Ashes to ashes, dust to dust."

"You don't believe in a hereafter?"

"No coon who can think for himself ever does. God is for those bred on fairy tales, McNair. It's for those who wet their pants at the notion of being no better than bugs."

Shakespeare swept a hand at the glittering stars that

bedecked the firmament. "Look up there, friend. Notice how they all have their place, how orderly they are? Think of how organized life is, how the air is just right for us to breathe, how the seasons change as regular as clockwork, how our bodies heal when we're hurt. That should tell you something."

"What? That a higher power planned it this way?" Galt grunted. "It's just how things are, McNair. Coincidence." He plodded toward the campfire. "You go on believing in fairy tales if you like. Me, I'm going to have some coffee. Enjoy myself while I can, that's the saying I live by."

Shakespeare had picked a spot far enough from the fire for him to be cloaked in shadow. Bending his legs up to his waist, he worked the quartz out and applied it to the rawhide binding his ankles. He had to be careful not to disturb the blanket and to stop whenever any of the cutthroats gazed in his general direction.

Soon the rawhide parted. Shakespeare sliced the rest of the way through the strip binding his wrists, then replaced the quartz for safekeeping and pretended to doze. Through cracked lids he saw Galt join Flynt and the two of them stare at him awhile. Did they suspect? Or were they plotting what to do with him once they had what they were after? As if there was any doubt. They dared not leave witnesses. Anyone who could identify them must be slain.

An hour dragged by, each second a week in itself. None of the scouts came back. Two of the cardplayers stepped to the rim, which left a solitary man by the fire, and he had his back to the horses.

Shakespeare reached out, gripped a parfleche, and pulled it under the blanket. Flattening it, he slid it close to his hips. He did the same with a second one, which he positioned beside his left shoulder. His saddle he pulled closer, draping the upper part of the blanket over it. The combined effect gave the illusion that he was curled up asleep.

Crawling out from under, Shakespeare snaked toward the horses. He regretted having to leave his personal effects, but he was sacrificing them for a worthy cause: his life.

The white mare was in the middle of the string. To reach her he would have to pass Flynt's mount and one other. The second animal could not have been less interested in him if it tried to be, but Flynt's was a wary critter that twisted its head to stare and nicker.

Shakespeare stopped, thinking that the animal would lose interest. But the horse kept on staring. And staring. He feared that one of the renegades would notice. Shortly thereafter, the cardplayers returned to the fire. Neither was very observant even in broad daylight; at night they were worse.

Then Flynt himself walked over, giving Shakespeare's blanket a long, searching look.

Had something aroused Flynt's suspicions? Shakespeare was not inclined to wait around to find out. Sliding to the rim, he crawled over the edge and into the inky night.

Chapter Fifteen

The Varga expedition crossed the St. Vrain at a ford Nate King selected. Like the majority of high-country waterways, the St. Vrain was narrow and fast. Countless deep pools were separated by stretches of foaming rapids. The spot Nate picked was a bend where the current slowed and the water rose no higher than a man's knees.

Paralleling the west bank, the expedition backtracked, traveling generally northeast until they came to a creek notable for its sandy bottom. Up this they turned, bearing to the northwest, climbing steeply. On their right towered Long's Peak and its sister, Mt. Meeker. On their left rose a high ridge covered by thick forest.

They rode mostly in shadow—the shadow of the ridge early in the day, the shadows of the mountains in the afternoon, the shadows of pines and firs the rest of the time.

The air was thin and clear and should have been

invigorating, but the column moved in tense silence, the profound quiet of the wilderness broken only by the dull thud of hooves, the creak of harness and saddle leather, and the clatter and jingle of supplies on the pack animals.

Manuel de Varga insisted that Nate always ride at the head of the column with him. Nate's hands were no longer tied, but he was denied a gun or any other weapon. It was unnerving to travel though the deep woods totally defenseless, never knowing when a painter or a grizzly or hostiles might pounce.

Varga refused to give Nate an answer to his proposal. Bothered by a bad feeling that something was going to go terribly wrong, and not wanting his family to have any part in it, Nate badgered the man.

Don Varga had grown increasingly tense and irritable the closer they drew to their goal. He had so much riding on the outcome that it affected his state of mind. He took to snapping at servants and *vaqueros* who did not perform their tasks well enough to suit him, or who were lax in obeying commands.

Even Diego, his pride and joy, earned a rebuke when the boy wandered off alone to admire some wildflowers. In front of the whole company, Don Varga subjected his son to a tongue-lashing that turned the boy's cheeks flaming red and caused murmuring among the *vaqueros,* among whom Diego was a favorite. Ignacio treated them too sternly, and Martin—well, Martin was so bland, he inspired neither respect nor dislike. Or so Nate assumed.

The big trapper grew anxious. They were putting more distance between them and the Twin Sisters; it would take his family that much longer to reach home. With that in mind, he turned to Varga as they wound along the gurgling creek and said, "What about the proposal I made you?"

"Which one?" Varga asked distractedly. More and

more he withdrew himself, speaking only when there was a need, or when he was addressed.

"You remember," Nate said. "I gave you my word to go along peaceably and stick with your outfit until you're done mining ore if you'll agree to let my family go."

"Oh. That." Varga started when a jay squawked in a nearby tree. "Damned animals," he grumbled. "They are forever making a person jump."

Nate studied his captor without being obvious. The strain was taking a severe toll. Gone was the affable, easygoing *patrón*. Varga grew more temperamental each day. They had better reach the mine soon, for all their sakes.

"I have still not decided, *senor*."

"But it's been days," Nate noted. "Make up your mind now, so they don't have so far to go."

Like a hissing viper, Don Varga spun in the saddle. "Who are you to tell *me* what to do? *I* am in control here! And I will make up my mind when I am good and ready, not before. Do you understand?"

The venomous outburst still rang in Nate's ears when the column stopped an hour later for a brief midday rest. He rode back down the line to his family.

Winona was rummaging in a parfleche for pemmican. They were about out. She had a few pieces of jerky cached for future use, in case they were ever able to slip away.

Don Varga was not the only one on whom the strain was beginning to tell. Winona would never admit as much to her loved ones, but she was more despondent than she could remember being in many winters. She feared not so much for herself as she did for her daughter and son and husband. They were her life. They were her reason for breathing. Should anything terrible befall them, she would not want to go on.

For their sake Winona put up a brave front. She smiled a lot and offered encouragement when Zach and Evelyn were depressed. She was always there for Nate to lean on.

But in the silent hours before dawn, when the camp was still and the wind had died and the forest itself slumbered, inwardly she wept in grating despair.

How long could this go on? she would ask herself. How much more must her family endure? She was thankful that none of them had been harmed. But she was also aware that the violation of Ute territory would be costly, and she did not care to have her family added to the toll.

Now, as Nate dismounted, she brought pemmican and said, "I saw Don Varga snap at you. What was that all about?"

Nate had not told her about the offer he had made Varga, because he knew how she would react. But faced with a direct question, he could not hide it any longer. In all the years they had been together he had never lied to her, and he never would. So he told her.

"You did *what*?" Winona exclaimed, stepping back in dismay. "How could you? We will never desert you, even if he were to agree."

"That's right, Pa," Zach declared, as upset as his mother. The very real likelihood of a clash with a war party had him excited to be part of it. "I'm not leaving if you don't. You taught me better than that."

Nate did not hide his exasperation. "If I want you to, you'll go. What I'm trying to do is for the best. I don't want any of you to be hurt."

"How could you shame us like this?" Winona said. "A Shoshone woman always stands by her man. In good times and bad. In peace and during war." She straightened. "I am not leaving, either. Not without you, husband."

"You're being pigheaded," Nate said. "What

192

about Evelyn? She's more important than your pride. We have to get her out of here before it's too late.''

Evelyn was hunkered by the creek, playfully poking a stick in the sand. Rising, she stepped between her parents, neither of whom saw her, and clasped her father's callused hand.

Nate looked down, annoyed by the interruption. ''What is it, little one?''

''I'm not that little any more, Pa,'' Evelyn said. ''I can make up my own mind about things. And it's best if we all stick together.''

''Let your ma and me work this out,'' Nate said, patting her on the head.

But Evelyn had more to say. ''We're a family, aren't we? And don't you always say that nothing is more important than family?''

''Yes, but—''

''We should always pull together, you tell us. We should always be there for each other. Like the time that evil lady and her wicked brother from the big city tried to murder us. And when the Bloods tried to rub us out.'' Evelyn squeezed her father's fingers. ''So long as we stand by one another, we'll be all right. Isn't that what you've told us over and over?''

Nate's words were coming back to haunt him. How could he make her see it his way without upsetting her? ''There are times, Blue Flower, when we have to do things we don't like, things we would never do normally. This is one of those times. If Varga agrees, I want you to take your ma and brother back to the cabin. I'll be along as soon as I can.''

Evelyn moved to her mother's side. ''No.''

''See what you've done?'' Nate said to Winona, and walked to a log. Slumping onto it, he morosely chewed his pemmican. They would never leave, not of their own free will. And since he was not one of those men who beat their wives or took a switch to their children when they bucked, he could not force them. It had always been his belief that differences could be talked out. When he put his foot down, he did so without being brutal.

Winona motioned for the children to stay put. Her husband did not sense her until her hand fell on his shoulder. "Do not tear yourself apart over this," she said softly.

"You're making a mistake," Nate said.

"Perhaps. I have made them before. I will make them again." Winona sat. "But how can I do otherwise, when I know in my heart what is right?"

"And what of the kids? How right will it feel if you have to bury one or both of them? What will your heart be telling you when you're standing over their freshly dug graves?"

Winona did not answer immediately. The issue was too important to be treated lightly. "No one wants to die," she began slowly. "Just as no one wants someone they care for to die. But dying is as much a part of life as living. Always being afraid of death makes us enjoy life that much less."

Nate did not butt in. She was entitled to her say, and he would hear her out.

"You fear for our safety. So you ask us to do that which we would never do on our own. You ask us to go against everything we believe, and everything you believe."

"Sometimes we have to. It's called compromise."

"Should anyone ever let their fears destroy their convictions?" Winona countered. "Is it not the mark of cowards to run away from hardship?" She paused. "Would you have us behave as cowards do? You should be proud that we are willing to stand by your side." She paused again. "How can we compromise that which makes us who we are?"

"I've always been proud of all of you," Nate said to defend himself.

"Prove it, husband. Being proud is easy when life is easy. Be proud of us *now,* when life is hardest, when we must rise up against those who would destroy us. Make us as proud of you as you are of us."

Nate stared into her eyes and felt his insides melt. "I'm sorry," he said, draping an arm over her shoulders. "Through thick and thin it will be."

Winona glanced at the nearest *vaqueros,* none of whom was watching. Impulsively, she kissed her man full on the lips, a display of affection she rarely indulged in when there were strangers around.

A shout at the head of the column was the signal for the expedition to resume its tired march. Nate pecked Evelyn on the cheek, advised Zach to always stay close to them, and trotted to the front where Don Varga waited. The Spaniard was consulting his map.

"How soon until we reach the big lake, *Senor* King?"

"By tonight."

Varga gazed at the lower slopes of Long's Peak. "Then, if all goes well, by tomorrow night we will be at the mine."

Finally. Nate was relieved. But they had to be realistic. "Let's just hope it's there."

"Why wouldn't it be?"

"The map could still turn out to be wrong about the exact location. And what if the Utes sealed the tunnel after they drove off the soldiers?"

"Sealed the tunnel?" Don Varga said, shocked. "Mother of God! No! Surely simple savages would not be clever enough to do such a thing?"

"Those savages, as you keep calling them, are as smart as the two of us."

The Spaniard chewed on his lower lip. "It would add weeks, perhaps months, to our effort. Why, if we are not finished by the change of weather in the fall, we might have to stay the winter."

"Don't even think it," Nate said. "You have no idea of how bad the winters are. Snow piles up higher than my cabin. And the temperature drops to thirty or forty below zero. You'd lose half your people to cold and hunger."

"How many winters have you survived?"

"That's not the point."

Don Varga, in the act of folding his map, jabbed it at Nate as if it were a knife. "It is *precisely* the point, *senor*. I should have thought I had made my intentions clear by now, but apparently I have not." His voice lowered to a throaty growl. "I will not let *anything* stand in my way. Not these mountains, not the Utes, not all the wild animals alive, and certainly not a single *winter*."

Nate was saved from having to comment by the arrival of the Maricopas. Chivari gestured to the northwest. "Big water not far," he reported in his heavily accented English. "Many ducks, many geese."

Varga frowned. "You came all the way back to tell me you saw the lake and some birds?"

"Saw heap plenty warriors."

Nate's heart seemed to skip a beat. The moment he had dreaded most of all had come. Somehow, to avert mass bloodshed, he had to influence the outcome. "They must be Utes," he remarked.

"How many?" Don Varga asked.

"We count," Chivari said, and held up all his fingers and thumbs two times, then another three fingers.

"Twenty-three," Varga said pensively. "That's more than I would like, but we still outnumber them two to one. The odds are with us if we can take them by surprise."

Nate swore that he could feel the blood drain from

his face. "You can't be thinking what I think you're thinking!"

Turning his handsome Arabian to face the column, Don Varga sniffed in contempt. "Why not, *senor*? Have you not warned me again and again that the Utes will rise against us once they learn we are here? Out of your mouth has come their judgment."

"Don't do this," Nate pleaded.

Varga acted as if he had not heard. "As I see it, our main objective is to prevent them from alerting the Ute villages. So, it is simple! We must not let a single heathen escape alive."

"Please, no."

Ignacio, Martin, and Diego converged at a gesture from their father. So did two of Varga's most trusted *vaqueros*. A hasty conference in Spanish resulted in the *vaqueros* moving back down the line, relaying instructions. Rifles were checked, pistols loosened, swords and knives flourished in preparation for the attack.

Nate could not help himself. He grasped the Spaniard by the wrist. "In heaven's name, think of what you're about to do! So long as you don't kill any Utes there's a chance—a slim one, I'll admit—but a chance that they'll let you go on about your business unmolested. But kill just one of them and there will be no holding them back. They'll rally from every village. Hundreds and hundreds of warriors will mass against you. They'll sit in council, pass around the pipe of war, then tear into you like a hailstorm. There will be no stopping them."

"You exaggerate, I am sure," Don Varga said. "I have enough men and guns to hold off an army. We will mow them down like wheat under a scythe. In the end, they will regret their folly and let us get on with the mining without being hindered."

How do you convince someone who has closed his

mind? How can you persuade a man who thinks he has all the answers that he is on the road to perdition? Nate tightened his grip. "I won't let you get away with this," he said grimly.

"You can't stop me" was the Spaniard's rejoinder. At an imperious nod, three *vaqueros* closed in, unlimbering pistols. Varga issued directions in Spanish, then said in English for Nate's benefit, "I have ordered them to shoot you if you do not release me by the time I count to four."

"Is there no making you understand?" Nate said earnestly.

"Uno."

"You're dooming everyone in your party."

"Dos."

"Damn it, Varga! Is the gold worth your lives?"

"Tres."

So mad that he burned with a desire to pound the Spaniard's face to a pulp, Nate jerked his hand off. "There? Happy? Because you won't be once this is over."

In rapid order, thirty of the *vaqueros* were selected to accompany the *patrón* and his sons. The rest were to stay behind and safeguard the servants and captives. Nate took it for granted that he would stay also, and turned his horse to go be with his family.

"Where do you think you are going, *senor*?" Manuel Varga was quick to ask. "I insist on the pleasure of your company."

"You're taking me along? Why? I won't lift a finger against the Utes," Nate stressed.

"How noble," Ignacio said scornfully. "We should leave him here, *padre*. The *gringo* will be of no use to us."

Don Varga was forming the *vaqueros* into a column of twos. "That is where you are wrong, my son. A true leader learns to make use of all his resources.

The mountain man will not attack the Utes, but I warrant he will not sit still for *being* attacked. If they catch wind of us and stalk us, he will spot them first."

"That is what we have the Maricopas for," Diego reminded him.

"Indians cannot always be trusted to turn against other Indians," Don Varga said. "Always have a plan you can fall back on in case your first one fails through no fault of your own."

"*Sí, mi padre.*"

While all this transpired, Winona, Zach, and Evelyn were herded toward a clearing, along with the servants. Maria, Francisca, and Luisa were shunted to a sunny spot close to them.

Evelyn was disturbed by the burst of activity. "What's going on, Ma?" she asked, fingers entwined in her mother's buckskin dress.

"I do not know, daughter," Winona answered. She did not speak Spanish, but the flurry of commands and commotion signaled something important was about to happen. Were they near the mine?

Maria Varga happened to hear Evelyn's question. "Our men go to attack the Utes," she divulged. "Do not worry, though. We will be well guarded while they are gone. You are welcome to join my sisters and me if you would like."

Attacking the Utes! Winona rose onto the tips of her toes to see the front of the line. Nate was hemmed in by a trio of *vaqueros*. The set of his features testified to his feelings. Before she could catch his attention, he was ushered off into the woods. "Do they know what they do?" she said in her own tongue.

"Why are they bothering the Utes, Mother?" Evelyn asked in the Shoshone language. "The Utes have left us alone for a long time. This will stir up trouble."

Winona nodded absently. "Trouble" was an understatement. The Utes would go on the warpath, wiping out every Spaniard, Mexican, and white they could find. That might include her family, for while the Utes were grateful for the truce they had negotiated with her people, the Utes would not forgive their having an indirect part in the slaughter of Ute men.

"Won't you join us, *Senora* King?" Francisca coaxed.

Taking Evelyn's hand, Winona ventured to their blanket. She beckoned Zach, but he shook his head. Sitting so she could see the column leave, she said boldly, "Your father makes a grave mistake, *senorita*. Many will suffer."

Francisca scoffed. "My *padre* is very clever, *senora*. He is always two steps ahead of everyone else. Trust him. He will show the savages that we are a force to be reckoned with."

The other sisters nodded agreement. Winona just stared at them, overcome by sorrow. They were so sure of themselves, and so terribly, utterly wrong. They were innocents about to stick their heads in the gaping maw of a ravenous bear. They were fools.

"If you truly love your father and brothers," Winona said, "you will jump on a horse and fly after them. Convince your father to change his mind before it is too late."

Maria laughed. "Are you seriously suggesting we tell our father that we believe he is wrong?" She laughed louder. "*Senora*, we are women, remember? And his daughters. It is not our proper place to question his authority."

A sharp reply was on the tip of Winona's tongue, but she held it in. Who was she to criticize, when among her own people the women had little say in important affairs. It was the warriors who sat in council, the warriors who decided when to go to war, the warriors who policed the villages, and always it was a warrior who led the tribe.

Shoshone women tended their tepees, cooked and sewed and foraged for berries, and the like. They did not sit in council. Rarely did they go to war. Whatever influence they had was exerted in the privacy of their lodges.

Once, she had thought that was as it should be. But living with Nate had changed her outlook. He insisted that she have her say in every decision. He treated her more as an equal than any man ever had. Even among whites, that was unusual. Most browbeat their women, never letting them make a decision.

It had taken time for her to change. At first, when Nate had asked her opinion, she had always said, "I don't care. Whatever you want is fine." Later, it had dawned on her that he really *did* want to know how she felt, and that she put an extra burden on him when she put it all on his shoulders.

"Isn't this marvelous!" Luisa said. "What a grand adventure! We will have much to tell our friends and relatives after we return to Spain."

You should live that long, child, Winona thought. *We all should!*

Chapter Sixteen

Sandy Lake, as some of the trappers had taken to calling it, was two miles above sea level. Its rich blue water was sterling pure and crystal clear. A haven for wildfowl of all kind, it was ringed by thick forest that gave the Spaniard and his *vaqueros* ample cover as they advanced stealthily on the unsuspecting Utes.

Nate King's wrists were bound again, and a *vaquero* was assigned to ride directly behind him and shoot him dead if he tried to get away.

The Ute camp was on the northeast shore. On a broad sandy strip were scattered more than a dozen temporary conical lodges constructed of long trimmed limbs and brush.

It was a large hunting party, out after elk. They had already brought down quite a few. Hundreds of pounds of meat, cut into thin strips, hung drying in the sun on crude racks. Hides were being scraped with fleshing tools, and cured. Many had been stretched taut and tied to big frames.

Spanish Slaughter

Don Varga halted his party several hundred yards from the shore. Accompanied by his sons, the Maricopas, and Nate, he crept closer for a better look.

Nate wished there were some way he could warn the Utes. But what could he do, with a pistol muzzle jammed against his spine? Any outcry, and the *vaquero* would blow a hole in his back as wide around as a walnut.

He did not see any warriors he knew among those engaged in various jobs, but he was horrified to find that four women were present.

The Utes were joking and laughing, totally at ease. They had no reason to fear enemies this far into their territory. No doubt, no one had ever attacked them here. They felt safe, secure. So secure that they had not bothered to post sentries. Bows and quivers had been left in the lodges, for the most part. Not a single warrior was armed with a rifle or pistol. They were easy pickings, and Varga knew it.

The Spaniard's brow glistened with sweat. His eyes held a peculiar gleam as he bobbed a finger, counting them. "Twenty-three warriors," he said with satisfaction. "Just as Chivari told us."

Nate noticed that the women did not rate a mention. He saw that the mounts and pack animals were tied near the lodges. The Utes did not mix their horses; each warrior kept his close to his lodge. There had to be more than fifty animals, and that was disturbing. "What if there are more?" he whispered.

Don Varga turned. "How is that again?"

"Maybe some of the warriors are off hunting. They'll hear the shots, and never show themselves."

Ignacio scowled. "They are all there, Father. He tries to scare us off, to make us change our minds."

"Perhaps," Don Varga whispered, "but it is not a chance we can afford to take, my son. We will wait and see if other savages show up."

Nate had bought the unsuspecting Utes a little time, at least. He was ordered to sit. The Vargas made themselves comfortable. Martin and Azul were sent back to tell the *vaqueros* to lie low and keep absolutely quiet.

Nate was tense with foreboding. It was his fervent prayer that a roving hunter would stumble on them and sound an alarm. The Utes could reach the trees before the *vaqueros* reached the shore, and most would escape.

Knowing Manuel de Varga, though, the setback would not stop him. The expedition would forge on to the mine, with appalling consequences for all involved.

Time dragged. Nate anxiously scanned the lake and the woods, longing to see Utes approach. None did. None of the warriors even left camp.

Then, about an hour later, three more strode out of the undergrowth to the north, two of them carrying a black-tailed buck on a long pole between them. On their arrival at camp, the women took charge of the deer, setting to work butchering it for the evening meal.

"So," Don Varga said softly. "That is the last of them, I do believe."

"You don't know that for certain," Nate whispered. "My advice to you is to wait a while longer."

"And how long would be long enough to suit you?" Varga responded. "Another hour? Another day? No, *Senor* King, you are trying to stall us. We go in now, while the light is still with us."

"At last," Ignacio gloated. "I will bring our men and have them fan out to surround the camp."

Varga snatched his son's sleeve. "Make it plain that they must move like ghosts. The man who gives us away will answer to me personally. Tell them not to shoot until I give the signal. We will fire a volley into the savages, then rush in and finish them off.''

Ignacio started again to leave, but his father held on to his arm. ''Above all, my son, impress on them that not a single heathen must escape us. The women, too, must be shot down like the animals they are. If any of the Utes are able to mount up, our men must shoot their horses out from under them.''

''It will be done, Father.''

The next half an hour was one of the most awful in Nate's whole life. To know that thirty innocents were about to be slaughtered, and that he was powerless to prevent it, tormented him in heart and soul. His only recourse was to give a yell at the right moment. It would earn him a rap on the noggin, or much worse, but he could not just sit there and do nothing.

The Spaniard glanced at him, then leaned toward Chivari and whispered so that no one else could hear. Nodding, the Maricopa rose and began to go in the same direction Martin and Azul had gone.

Nate did not think much of it until suddenly he was gripped by the shoulders and flung to the ground. Chivari pinned his chest, while the *vaquero,* acting under Don Varga's directions, viciously punched him on the jaw. Bright points of light pinwheeled before Nate's eyes. He remained conscious but groggy. He was dimly aware that his mouth was being pried open and that something was being stuffed into it. He tried to swallow and nearly gagged.

A gag! Nate realized. They were ensuring he could not warn the Utes! He struggled in vain. When the *vaqueros* and Chivari rose, he had a bandanna stuffed into his mouth and another tied around the lower half of his face, holding it in place.

''There,'' Don Varga said. ''In case you had any silly ideas of letting the Utes know we are here.''

Could the man read his thoughts? Shaking his head to clear it, Nate sat up. The *vaquero* sat next to him, the cocked pistol wedged against his ribs.

"Try anything, *senor*," Don Varga whispered, "and you assuredly die."

Impotent fury brought tears to the mountain man's eyes. He had to sit and watch as the *vaqueros* filed past and spread out to enclose the encampment in a crescent of rifles and pistols. For once, the Utes had their guard down. The women were about ready to cook the buck, and the hungry men gathered to talk and relax.

Don Varga and his sons moved in. The skinny *vaquero* prodded Nate forward. Nate intentionally stepped on a dry twig that cracked loudly, but not loudly enough to be heard at the lake. For his ruse, he was hit across the back of the head. His legs nearly buckled, and it was a minute before he could go on.

By then the Mexicans were ranging wide to the left and right. Silently, they stalked their prey, the whole line freezing when one of their number accidentally smacked the stock of his rifle against a pistol tucked under his belt. The offender withered under Don Varga's glare, but no harm had been done. The Utes did not hear the noise.

Advancing more carefully, the *vaqueros* took up positions within twenty feet of the sandy shore. A few horses lifted their heads, but none whinnied. The wind was blowing from west to east, bearing the scent of the attackers away from the camp.

Nate was made to kneel near Don Varga. The Spaniard was staring at a petite woman roasting a haunch over a crackling fire. Was it Nate's imagination, or did Varga's face soften?

For the longest while the *patrón* simply stared. With a toss of his head, he snapped out of it. The peculiar gleam returned. Perspiration coated him from his hairline to his neck. He glanced at the trapper.

Nate could not speak, but he could convey his feelings with his eyes. *Don't do it!* he yearned to shout. Varga was about to cross the invisible line that separated humanity from the beasts, and once across, there was no turning back.

Ignacio eagerly hefted his rifle and nudged his father. Don Varga nodded. All along the line, rifles were leveled and quietly cocked. Cheeks were bent, sights aligned.

Nate's blood boiled. He looked at the Utes and began to rise. Immediately, the skinny *vaquero* and one of the Maricopas seized him and held him fast.

Part of him wanted to close his eyes and blot out the slaughter to come, but another part of him overrode the impulse. He must be a witness to the atrocity so there would be someone to speak out against Varga should the opportunity arise. Justice demanded that he do all in his power to see that the Spaniard paid in full for the heinous act.

Don Varga was squinting down his barrel. Opening his right eye, he looked at Nate, his expression unreadable. It appeared as if he were going to say something. Then, abruptly squaring his jaw, he took aim once more.

Nate attempted to rise, to crash through the brush, to alert the Utes, but the *vaqueros* and the Maricopa held him in grips of iron. As if in slow motion, he saw a Ute warrior smile, saw one of the women throw back her head and laugh, saw the petite one bend to run a finger over the top of the roasting deer haunch.

A single word was roared in Spanish. At Don Varga's command, thirty-six rifles boomed, belching lead and smoke. The combined retorts echoed off Long's Peak, rumbling like thunder.

About half the Utes dropped at the first volley. Many were struck by more than one ball. Nate saw a husky warrior lurch backward as a ball cored his chest, another his neck, and a third his thigh. The man was dead on his feet. Oozing blood, he melted to the sand.

Bloody bodies littered the ground. A woman thrashed and moaned, a gaping wound high in her shoulder, her left knee shattered.

In the time it took the *vaqueros* to bring their spare rifles into play, the Utes scrambled for their bows or bolted toward the trees to the north and the south. One man ran to the lake and dived neatly into the water.

Standing, Don Varga bellowed. The entire line closed in. The Spaniards, Mexicans, and Maricopas all fired at will, as targets presented themselves. Guns blasted in a steady cadence, punctuated by screams and war whoops.

An arrow sizzled out of the blue to transfix a *vaquero* on the left. Another shaft caught Diego in the right leg and he dropped, yowling. Don Varga instantly halted and knelt by his youngest. When the rest of his men likewise stopped, he waved them on with angry commands.

Ignacio took charge. Boldly stepping into the open, he fired his spare rifle, handed it to a Maricopa, and drew two pistols.

Nate's eyes were glued to the Utes, who had rallied and were ferociously fighting back. From behind their conical lodges, warriors sent arrows whizzing into the woods. Two women were still alive and passing out arrows to the men as fast as the men could shoot.

Three Mexicans were down, either dead or severely wounded. The line wavered, trading lead for barbed-tipped shafts. Hot lead tore into the lodges like molten sleet, sending slivers flying everywhere.

For a few moments it seemed as if the *vaqueros* would break and retreat. Then Ignacio shrieked like an angry eagle and charged. Taking their cue from him, the Mexicans spilled onto the shore, shooting madly.

Arrows and spears whistled through the air. Another four *vaqueros* fell, one with an arrow through his left eye, another clutching a spear that had pierced him below the sternum.

In a collective rage, the *vaqueros* rushed the lodges. Venting howls and whoops, the Utes bounded out to meet them. War clubs and tomahawks were met by swords, knives, and pistols. The combat was man to man.

Outnumbered, the Utes fought fiercely. Two or three *vaqueros* would jump a single warrior, seeking to batter him down through sheer weight of numbers.

Nate could not have closed his eyes now if it meant his life. The Utes had long been his enemies, yet he was overcome with pride. They resisted valiantly, battling with more than human desperation. Gradually, though, they were whittled down.

Soon only six warriors and the petite woman were left. Clustering together, side to side and back to back, they sought to break through to the trees. In a solid breast, cutting and bashing and hacking, their wedge parted their enemies like the prow of a canoe slashing through water.

Above the bedlam rose Don Varga's voice. The words were in Spanish, but Nate did not need to have them translated.

"Stop them! Do you hear me? *Stop them!*"

Two of the Utes sprawled, pierced by a dozen wounds. Another had his throat cut. A fourth took a sword in the back. The last pair and the petite woman paused, too exhausted to take another step. Covered with blood, their garments gashed and rent, they panted and gasped, held at bay, waiting for their adversaries to end it.

Ignacio pointed at the tallest Ute, and four pistol

balls shattered the man's skull. The last warrior stepped in front of the woman to shield her. Ignacio's finger stabbed again. A burly Mexican, wielding a sword, sprang, the curved steel shearing into the warrior's temple like a knife through soft wax.

Only the petite woman was left. In her scarlet-stained right hand was a long knife, in her left the broken haft of a lance. She jabbed at a *vaquero* who skipped in close. Another attempted to grab her from the rear, and she whirled, opening his arm with her blade.

Stepping forward, Ignacio pointed his pistol at her head. She faced him, slowly straightening. Weariness and resignation etched her lovely features. And so did something else. Squaring her slim shoulders, she met Ignacio's gaze in bold defiance.

Nate's heart went out to her. She reminded him so much of Winona. He wanted to scream in rage, but all he could do with the gag wedged so tight was groan.

Some of the Mexicans and Maricopas were equally impressed. They lowered their weapons, bestowing looks of respect on the blood-drenched figure who so calmly awaited her doom.

Ignacio took another pace. Extending his pistol, he laughed, whether in glee or scorn it was hard to say. And as the cold mirth died, he casually stroked the trigger.

Nate bowed his head, unable to bear the sight of the twitching form or the gruff mirth of several of the *vaqueros*. He let himself be hauled to his feet and shoved toward the shore on the heels of Don Varga and the two men supporting Diego.

Manuel Varga barked orders. His men went from body to body, finishing off the wounded Utes and helping fallen companions. Suddenly a yell brought them in a rush to the water's edge.

The warrior who had dived into the lake was hundreds of feet out, stroking smoothly, bound for the opposite shoreline.

"Martin!" Don Varga shouted. "He is yours. Take him."

The middle son took four or five steps into the lake, the water rising up to his knees. Tucking his rifle to his shoulder, he fixed a bead on the swimmer.

Nate prayed that Martin would miss. It was a difficult shot; even Shakespeare, who was generally acknowledged as one of the best marksmen in the trapping fraternity, might not be able to make it.

The warrior slowed. Nate tried to push the gag from his mouth with his tongue so he could shout a warning, but it was hopeless. He watched, aghast, as the Ute tread water to catch his breath and glanced shoreward.

Spotting the massed Spaniards and Mexicans, the warrior bent and fairly streaked toward the far side. He was a marvelous swimmer, his arms and legs superbly coordinated. Spray swirled around him and spewed from under his feet.

"He is a fish," Don Varga commented.

Martin had not twitched a muscle. Now, inhaling and holding the breath to steady his aim, he thumbed back the hammer, then lightly touched his forefinger to the trigger.

Nate sidled toward him, thinking to ram his shoulder into Martin's at the very moment Martin fired. But the *vaquero* guarding him was too clever. The man grasped him by the back of the shirt and held him where he was. Nate drew back a leg to kick.

Martin's rifle spat lead and flame, the recoil snapping the barrel upward. Three hundred feet out on the lake, the Ute warrior raised both arms into the air, turned completely around, and sank like a rock. All eyes were fixed on the spot, waiting for him to reappear. He never did.

Martin looked expectantly at his father, apparently anticipating a compliment. If that was the case, he was severely disappointed. Don Varga, grunting, walked into the camp. Martin's cheeks flushed, and he clenched his fists until the knuckles were white, but he did not say anything.

Nate surveyed the carnage and felt his stomach curl up into itself. The massacre had been a success. Every Ute, every last man and woman, was either dead or dying. *Vaqueros* were dispatching those who still clung tenaciously to life.

Don Varga came over. "There is no need for this anymore," he said, and unfastened the bandanna that held the gag in place. "I trust it was not too much of an inconvenience."

Wriggling his tongue, Nate spat the gag out. His mouth felt dry and rough. Swallowing, he moistened it enough to rasp, "Go to hell!"

"I most likely will," Don Varga said soberly, staring at a Ute woman whose brains formed a gory halo around her broken body. "I most likely will."

Revulsion and hatred waged a bitter war in the depths of Nate's being. If only his wrists were free! He would hurl himself at the Spaniard and throttle the life from him with his own two hands.

Harsh laughter came from a trio of *vaqueros* who had surrounded a warrior trying to sit up. The Ute had a hole in his torso, another in his arm, a third in his leg. A pool of blood framed him as he unsteadily propped an arm and struggled to rise. A *vaquero,* chortling, kicked the arm out from under the Ute, and the man pitched onto his face.

"Enough! Kill them, don't torment them!" Don Varga yelled in English, forgetting himself. Repeating the command in Spanish, he walked northward alone.

The same *vaquero* who had kicked the Ute now produced a dagger and plunged it into the warrior's unprotected back, between the shoulder blades. The Ute exhaled once loudly, convulsed, and died.

Nate could not stand to see any more killing. Sick to his spirit, he shambled off, head bowed. There would be no stopping the Utes now. Once the bodies were discovered, the tribe would rise up in righteous wrath and launch a campaign of extermination that would make the bloodthirsty campaigns of the Blackfeet pale in comparison.

Varga's only hope was to find the vein, mine enough ore to suit him, and vacate the territory before the Utes learned of the slaughter.

"What have I done, *senor*?"

Nate stopped. Don Varga was a few feet away. Self-loathing marked the haughty Spaniard's swarthy countenance as he stared at a Ute no older than Diego whose right cheek was gone. "What have I done?"

"What you set out to do, as I recollect," Nate snapped. "Remember this day well, mister! Sear it into your brain, so at night when you're asleep you'll hear the screams of the dying and see the faces of those women as they were shot to pieces."

Nate took a step and would have cuffed Varga if not for the *vaquero,* who seized his arm. "I want you to recall every detail!" he declared, his anger swelling like a river in a torrent. The floodgates had been lowered, and his pent-up emotions roiled out. "I want you to have nightmares for the rest of your life! I want you to suffer! To suffer as few men ever have!"

Suddenly shoving the *vaquero,* Nate hiked both arms to bash the Spaniard full in the face. Don Varga, though, did not try to defend himself. His haggard visage had grown pasty, his eyes glazed. Deaf and dumb to events around him, he stood there like a dumb cow about to be butchered. Nate banded his muscles, then hesitated.

"What have I done?" Don Varga repeated, gazing out over the scarlet-spattered battleground at the scores of crumpled figures.

Nate peered into the Spaniard's dull eyes. Like a branch that breaks after being bent too far, something had broken deep within Manuel de Varga. Nate stepped back without swinging.

"Patrón?" the *vaquero* said.

Don Varga tilted his face to the heavens. His lips trembled and he took a halting step. "I had to do it," he said, but to neither of them. Thrusting his hands at the sky, he contorted his fingers into claws and roared, "I had to do it!"

The cry echoed off the peaks, growing fainter and fainter until it was swallowed altogether by the vastness of the shadowed mountains.

Chapter Seventeen

Blue Water Woman was glad that Flathead saddles did not have large saddle horns like those some whites used. She was jostled and jolted every few steps as her captors led the sorrel through the darkening woods. After they had traveled a quarter of a mile, her belly was terribly sore.

It was not the sorrel's fault. The three Utes were in a hurry to reach their dead companion before sunset. So they pushed their animals, not caring how rough the terrain was.

Bands of pink and yellow painted the western horizon when they finally reached the ridge. The dead man was right where he had fallen, but he was not alone.

Several buzzards were perched on the corpse, one pecking at the neck. Stout howled in anger and trotted toward them, waving an arm. One bird hissed in protest, but vultures were not renowned for their bravery. Flapping ponderously, they rose into the sky and circled overheard, waiting for another chance at their supper.

Hook Nose was more upset than Stout. Galloping up, he dismounted and knelt by the dead warrior. Tenderly placing a palm on the man's chest, Hook Nose said something in the Ute tongue. Then, unslinging his bow from his shoulder, he nocked a shaft and sent it whizzing at the buzzards. The arrow clipped a wing on one of them; marvelous skill, considering how high they had climbed.

Without further ado, the buzzards left to find food elsewhere.

Rope drew rein and dismounted, leaving his end of the rawhide dangling across his animal. He did not bother to lower Blue Water Woman down.

Another dispute broke out. Judging by their gestures, Blue Water Woman gathered that Hook Nose wanted to take the dead warrior with them but Stout and Rope did not. She figured that they had made up their minds when the horses were ushered beyond the boulders and camp was set up. Rope roughly yanked her off the sorrel and practically threw her to the ground.

Sore and bruised, Blue Water Woman moved to a boulder and sat with her back to it. The Utes ignored her at first. Hook Nose got a fire going. Rope stripped the horses and tethered them. Stout went off down the slope and did not come back until well after the sun had relinquished the sky to the stars.

When the other two looked at him hopefully and Stout frowned, Blue Water Woman guessed that he had gone in search of the dead warrior's mount and not found it. That would pose a problem if they were determined to take the body along. They had only the four animals. In order to cart the corpse, one of them would have to walk, slowing them considerably.

Their evening meal consisted of pemmican taken

from a parfleche belonging to Hook Nose. None was offered to her. Nor was she given any water. Her throat was parched, and she sorely craved a drink. Making bold to slide toward them, she said aloud in her own language, "I thirst. Please share your water with me."

Rope glanced at her as if surprised by her presence. Standing, he walked up and stared a few moments. She could not tell what he was thinking, but it became apparent the next second when he grabbed her by the hair and dragged her back to the boulders. She clutched at his wrist and received a swift kick in the shins for her effort.

Muttering spitefully in Ute, Rope unwound the rawhide rope from her neck and coiled it tightly around her ankles instead. After giving it a jerk to ensure it was secure, he straightened and smirked.

"You are a heartless bastard," Blue Water Woman said in English. "I did not mean to kill your friend. It was an accident. Do you understand? An accident."

She was wasting her breath. Rope kicked her again, although not very hard, and sauntered to the fire. She was left alone with her bitter thoughts and her misery.

The night was endless and cold. At that altitude the temperature dropped quickly once the sun went down, so by midnight she was shivering and strongly tempted to crawl to the fire, where Stout sat up keeping watch while the other two slept. But she held no illusions about what would occur, and she had been beaten enough for one day.

By the middle of the night, Blue Water Woman changed her mind. She could not sleep, it was so cold. Without a blanket, the chill had seeped through her dress into her bones.

Marshaling her nerve, Blue Water Woman crawled toward the small fire. She had to move much as a snail would, by hunching her shoulders and hips and then straightening. It was painful and it was slow, but she eventually came close enough to the flames to feel their warmth.

Stout looked at her. He made as if to stand, then settled back. Glancing at Rope, he pursed his thick lips in thought. With a shrug, he folded his arms and gazed off across the mountains as he had been doing.

The message was clear. Blue Water Woman was intensely grateful. She scooted a little closer, relishing the warm sensation that spread throughout her body. In her exhausted state, she was asleep within seconds, totally oblivious to what went on around her. If a grizzly had wandered into camp and stood on her, she might not have woken up, so soundly was she asleep.

That all changed when pain lanced down her skull into her neck. Startled, she blinked awake, her mind sluggish.

It was dawn. The Utes were preparing to leave. Rope had her by the hair and was dragging her to the horses. Once again she was thrown over the back of the sorrel and the rawhide looped around her neck. She objected but was ignored.

The warriors rode down the slope in single file. The previous evening they had brought the body onto the ridge, and Blue Water Woman was greatly surprised that they now left it there, covered by a blanket.

She understood their purpose when they came to where she had last seen the dead warrior's mount, and Stout and Rope climbed down to inspect the grass. They were going to track the bay, which meant she was in for a long, agonizing day of being bounced and battered.

Her prediction proved accurate. The bay had wandered aimlessly over some of the roughest patches of ground around. By noon she was queasy. She tugged on the rope to get Rope's attention.

"Let me ride," she requested in Flathead.

The warrior did not react.

"Please!" Blue Water Woman said, gesturing at her stomach and grimacing to show how bad off she was.

Rope grinned and kept on going.

Furious, Blue Water Woman gripped the rawhide with both hands at the point where it was coiled around her neck. Bracing herself, she pulled with all her might. It was torn from Rope's grasp, and he reined up, calling out to the others.

Twisting, Blue Water Woman slid from the sorrel. Her legs were wobbly but held her up long enough for her to grip the sorrel's mane and swing astride it. Rope was moving toward her. She quickly wound the rawhide, smiled sweetly, and offered it to him.

Coarse laughter erupted from Stout and Hook Nose. Stout made a comment that caused Rope to look as if he had just sat on a thorn. With a sharp snap of his arm, he snatched the rawhide, wheeled his horse, and rode on.

Blue Water Woman kneed the sorrel, keeping pace. They would let her ride! It was a small boon, but it made all the difference in the world to her.

Late in the afternoon, Hook Nose gave a yip and pointed. On a slope below grazed the bay. It heard the shout and regarded them warily, its ear pricked. Slapping his legs, Hook Nose trotted lower to claim it. He had gone half the distance when the bay snorted, pranced, and galloped eastward.

Instantly, the Utes gave chase. Blue Water Woman was hard pressed to stay close enough to Rope to keep the rawhide from biting into her neck. He yanked on it every now and again, even though there was no need.

The bay plunged over a crest. When they reached the spot, the horse was gone, having vanished into heavy timber. Rope made a harsh comment, but Hook

Nose motioned and galloped on into the pines.

Once among the trees, Blue Water Woman was constantly jerked and tugged. Rope would change direction without warning, and unless she promptly did likewise, the rawhide would grow so taut that it dug into her neck.

Rope was so intent on catching the bay that he rarely checked on her. So when a meadow broadened before them and they were speeding across open ground, Blue Water Woman slipped her fingers under the noose, wrenched at it until the rawhide loosened, and slid it up and over her head.

Rope never noticed. There was now an added two feet of rawhide between them, making it easier for her to keep up with him. She toyed with the notion of undoing her wrists, but that was bound to rouse his wrath.

The bay ran them a merry chase. Having tasted freedom, it resisted being caught. Mile after mile fell behind them, and still the animal maintained a wide lead.

They were winding into a lush valley when Rope hollered and slowed. Hook Nose and Stout imitated him, their quizzical expressions showing that they did not know what he was up to.

Rope shoved the end of the rawhide into Stout's hands, then took off as if shot from a cannon, his speckled horse proving once again that it was as fleet and nimble as any alive.

They stayed where they were, watching the pursuit. The bay ran its heart out, its mane and tail whipping in the wind, but the many miles they had already covered had taken a toll, and its sides were slick with sweat.

The shaggy speckled bolt of lightning narrowed the gap rapidly.

Despite herself, Blue Water Woman was impressed

by Rope's horsemanship. He was as skilled as any man she had ever seen, including the Comanches, who were widely regarded as the best horsemen anywhere. He jumped obstacles and avoided others with uncanny mastery. When the bay angled down a sheer slope, Rope never hesitated. He hurtled down too, leaning far back to better balance his body and make it less taxing on his mount. At the bottom, they flew onward even faster than before.

The bay was running on shreds of stamina. Its coat was lathered white, its head drooping. At long last it halted, unable to run another step. Game to the last, it shied when Rope caught up and tried to grab the reins. He had to virtually ram his mount into the bay in order to lay his hands on the rope. Victorious, he glanced up the mountain at them and yipped like a coyote.

They could not start back right away. The bay was too winded. So Rope tied it to a tree, then turned toward the sorrel. Only then did he discover that the rawhide was no longer around her neck, and an inarticulate growl escaped him, the closest an Indian came to swearing.

Stout and Hook Nose turned. The latter moved toward her as if afraid she was about to bolt, but Stout put his hands on his ample stomach and laughed hilariously. Taking the rawhide from Rope, he shook it and offered a remark that brought a huge smile to Hook Nose but a scowl to Rope.

Much to Blue Water Woman's surprise, Rope did not press the issue. Throwing his end of the rawhide to the ground, he let her climb down on her own and did not bother her as she stepped to a log and sat.

The Utes held a council. Having no idea what it was about, Blue Water Woman contented herself with licking her fingers and rubbing them across the nasty raw furrow in her skin where the rawhide had bit deep. She stiffened when someone appeared at her side.

It was Stout, carrying a parfleche. Squatting, he rummaged in it and brought forth a buffalo horn covered by a circular strip of buffalo hide. He held it out to her.

Not knowing what he was about, she accepted uncertainly. The horn was heavier than it should be. Something was inside. He gestured, indicating she should remove the hide. Loosening the cord that bound it, she learned that the horn contained a greenish salve similar to herbal medicines her own people relied on. She caught the scent of bear fat.

Stout acted out dipping a finger into the horn and applying some to his neck.

Nodding, Blue Water Woman did so. Almost immediately the burning subsided. Whatever plant had been mixed in with the fat was remarkably potent. After she was done, she handed the horn back, smiling to express her gratitude.

Rope did not appear any too happy. Nor did Hook Nose. They held her to blame for the death of their friend, and they were not the forgiving kind. Why Stout was being so friendly, Blue Water Woman could not guess. Maybe he was just that way by nature. Or maybe he had designs on her and intended to make her his woman.

The sun was low in the sky when the Utes moved to their mounts. Hook Nose examined the bay, which stood with its head low, blowing softly. The rest had not done it any good; the animal was in no condition to go anywhere.

Reluctantly, the warriors made camp where they were. This time, Blue Water Woman was allowed to sit near the fire. And this time, Rope himself brought her a small piece of pemmican.

It had been so long since she tasted food that Blue

Water Woman almost crammed it into her mouth and wolfed it down. Reason won out, however, and she chewed slowly, nibbling so it would last longer. Pemmican had never tasted so delicious. When she was done, she felt as if she had partaken of a fine feast.

Hook Nose brought her water. Blue Water Woman thanked him in the Flathead language and he replied in Ute. That they were treating her better was encouraging, but she did not fool herself. Essentially, she was no better off than before. She was still a captive, still fated to be taken to their village, and still helpless to aid her husband, who might already be dead.

Despondent, Blue Water Woman curled up on her side as close to the comforting flames as she could without being singed. She slept soundly enough, although she awakened when one warrior relieved another to stand guard, and later, when sinister snarls from a thicket to their south alerted them to a prowling predator.

Hook Nose added wood to the fire. In the light of the dancing flames they saw a pair of fiery eyes blaze at them from the depths of the thicket. Whether it was a bear or a panther was hard to say. That it would make so much noise hinted at a grizzly, but when it departed, it did so with spectacular stealth. One moment the burning eyes were there; the next, they were gone, and not so much as a rustling leaf marked the creature's disappearance.

Morning was brisk and windy. The Utes wasted no time, mounting and heading out before the sun rose. Blue Water Woman was no longer led around as if she were a dog on a leash. Rope cut the rawhide a few inches from her wrists, but he was more watchful from then on. They all were. They were not going to let her escape if they could help it.

Noon found them approaching the boulder-strewn

ridge. The sight of black specks spiraling above it spurred the warriors into a gallop, Hook Nose frantically lashing his mount up the slope. A piercing cry heralded the panicked flight of more than a dozen buzzards who rose heavily, their long wings beating lethargically.

Blue Water Woman was last on the scene. Even though the Utes were her enemies, she shared their disgust at the wreck the vultures had made of their fellow. Somehow the birds had learned the body was under the blanket. Perhaps a wayward gust was to blame.

In any event, his eyes, nose, and lips were gone, one ear was missing, the other hanging in tatters. Both cheeks were ripped wide. And that was not the worst. From the neck down was indescribable. The foul birds had eaten to their heart's content before they were interrupted.

Another dispute was born. Hook Nose insisted on taking the body with them, but Rope objected. Stout stayed out of it this time; maybe he was tired of the constant bickering.

Presently, Hook Nose wrapped the remains in the blanket and tied the blanket at both ends so the body parts would not slip out. But when he tried to place the dead man on the bay, the bay would have none of it. Sorting and bucking, the animal forced Hook to step back or be trampled.

Stout lent a hand. The heavyset warrior held the bay steady while the body was draped over it and tied down.

Blue Water Woman perked up when they headed to the south. The last she had seen of Shakespeare, he had been on a shelf a mile or so in that direction. With any luck, the band of cutthroats was still there. The Utes were bound to spot them and spy on them. Somehow, someway, she would contrive a means to embroil the Utes in conflict with the cutthroats so she could spirit her man away during the confusion.

In under an hour, as the whites reckoned time, the shelf appeared. It was higher than they were, the rim open and stark and empty of movement. Blue Water Woman looked long and hard, but there was no one to be seen. The white men were gone. With them went her last hope of saving Shakespeare.

On they rode, holding to a brisk pace but not so brisk that it unduly tired their mounts. Late in the afternoon the Utes grew mildly excited. They joked with one another as they entered a low pass that connected to a magnificent valley dominated by a broad lake.

The lake was much lower and far away, but Blue Water Woman's keen eyes picked out the lodges that dotted its northeastern shore. Her anxiety worsened. Had they reached a village so soon? She had not heard of one in that area, but individual bands were forever moving around. It must be a summer encampment.

Too depressed to pay much attention to her surroundings, Blue Water Woman did not look up again until a strident yell was voiced by Hook Nose, who was well in the lead with the bay.

Rope wasted no time catching up. His intake of breath was like the wheeze of a bellows. Stout gawked, his skin as pale as a white man's.

Blue Water Woman hardly noticed the makeshift lodges or the meat drying on racks or the elk hides stretched out on pole frames. She could not tear her gaze from the scores of bodies scattered on the sand. Stiff, pasty bodies, some starting to bloat. All were partially consumed, either by coyotes or the black flock of ugly carrion eaters that had assembled from miles around.

Hook Nose seemed to go crazy. Howling wildly,

he galloped in among the lodges, scattering buzzards right and left. Three dropped with arrows in them. The rest leaped into the air and winged upward on ascending currents. Soon the sky was choked with birds, all waiting for the newcomers to leave so they could resume their feeding.

Stout and Rope climbed down. They were shocked, so shocked that they shuffled among the bodies as if they were dead themselves.

Blue Water Woman had been completely forgotten. A crack of her reins, and she could flee into the pines. The question, though, was whether she could make it before one of the warriors put an arrow into her. Deciding she could not, she slid off.

Breathing was a trial. The stench was awful, the worst she had ever encountered, the sweet, sickly smell of putrefaction mixed with odors so foul they were an abomination to the senses. She saw a woman whose dress had been ripped open by ravaging beaks, whose flesh had suffered even worse.

Turning toward the lake, Blue Water Woman walked to the water and splashed some on her face. All the dead were Utes. The crude lodges and the meat told her that it was a temporary hunting camp. Hook Nose, Rope, and Stout, she surmised, were three of the hunters. Only the fact they were gone when the camp was attacked had spared them.

Who could have done it? Blue Water Woman wondered. The Blackfeet were known to raid this far south on rare occasions, but she doubted they were to blame. The bodies had been literally shot to ribbons. Only whites had that many guns. She thought of the band who had abducted Shakespeare, and just as quickly dismissed them. They had been too few to wipe out a camp this size.

Who, then?

A shout caused the vultures to rise higher. Rope

had found something he was brandishing for the others to see. Blue Water Woman moved closer.

It was a shirt. A bloodstained garment discarded because it was caked with blood and had a huge tear in the back.

Blue Water Woman recognized the style. It was the same as that worn by the *vaqueros* who had been in Manuel de Varga's camp. Leaping to the only possible conclusion, she tried to imagine why Varga would have made so monumental a blunder.

Another shout, this time from Stout. He had found footprints leading into the trees.

Hurriedly, Hook Nose and Rope carried the body of the warrior whose horse had fallen on him into a lodge. Then they dashed to their horses, Rope gesturing for Blue Water Woman to follow suit.

No sooner was she on the sorrel than the three grim warriors raced into the forest on the trail of those responsible for the slaughter.

Chapter Eighteen

Barely ten seconds after Shakespeare McNair slid over the rim of the shelf, he heard Jasper Flynt bellow.

"Galt! What the hell are you doing sittin' down? Go check on that old coot you're supposed to be guardin'. There's something mighty strange about the way he's lyin' there. I don't like it."

Shakespeare had been crawling, staying low in case any of the cutthroats peered over the edge to look for sign of the men who had been sent out to find the Varga expedition. Now he flung himself erect and ran, praying he wouldn't trip over a rock or step into a rut.

There was no moon. It was so dark, he could not see his hand in front of his face. Fortunately, boulders and other objects loomed as shadowy bulks even blacker than the night. He swerved aside again and again, refusing to slacken his speed even at the risk of a broken leg or twisted ankle.

Ahead, a seemingly solid ebony wall hove up out of the earth. Shakespeare knew it for what it really was, and ran faster. He was almost there when angry shouts and curses informed him that the renegades had discovered he was gone.

Torches lit up the rim, but two more bounds brought Shakespeare to the trees. He barreled into the growth, raising both arms in front of his face to protect his eyes from the raking limbs and rapierlike branches that thrust at him from all sides.

His plan had worked to perfection! The key had been persuading Flynt to send out most of the cutthroats in search of the Vargas. Now only a handful remained. He stood a much better chance of eluding them than he would the whole band at once.

Slowing, Shakespeare listened to the nicker of horses and Jasper Flynt roaring curses. They were saddling up. He jogged eastward, the ground spongy thanks to a thick layer of fallen needles that muffled his tread.

It worried him that the only weapon he had was a short piece of jagged quartz. Against a grizzly or a painter it would be useless. He might as well throw peas at them.

Hooves drummed, growing steadily louder. The killers were making their way down the slope. He counted three, four, five torches. Flynt had ordered every last man to take part in the hunt. They were zigzagging back and forth, yelling to one another.

Shakespeare came to a dense patch of brush and veered to the left rather than barrel on through and be lashed and torn. Suddenly something snorted. A large shape materialized, and he drew up short, crouching, fearing he had blundered onto a bear.

The creature did not move. Neither did he. Its heavy breathing confirmed its massize size. Behind him, the undergrowth crackled. At least one of the cutthroats had reached the forest. He could not afford to stand there much longer, yet if he moved, he might provoke an attack.

The animal snorted. Recognizing the sound, Shakespeare straightened and said softly, "Boo!"

Uttering another snort, the elk pivoted and fled, plowing on through the vegetation like an out-of-control steam engine. Shakespeare could go on now, but he didn't. Darting to the right, he dropped onto his hands and knees and scooted in among high weeds.

"Do you hear that, boys?" a grating voice bawled. "Flynt! He's down here! Hurry!"

Two torches moved toward McNair, bobbing and weaving as the riders wound among the boles. In the flickering glow, the grimy, bearded faces of the two men resembled disembodied specters. They reined up less than fifteen feet from where McNair lay to cock their heads and listen.

The elk was still making plenty of noise.

"We've got him!" gloated one of the killers.

"Flynt! Flynt! This way!" shouted the other, and the pair sped off.

Shakespeare started to stand, then ducked down again. The rest were closer than he had realized. Within moments, Flynt, Galt, and the last man drew abreast of his position.

He grinned to himself. Once they had gone by, he would retrace his steps to the shelf. His white mare and personal effects had been left unguarded. In no time he would be in the saddle and out of there.

Then Jasper Flynt unaccountably reined up. Galt and the other man followed his example. Galt asked, "What is it, Jasper? Why'd you stop?"

Shakespeare tensed. Had Flynt seen him? No, that was not possible. But Flynt might have *sensed* him. Men who lived in the wilderness long enough often developed heightened senses much like those of the wild beasts with whom they lived in such close proximity.

Flynt swiveled in the saddle, his gaze passing right over Shakespeare. He looked toward the shelf and frowned. "Galt, I want you to go back and keep watch."

"By my lonesome?"

"You afeared of the dark, fat man?" Flynt said.

"No, it's just that—"

"I ain't got time to bandy words, damn you!" Flynt growled. "It's your fault the old-timer got away from us. I ought to take a switch to your head. Or maybe hack off one of your fingers. Maybe that would learn you to do as I tell you from now on."

The tip of Galt's tongue nervously licked his thick lips. "There's no need for that, Jasper," he whined. "I was stickin' close to him, just like you said. How was I to know that he untied those cords?"

"Untied them, hell!" Flynt declared. "Those knots were too tight for anyone to unravel. I should know. I tested 'em myself."

To the northeast one of the pursuing riders hollered, "Jasper! Jasper! We've got the varmint cornered in a wash! Come on! We need some help!"

Flynt jabbed a finger at Galt. "You don't know how lucky you are that McNair didn't get away. Now, get your fat ass back to camp and don't budge until we return. Savvy?"

Galt's double chin bobbed.

Flynt raised his reins, then paused. "So help me, if you let anything happen to our pack animals and supplies, I'll skin you alive and stake you out over a hill of red ants." With that, he was gone, flying toward the two points of light in the middle distance.

Mopping his forehead, Galt wheeled his animal and did as he had been instructed. "Damn that man!" he grumbled. "One of these days he's going to push me too far, and that will be the end of Mr. High-And-Mighty Jasper Flynt!"

Shakespeare rose to his knees. His scheme had not worked out, after all. Galt would be extra alert, afraid of incurring Flynt's wrath. To try and claim the mare might get him shot.

He glanced at the torches of the others, visible through the trees. It would not take Flynt and company long to learn that they had trapped an elk, not him. The first thing they would do was retrace their steps, seeking sign. He had to leave.

Bearing to the southeast, Shakespeare held to a pace that would have exhausted most men half his age. After an hour he slowed to a walk. Another hour, and a haven appeared, a deadfall at the edge of a meadow. It was a tricky proposition climbing to the top, what with the gaps and cracks where an arm or leg could slip. But he managed it.

Resting on a wide log, Shakespeare propped his arms on his knees. He was tired. Powerful tired. It had been a long day, and the next promised to be longer. He had no rifle, no pistol. No belt knife, no tomahawk. His ammo pouch and powder horn were gone.

So was his possibles bag. He missed it the most, since it held, among other useful items, his flint and steel. Also a small clasp knife. With them, he could make do fairly well. Without them he would have to scrape up food as best he could, and starting fires would be a chore.

Or would it? Fishing under his moccasin, Shakespeare pulled out the flint. All he needed was another piece. Striking them together would set sparks to flying. With the right kindling—an old bird nest, for example—he could get a fire going in no time.

But it would be dawn before he could think of doing anything. Replacing the flint, he reclined on his back, his arm on his forehead. Glumly, he stared at the stars. Normally the celestial grandeur was inspiring. Not tonight.

He was glad to be shed of the renegades, but he had a greater worry that had been eating at him for days. Namely, what could have happened to his wife and the Kings? He was sure it had been something awful. That they had not shown up to rescue him was proof.

Hadn't he trained Nate himself? The younger man could track like an Apache, and his wife was no slouch in that regard, either. It should have been simple for them to trail the renegades.

What if they were . . . dead? The notion was unthinkable, yet he had to be realistic. As the old cliché went, no one lived forever. His white hairs belied the fact that most trappers wound up as worm food within three years of coming to the mountains.

At the last rendezvous, he had been astounded at how few faces he knew. Of the three hundred or so mountaineers who had been around when beaver trapping commenced, less than a score were still alive.

He was one of the supremely lucky ones. Nate had also lasted longer than most. They were overdue, as it were.

Shakespeare did not know if he could go on without Blue Water Woman and the Kings. They brought lively sparkle to his life, zest to his weary old frame. Losing them would plummet him into a state of unbearable loneliness.

"To be, or not to be," Shakespeare quoted, and closed his eyes. It had been a spell since last he prayed, but he prayed now, prayed long and hard that his wife and the man he thought of as his son were still alive. He fell asleep praying, not intending to rest more than a couple of hours.

Bright, warm sunlight tingling his skin awakened him. Shakespeare sat up, annoyed that he had overslept. The sun had been up half an hour. A deplorable lapse, he mused, and blamed his advanced years.

Stretching, Shakespeare took note of his surroundings. The deadfall was wider than it had appeared in the dark, the meadow that bordered it ripe with green grass. Somewhere in the woods a squirrel chattered. Elsewhere sparrows chirped gaily.

Serenity sublime, Shakespeare reflected as he clambered carefully to the ground. The pristine beauty of the wilderness had entranced him from the moment he first beheld virgin territory.

The majestic Rockies were Creation in its purest form, Creation as the Almighty meant the world to be. Here a man could live unfettered by the silly rules and tyrannical laws of civilization. Here a man could breathe deep of air not choked by wood or coal smoke, wander where he pleased, live as he saw fit.

Here a soul could revel in the glories of Nature. The rivers and lakes were as pure as gold. The forests had not been rendered a wasteland by the woodman's ax. The prairie had not yet been tilled by plows. It took his breath way, sometimes, to gaze out over so much splendor.

Occupied by his thoughts, Shakespeare headed across the meadow. Lower down would be lush valleys abundant with game and watered by babbling creeks. He glanced over his shoulder at the slopes above but did not see any evidence of the renegades. His stomach reminded him that he had not eaten since the evening before, and he gave it a playful swat to shut it up.

Shakespeare was at the middle of the meadow when a loud grunt to the southwest stopped him cold. A large animal moved in murky shadow under some trees. Another elk, he guessed, and walked on. As big

as they were, elk were harmless. They would rather
run than fight.

The animal shambled into the open. Shakespeare
halted again in consternation. He had erred. Badly.
The massive brute glaring at him out of beady dark
eyes was not an elk. It was a bull buffalo.

Few easterners were aware that there were two
types of bison west of the Mississippi. Most people
had heard of the immense herds of Plains buffalo,
herds of a million or more that yearly migrated from
Canada to Texas and back again. The second variety
had not been met with as often, and was less widely
known.

Indians called them mountain buffalo. They were
shaggier, darker, and slightly smaller than their prai-
rie-dwelling kin. One trait both breeds shared was a
fiery temperament, with those that lived in the mountains being rated more dangerous.

Shakespeare could remember being skeptical when
he was first told about the high-country breed. He had
been so much younger then, and cocksure of himself,
as were most that age. Only youth could explain his
audacity in thinking that he knew more about wildlife
than the Indians. Eventually he had been proven
wrong, and ever since he had given mountain buffalo
a wide berth except when he was specially hunting
them.

More appeared behind the bull that was glaring at
him. Four cows and two calves shuffled closer to their
lord and master, as if for protection.

Shakespeare did not move. Buffalo had a keen
sense of smell but poor eyesight. If he pretended to
be a tree, the brute might lose interest and stray into
the woods. The animal had its hairy head low to the
ground, but it was not behaving belligerently.

As if to prove him wrong, the bull snorted again
and tossed its great head. Wicked, curved horns that

could rend another bull wide open glinted dully in the sunlight.

Shakespeare shifted his eyes toward the deadfall without turning his head. It was too far off. The beast would run him down before he made it two-thirds of the way.

To the north grew tall pines. They were the closest available cover, but they were not close enough to suit him. He glanced at the bull as it rumbled deep in its huge chest and lumbered a few feet nearer. Its nostrils were flared to test the breeze.

Shakespeare was all right so long as he stayed calm and quiet. The wind was blowing from the northwest to the southeast, bearing his scent away from the small herd. He saw the bull sniff a few more times. Grunting, the monster began to turn.

As fate would have it, the wind chose that instant to change direction. Where it had been caressing his right cheek, now it fanned his back.

One of the calves bawled. The cows hurried toward cover, their short tails flicking. But the bull vented a bestial snort and swung around with incredible agility for an animal its size. The grotesque head tilted. It advanced, testing the breeze. The muscles on its sides and those that layered the broad hump on its front shoulders rippled and surged.

"No," Shakespeare said under his breath.

The bull paused to paw the ground. Clods went flying. Its head dropped lower, its shaggy beard almost brushing the soil. Nearly six feet high at the front shoulders and heavier than a stallion, it was not an adversary any sane person would care to tangle with.

It charged.

Shakespeare sprinted toward the tall pines. He was pumping his legs madly, yet it seemed as if he were wading through thick molasses. He could not move fast enough to suit him.

Huffing and puffing, the bull bore down on the mountain man. A wide swath of grass was left flattened in its wake, the ground scarred by deep hoofprints and chunks of ripped earth.

It was as if Nature had spawned a living engine of destruction, a creature that knew no fear and had no equal. Buffalo had ruled their vast domain for untold ages, and according to many Indian tribes they would endure forever.

For the Sioux and the Cheyenne, for the Arapaho and the Shoshone, for the Blackfeet and many others, the buffalo was as much a part of their lives as breathing and eating. They depended on the well-nigh limitless herds for their clothes, for their utensils, for the very dwellings in which they lived.

Buffalo hunts were held regularly. When a herd was spotted, warriors mounted their fleetest, most dependable steeds and gave chase. It was not uncommon for lives to be lost. A warrior might be thrown from his mount and be buried by an avalanche of plunging bodies. Or his mount might be gored, and down he would go under a flurry of hammering hooves. Or a bull might decide to turn and attack.

Small wonder that Indian women dreaded the aftermath of a hunt. It was not the backbreaking labor, not all the skinning and butchering they had to do. It was the constant fear of having the hunters return and their man not be among them. Buffalo had made widows of more women than all the guns of the white men combined.

Shakespeare McNair had been on his share of hunts, most of them when he was much younger and did not know any better. Each had been a bedlam of noise and motion and dust. He had lost friends. He had seen men stomped to a gory pulp, seen warriors torn by horns. After every hunt he had vowed that he would never go on another, yet he always did when invited.

He had been charged before. Once, a bull had chased him and his horse for pretty near two miles, which was unusual given that buffalo were not endowed with much stamina. On another occasion, a pair of young bulls had tried to box him between them and nearly succeeded. The horse he had owned at the time carried a jagged scar on its hindquarters ever after as a reminder of exactly how close a shave it had been.

But none of those times could hold a candle to the unbridled terror of being pursued on foot. A quick look showed Shakespeare that the bull was gaining with uncanny swiftness. He would never reach the trees. Not alive. Not unless he did something.

The pounding of hooves grew louder and louder. Shakespeare swore he could feel the deep breaths of the buffalo on the back of his neck.

Just when it seemed that the monster was about to run him down, Shakespeare leaped to the right, throwing himself prone. The bull chugged on by, brushing his leg. He rolled when he hit, over and over and over, and when he came to rest, he hugged the ground as if trying to melt into it.

The bull turned and came back. Shakespeare could feel the vibrations under him, could hear the rustling of the high grass and the animal's angry snorts and grunts. He was as still as a rock, refusing to twitch even when a hulking brown shape reared on his left.

Stems at his elbow crackled. A dark hoof was planted an arm's length from his head. Out of the corner of his eye he saw the bull plainly. Its own eyes were roving over the grass beyond. Saliva dribbled from its chin, spatting his hand.

Shakespeare stared at the hooves. If they came any closer, he must roll aside or be stomped.

For an eternity the bull stood there, sniffing and snorting. Then, with a jerk of its head, the brute lumbered to the southwest, nearly stamping on McNair's arm. He lay low until the crash of underbrush assured him that the monster had rejoined its harem.

Sitting up, Shakespeare swatted pieces of grass from his buckskins. There was no doubt about it. Obtaining a weapon was crucial.

Once a suitable period had gone by, the mountain man cautiously rose. The meadow was tranquil, the woods were peaceful, but that did not mean a thing. In a crouch he continued on, not really feeling safe until the forest shielded him.

He was more hungry than ever. His stomach sounded like an agitated painter, the way it carried on. A rabbit added insult to injury by letting him get so close that he could have beaned it with a rock had there been one handy.

Always Shakespeare traveled lower. He had not been through this area in ten or twelve years, but he had a fair idea of where he was. The spectacular view from a rocky spine proved him right. To the southeast glistened a large body of water. Sandy Lake, some called it, which fed into Sandy Creek.

As he descended the spine along a trail favored by mountain sheep, glittering rock detoured him to a vein of quartz. Broken pieces lay thick on the ground. All he had to do was select the one that suited him. It went under the top of his other moccasin. Now he could start a fire whenever he so desired.

Most of the morning was spent reaching a slope that overlooked the lake from the northeast. Intervening trees prevented him from seeing much of it.

Coming up on a path frequented daily by deer and elk, Shakespeare made good time. He planned to fashion a spear, use it to kill a deer, then fashion a bow and use *it* on the renegades if they tracked him this far.

At the bottom, when still a quarter of a mile from the lake, Shakespeare noted that the ground had been torn up. Ascribing it to buffalo, he did not give it much attention until he started across and the imprint of a shod hoof stood out like the proverbial sore thumb.

Dozens and dozens of riders had gone by, no more than a day or so before. It had to be the Varga party, Shakespeare guessed. What a stroke of luck! Don Varga would help him out, maybe outfit him with a horse and rifle. And Varga might even know what had happened to Blue Water Woman and the Kings.

Gone was any thought of food or water. Changing direction, aglow with his good fortune, Shakespeare hastened after the expedition.

Chapter Nineteen

"It is here somewhere!" Don Manuel de Varga declared. "It has to be!" Anxiety contorting his features, he intently scanned the sheer walls of the gorge through which they were riding. "The map says so!" he added, shaking the parchment at the mocking heights.

Nate King did not reply. Varga was beyond caring what he or anyone else said. The change that had come over the Spaniard was appalling.

Gone was the smug confidence, the air of self-righteous authority, the aspect of power and elegance that Varga had worn like a suit of armor. Little by little, day by day, cracks had appeared in that armor, cracks that widened and lengthened until the armor began to peel from Varga like the skin from an orange.

Don Varga was a shell of his former self. He had not slept decently in days. He rarely ate anything, and even then, he would only nibble on a piece of bread or cheese. Dark bags under his eyes accented his haggard appearance.

At times Varga had a feverish gleam in his eyes. But Nate doubted that it was due to illness. No, the fever was of another variety, the kind that men suffered when their lust for riches eclipsed all else. "Gold fever" was how some folks referred to it. And Varga had the worst case that Nate had ever seen.

"I will find it!" the Spaniard grated through clenched teeth. "After coming so far, I will not be denied!"

Three days had gone by since they left the lake. Three days had been spent scouring the lower slopes on the south side of Long's Peak, without results.

It was a maze. Here nature had carved mighty gorges and sculpted sheer cliffs. Ravines and ridges crisscrossed one another. Talus slopes were deadly traps for riders and pack animals alike. In wooded areas deadfalls were common, tangles so thick that it took forever for the expedition to find a way through.

Varga raised his glistening face to the afternoon sky. "You won't thwart me!" he railed, shaking the map again. "Not even you can stop me!"

Nate did not ask who Varga was talking to. Sadly, he turned away, shifting to check on the column.

Immediately behind them rode Ignacio and Martin. The older brother wore his concern for his father on his face, but Martin was oddly composed and calm, unaffected by his father's slow disintegration.

Farther back were Winona, Zach, and Evelyn. Evelyn saw Nate looking at them, smiled cheerily, and waved.

The mountain man waved back. How amazing small children were! he reflected. They did not let despair weigh them down. When beset by hardship, they always bounced back much faster than adults.

Their soaring spirits could not be bound in chains of worry and desperation.

Zach was not taking the ordeal nearly as well. Nate was troubled by the sullen mood his son had fallen into. It was not like the boy, and he did not know what to make of it.

If the strapping trapper could have peered into his son's mind at that moment, he would have discovered the cause. Zach was upset with himself for letting his family down when they needed him the most.

Back when Varga first took them captive, Zach had harbored the notion that he would soon find a way to free them from the Spaniard's clutches. But as day after day went by and no opportunities arose, he grew more and more upset. The failure, he felt, was his.

If he were a true warrior, it should not be taking him so long. True warriors never failed. A true warrior, he had always believed, never gave in to enemies, never stopped trying to come out on top. True warriors succeeded.

It bothered him, too, that the Vargas treated him as if he were a mere child. Don Varga, Ignacio, Martin, even Maria and Francisca, they never addressed him as an equal, never spoke to him like they did to his pa and ma. For the most part, in fact, they ignored him, just as they did Evelyn.

To be fair, Zach had noticed that they did not treat him any differently than they treated Diego. Diego's opinion on things did not matter. In family councils around the campfire, he was never asked his viewpoint.

Zach did not like to be treated that way. By Shoshone standards, he was at the threshhold of manhood. He had counted his first coup, hadn't he? Why, in another few winters he could take a wife if he so wanted—and if his pa let him.

This was not like the time he had been captured by

the Blackfeet. It was strange, he thought, that the mortal foes of his mother's people had treated him more decently than the Vargas were doing. The Blackfeet had adopted him as one of their own, had valued his insights, had given him the run of their village. There had been a maiden who took a shine to him, which suited him just fine since he'd had a powerful hankering for her company, as well.

Thinking of maidens turned Zach's thought to Luisa. He often caught the youngest daughter giving him looks on the sly. Initially, she had turned away in embarrassment. But of late she met his gaze with a frank appraisal of her own. Her friendly smile was an invitation to talk, but the few times he had tried, either Ignacio or Martin had snapped at her to stay away from him.

Zach hated Ignacio. The man treated him the worst of all of them. Zach daydreamed of planting a lead ball in Ignacio's brain, or of slitting Ignacio's throat while he slept.

Especially galling was Ignacio's habit of referring to him as a ''breed.'' Bitter experience had taught Zach that many people despised him simply because he was part white and part red. Half-breeds, he had learned, were universally frowned on by his father's kind. Fewer Indians shared the prejudice, although still too many to suit him.

Zach never had understood why. What difference did it make if his father was white, his mother Shoshone? Why hold a grudge against him for something over which he had no control?

Zach had never confided in his parents, but one of the reasons he was more inclined to go live with the Shoshones than the whites once he was old enough had to do with this very issue. Why go live among people who would look down their noses at him just because his skin color was not the same as theirs?

Why subject himself to being called vile names, and spit on, and worse?

A few yards in front of him, Winona put a hand on the small of her back and arched her spine to relieve a kink. Her gaze rested on her children. Evelyn grinned, but Zach wore a dour mask that grew worse with each passing day.

It worried Winona. Until the previous winter, her son had always been so carefree, so full of vim and vinegar, as Nate would say. Of late, though, he had been prone to surly spells, most noticeably at the last rendezvous when he had almost gotten into a fight with a man who made a comment Zach did not appreciate.

An added burden was her son's growing lust for warfare. Zach yearned to be a mighty warrior, a trait shared by many Shoshone boys his age. But in him there was a subtle difference. Her motherly instincts told her that he was becoming *too* preoccupied with bloodshed and battle. The next time she visited her people, she would have Touch The Clouds and Drags The Rope talk to him. Two of the bravest warriors in the tribe, they could perhaps change his outlook.

"Ma, will we stop soon?"

Winona turned to her daughter. "I cannot say. It is not up to me." They had been in the saddle since sunrise. Don Varga had not rested at noon, as was his custom. Nor had he done so for the past three days. The closer they came to the mine, the harder the man drove himself and everyone else.

"Too bad it isn't," Evelyn said. She was sore from so much riding, which she never imagined could happen, not as much as she loved horses.

Ever since her parents had given her a frisky pony for her very own, horses were all Evelyn thought about, all she dreamed about. Her favorite toy was a horse crafted from buckskin, sticks, and real horse

hair, given to her by a Shoshone aunt. At home she
played with it for hours on end, straddling it with her
toy doll and pretending she was out riding like the
wind.

A harsh command from the front of the column
brought the weary men and women to a halt. Don
Varga glared at the world as if it were arrayed against
him, and swore in Spanish. In English he said, "The
map must be correct. We will find the Beak. We
will!"

Once more Nate made no response.

"Where could we have gone wrong?" Varga wondered, and unrolled the parchment. Aloud, he translated, "Due south of the highest peak is a gorge with
red rocks at the mouth. Up it is a landmark I call the
Eagle's Beak." Varga frowned. "That is all the captain wrote. What do you suppose he meant?"

Nate shrugged. He had never heard of any landmark by that name, and he had mingled freely with
Spaniards who came to trade at Bent's Fort, a trading
outpost to the southeast, the only one of its kind for
hundreds of miles around.

"What could he have meant?" Don Varga repeated. A curt gesture moved the column forward,
Varga craning his neck and constantly swinging from
side to side like a heron stalking frogs and fish.

Around a bend appeared four runners. The Maricopas were on their way back after having scouted
ahead, as ordered. Chivari was in the lead. Whatever
he told the Spaniard sparked more cursing.

"Why is this happening?" Varga asked the heavens. "Why have you turned against me?" To Nate,
he said, "Chivari tells me that the gorge ends several
hundred yards ahead. They did not see any sign of a
mine."

Nate glanced at the high walls. It occurred to him
that they had boxed themselves in nicely. With only

the one way out, they would be trapped like rats
should a hostile war party get wind of them. Being
hemmed in made him uneasy. "Let's try farther
west," he suggested.

"No!" Don Varga said. "We will check every
square inch. I must see that the mine is not here with
my own eyes." He nodded at the Maricopas. "Do
you honestly think I would trust the word of these
miserable wretches?"

Nate followed when the Spaniard put spurs to the
Arabian. He did not point out that this was the third
gorge they had searched, and that they were no closer
to finding the mine than they had been out on the
prairie. The map had mentioned a gorge with red
rocks, all right, but there were many gorges in that
area, and sandstone was common. Locating the right
one could take days, if not weeks.

Nate trotted around the turn. Varga was staring at
the base of the right-hand wall, which was as blank
as a child's chalk slate. Nate looked up, to the left,
and whistled softly.

Far above, perched on the smooth rim, was a stone
outcropping. Carved by wind and erosion, it bore a
remarkable resemblance to the beak of a gigantic bird
of prey.

"Look yonder," Nate said, pointing.

Manuel de Varga stiffened. Whipping his mount,
he galloped to a jumbled collection of boulders of
varying sizes that lined the base of the left wall. He
flew from the saddle, racing in among them.

Nate was only a few steps behind. He heard an
elated outcry, swept past one of the largest boulders,
then dug in his heels in astonishment.

A square black maw gaped darkly, framed by ancient timbers. An incline of excavated dirt led up to
it, while beside the opening sat two weathered

wooden ore carts. To the left of the entrance was a giant pile of discarded worthless rock.

Don Varga stood as one transfixed, mouth agape. Tears welled up in his eyes and seeped from their corners to moisten his cheeks. "I have done it!" he breathed. Then, pumping his arms at the blue vault that crowned the gorge, he shouted in near-hysterical triumph, *"I have done it!"*

Others were filing through the boulder field. Ignacio was foremost, and like his father, he shed tears of joy. Martin, as usual, was unfazed. Beyond an odd smirk, he showed no emotion. Maria, Francisca, and Luisa giggled and clapped their hands and hugged one another.

"Bring lanterns! We are going in!" Varga said, dashing up the incline with all the enthusiasm of a child who could not wait to open the gift he had just been given. His family and many of the *vaqueros* surged forward, a wave of greed washing against the rampart of stone.

"Wait!" Nate hollered, bringing everyone up short.

Varga was a few steps from the opening. "What is wrong?" he asked impatiently.

Nate shouldered through them, up to the entrance, and rose onto the tips of his toes. He pried at the overhead beam with his fingernails. A sliver the size of his little finger came off in his hand. "This wood is rotted. Go rushing on in, and you're liable to bring the whole tunnel crashing down on top of your heads."

The Spaniard took the sliver. It crumbled when he pressed it between his palms. Swallowing hard, he stared at the supports. "You are right. In my haste, I nearly got all of us killed."

Ignacio's brows pinched. "Why did you warn us, *senor*?" he asked. "All you had to do was keep quiet, and you would have been rid of us. You could have been free.''

"Yes, I could have," Nate said, and brushed past the perplexed eldest son to join his family. A hubbub broke out as Don Varga barked orders fast and furious and the servants and *vaqueros* hustled to comply. Nate strode to his wife, placing his hands on her shoulders. "I'm sorry," he said. "I couldn't do it."

"I am glad," Winona said, and she genuinely was. Other men would have let the Vargas be crushed without a second thought. But not *her* man. It was not in his nature.

From the moment they first met, Winona had known of her husband's inherent noble streak. Marauding Blackfeet had been about to slay her when Nate had appeared out of nowhere, putting his own life in jeopardy to save hers. Few would sacrifice themselves for a stranger. Fewer still would then dismiss their courageous act as "nothing special."

His nobility was one of the traits that most attracted her. Maybe he was not the smartest man alive, or the most clever, or the handsomest, but there was no denying that he was achingly decent and honest and true.

Other wives often worried that their husbands would be unfaithful. Or that their men would cast them aside for younger women. Not Winona. In her heart of hearts, she knew as surely as she did that the sun would rise each day and set each night that her man would never betray her trust, and never, ever discard her as if she were an old shirt that had outlived its usefulness.

Some believed she had chosen unwisely in picking Nate. She could have chosen any warrior in the tribe as her mate, they claimed, and lived in the grandest of lodges, owned many furs and more horses than she knew what to do with. She could have lived her life in relative ease and luxury, as her people measured status.

Winona would rather have Nate. She would rather have a man who adored her heart and soul than a warrior who valued his warhorses more than he did her. She would rather have a mate who would stand by her side through the worst of times than one who would run out on her on a whim. As silly as it sounded, Nathaniel King was everything she had ever wanted in a man, and more.

The mountaineer who had won her heart steered his family to a small clear space. Winona passed out pemmican. As they slowly chewed, frenetic activity swirled around them. Everyone except the three *vaqueros* assigned as guards was bustling this way and that. Either they were setting up camp, or they were picketing the horses, or unloading supplies. A group of ten men took axes and pack animals and rode off to find suitable timber to use as beams and supports.

Don Varga was rejuvenated. He was everywhere, snapping commands, giving detailed instructions, showing how he wanted certain chores done.

Nate leaned against a boulder and was about to doze off when the Spaniard moved purposefully toward the mine entrance, the four Maricopas tagging along. At the opening Don Varga stepped to one side and gestured imperiously. Chivari's response seemed to anger Varga, who shoved a lantern into the warrior's hands and gestured more sharply.

The Maricopas were none too happy, and Nate could not blame them. The rest were given lanterns of their own. Ignacio brought a rope, which was looped around the waist of each. Another rope was tied to the end of the first, yet another to the end of the second.

Chivari stepped forward but hesitated just inside. For that he received a push from Don Varga. The

Maricopa spun, livid, his hand on the hilt of his knife. For a moment the outcome hung in the balance as the warrior and the Spaniard locked blazing eyes. It was the Maricopa who backed down.

The Indians filed into the mine, a *vaquero* playing out the rope. Don Varga and his sons crowded forward. Nate rose and started to move closer, but a *vaquero* holding a cocked rifle motioned him back.

Contempt washed over Winona. Varga had forced the Maricopas to go in first because in his eyes the warriors were expendable. They were nothing but heathens, weren't they? So what if they were all killed? It would be no great loss.

Winona was not a naive innocent. She had met people before who insisted on having their way at all costs, people who were so wrapped up in themselves that they never gave a thought to the feelings of others.

Don Manuel de Varga was such a man. He would do whatever was necessary to achieve his goal, even if he had to slaughter unsuspecting women like those at the lake.

What did that bode for her? For the children?

The light reflected on the walls of the mine was growing dimmer. Ignacio cupped his mouth and shouted, getting only a few words out before his father cuffed him and berated him in Spanish.

Nate would have done the same. Shouting might cave the roof in on the Maricopas, and along with the servants, they were about the only members of the expedition against whom he did not nurse a grudge.

He could forgive many things. Being mistreated. Being called names. Being forced to accompany Varga against his will. But what he could not and would not ever forgive was the abuse his family had endured. That they had not been physically beaten or otherwise hurt was beside the point.

No one had the right to lord it over others. Politicians did it all the time. So did European royalty. In their own estimation they were special; as a result, they assumed special privileges to which they were not entitled.

The airs that people put on had always rubbed him wrong. If it wasn't his father acting as if God had granted him a special dispensation to run Nate's life any way he wanted, it had been his employer, making him work late without extra pay or belittling the job he did in front of fellow workers.

No one did that in the wilderness. Any man who presumed to tell another what to do had better be right handy with a gun or a knife. Frontiersmen cherished their freedom above all else, and woe to the jackass who did not respect the fact.

Politicians and their ilk were unwelcome west of the Mississippi, and if Nate had his druthers, they always would be.

A fuss at the mine returned Nate to the here and now. The rope had stopped playing out. By the antics of Varga and his sons, it was clear that the Maricopas had stopped for some reason and were not going on. Don Varga stooped and gave the rope a powerful tug to signal the warriors, but it still lay limp and unmoving.

Ignacio headed into the tunnel, brushing past Martin, who made no attempt to stop him. Their father did, though, calling Ignacio back. Then Don Varga surveyed the camp and smiled when he saw the big trapper. "*Senor* King, come over here. *Por favor.*"

Winona sat up. "Do not go, husband," she whispered.

"If I don't, he'll have me dragged there." Caressing Evelyn's cheek, he moved to the bottom of the incline.

"Up here," Don Varga said, beckoning. The icy

smile was branded into his skin, and the same strange gleam that had lit his brooding eyes at the lake was lighting them again. "I want you to do something for me."

"I'm not going in there," Nate said bluntly.

Varga chuckled. "Ah, but I think you will. You see, *senor*, now that I have found the lost mine, you are the one person I need the least." The Spaniard's pause was masterful. "That is, if we do not count your wife and children."

The thinly veiled threat fired Nate's temper to a fever pitch. But covered as he was by several guns, to throw himself at Varga would be pointless.

"Perhaps you would prefer for me to ask your son?" Don Varga added salt to the wound. "I am sure he would obey me, if only to spare you from having to do it. What do you think, *senor*?"

Not dignifying the barb with an answer, Nate snatched a lantern from Diego, who had to use a crutch to get around, and stepped to the opening.

"Off you go, *gringo*," Ignacio said.

Nate resisted an urge to smash the lantern against the hothead's face. Holding the lantern in front of him, he strode into the dank bowels of the earth.

Chapter Twenty

At that very moment, high on the gorge rim, Blue Water Woman was secretly rubbing her wrists back and forth while keeping an eye on the three Utes. The warriors were on their bellies at the very brink of the precipice, peering down. By their excited whispering it was apparent that they had located their quarry.

They had forgotten all about her. Blue Water Woman stopped rubbing, eased onto her hands and knees, and crawled to the edge a few yards from her captors to take a look herself.

The Varga expedition was down there, all right. They were swarming about like bees, engaged in a variety of tasks. Almost instantly she spotted Winona, Evelyn, and Zach. She did not see Nate, which worried her. Had something happened to him?

Don Varga and his family were gathered together almost directly under her. She did not understand why they were staring at the wall until it hit her that they must have found the mine. The Spaniard's party could not have been there very long, judging by the fires just being started and the horses not yet tethered.

Rope, Stout, and Hook Nose pulled back from the brink and crouched. An urgent exchange resulted in Stout dashing to his horse, mounting, and flying to the southwest as if he were pursued by a pack of rabid wolves.

Blue Water Woman knew that he would race to the nearest Ute village, there to rally his people against the invaders. Before long, a war party would be on its way. The word would go out to other villages. In no time, an army of vengeful warriors would be there.

It bothered her that Stout had gone instead of one of the others. He was the friendliest of the three, the one who had treated her the nicest.

As if to prove her point, Rope suddenly hissed and sprang to her side. Seizing her by the elbow, he yanked her back from the edge and shoved. She fell on her hip. Scrambling to her knees in case he came at her again, she brought up her arms to ward off blows.

But Rope did not pounce. Using gestures, he commanded her to stay away from the edge.

The Utes were afraid someone below would see her, Blue Water Woman reasoned. That would alert the Spaniard and his men, and the Utes did not want Varga to know he was being spied on. It would spoil the surprise attack the war party was bound to spring on the slayers of their brethren at the lake.

Blue Water Woman grew rigid with anxiety. What about Winona and her family? Although innocent of any wrongdoing, they were bound to be slain with the rest. Or more likely, they would be taken alive and tortured.

She could not allow that. Somehow, she must help them. To that end, she moved to a boulder well back from the brink and sat with her forearms between her legs. That satisfied Rope, who grunted and flattened to peer into the gorge again.

Gritting her teeth, Blue Water Woman worked on the rawhide. It was tight, but not so tight that it cut off the circulation. She had loosened it a bit already, at the cost of raw skin and a trickle of blood.

The situation had gone from bad to worse. Not only must she free herself, not only must she find Shakespeare and save him, now she must save the Kings.

Others might have said it was hopeless, that she could never achieve all that, but Blue Water Woman pushed pinpricks of despair from her mind. She would never give up, not so long as life animated her body.

Her upbringing had a lot to do with her resolve. Flatheads were pragmatic people. They took each day as it came, coping with problems as they arose. From her mother she had learned to adapt to the flow of life without complaint, to take the good with the bad, to meet hardship with courage and an iron will.

Now she applied that will to the cords. By constantly moving her wrists, by moistening the rawhide with her blood, she gained a little more slack. Not enough to slide her hands from the loops, but that would come.

Unexpectedly, Rope stalked toward her. Blue Water Woman sat perfectly still, fearful that he had figured out what she was up to. But no, he gestured at the woods that fringed the gorge, at the trees, and mimicked picking up things from the ground.

They wanted her to gather firewood! Blue Water Woman rose and walked into the growth. They must be supremely confident she would not try to escape on foot, she mused. And they were right. Afoot, she could not possibly do all that had to be done. She needed the sorrel.

She bent to grab a small fallen branch, resting it in

the crook of her elbows. As she unfurled, inspiration struck. What if she were to trick the Utes into thinking she *had* run off? They would probably jump on their horses and hunt for her, leaving the sorrel where it was.

Grinning, Blue Water Woman threw the branch down. She roved to the right, seeking a place to hide. She was among firs, tall pines with no low limbs. With her wrists bounds, climbing one was out of the question. She knew that—and so did the Utes.

Her grin grew positively devilish. Casting about, she ran to a waist-high boulder, jagged at the top. She pressed the rawhide against it and sawed vigorously, biting her lip when the rough stone scraped flesh.

It took forever. Rawhide was tough, which was why it was used to make ropes and the like. Both of her wrists were repeatedly gashed and nicked. When, at long last, the loops parted, she desired nothing so much as to plunge both arms into ice-cold water. But that would have to wait.

Sprinting to a fir, she wrapped her arms and legs around the trunk and shimmied upward. Her wrists protested. More pain seared her arms and shoulders. Refusing to be deterred, she did not stop until she was high above the ground.

Straddling a limb was precarious; firs did not have thick branches. She had to clasp the trunk in order not to fall. Looking down, she gulped. To slip would be disastrous.

Composing herself, Blue Water Woman leaned a shoulder against the bole. Now all she had to do was wait. And not that long, as it turned out.

She could not see the Utes from her vantage point. So she was startled when Rope appeared as if from out of nowhere in a clear space less than half an arrow's flight from the tree in which she roosted.

He was mad, and it showed. Glancing around, he

ventured westward, prowling noiselessly. Failing to see her, he increased his speed, swinging wide from north to south. He bent his head to the soil, but he was looking for tracks in the wrong area. Soon he stopped, smacked his thigh, and whirled.

At a run, Rope raced to the gorge. Presently, a horse snorted. Rope and Hook Nose rode into the woods, spreading apart to cover more ground.

Blue Water Woman almost laughed aloud. The tactic had worked! Clinging to the fir, she watched until the two warriors were out of sight, then she shimmied down twice as fast as she had climbed, scraping her arms *and* her legs but not caring.

She dropped the final seven feet. Steadying herself, Blue Water Woman sprinted to where she had left the sorrel. Lithely, she bounded astride its broad back, gripped the reins, and cut to the north.

Earlier, the Utes had reached the crest of the knobby spine that flanked the gorge along a game trail that approached from the south. Quite naturally, they would expect her to go back the way they had come. So she was doing the exact opposite.

Blue Water Woman could only hope that she was not making a grave error in judgment. She did not know if there was a way off the spine to the north or the west. She could get there and find impassable cliffs. In which case she must turn around and try to sneak past the Utes.

The trees were so thickly clustered that she could not hold to a gallop. Settling for a trot, she threaded steadily on until the pines thinned and rocky terrain unfolded. She hesitated to venture out. The ring of hooves on rock would carry quite a distance, perhaps to the ears of Rope and Hook Nose. But if she stayed where she was, the warriors might show up anyway.

Clucking to the sorrel, Blue Water Woman headed for what she hoped was a gradual slope that would take her safely down from the spine. She held to a walk to reduce the noise, avoiding flat rocky stretches.

Suddenly a gust of wind struck her full in the face. Dreading the cause, she clenched her jaw as she advanced. Another gust fluttered her long hair, howling up from the depths below.

She was on the verge of another precipice. This one was not as high or as sheer as the wall of the gorge, but there was no descending unless the sorrel were to sprout wings and fly.

Quelling a surge of panic that rattled her nerves, Blue Water Woman loped to the west. A sense of urgency pushed her, the clatter of hoofs like the beating of drums.

The cliff extended for as far as she could see. She raked her heels against the sorrel, breaking into a full gallop, aware that every precious moment wasted could mean the difference between escaping and winding up in the clutches of the Utes.

To her consternation, the cliff covered the whole north side of the highland spur. She swung south along the west rim, longing for a break or rift that would enable her to reach the bottom.

A feeling of helplessness came over her. She dismissed it with an angry shake.

Even if the Utes were watching the game trail, she might get by them. Jerking on the reins, Blue Water Woman made for it. She moved slowly, utilizing the shadows. The woods had fallen quiet. To her, every thud of a heavy hoof resounded like a clap of thunder. The Utes were bound to hear.

A lightning-scarred tree marked her goal. She reined up, head cocked. If the Utes were nearby, they were very well hidden.

Coming to a decision, Blue Water Woman slammed both legs against the sorrel and smacked the animals between the ears. It had the desired effect.

The horse exploded into motion. She was on the trail in the blink of an eye and swinging due south at a breakneck pace.

At her mount's top speed, Blue Water Woman streaked down the slope. The trail twisted and turned and she did the same, riding as she had never ridden before, expecting to hear an outcry at any second.

Soon the trail began to level off. She was almost to the bottom! Elated, she looked back, and into view burst Hook Nose and Rope, in hot pursuit. Hook Nose was in the lead, Rope trying to swing past to give the speckled horse its head. But the narrow trail hampered him.

She bent, slapping the reins against the sorrel's neck. Her mount responded as it always did, superbly. Fleeing onto the valley floor, she made for a band of woods on the other side. The open ground permitted her to go slightly faster.

Unfortunately, it also allowed Rope to pull ahead of Hook Nose. The speckled horse was a blur of motion, gaining rapidly.

The helplessness that had assailed Blue Water Woman up on the cliff enveloped her again. To have gone to so much trouble, only to be foiled! And this time the Utes might not be as forgiving. With Stout gone, there was no predicting what Rope would do. He might beat her. Or kill her.

Even so, she would not give up. She rode brilliantly, flawlessly, a credit to her tribe. But sometimes all the ability in the world was not enough.

The pounding of the sorrel's hooves seemed to grow louder. She did not bother to look back. The Ute would have to drag her from the saddle to stop her.

He did something else.

A flash of brown fluttered past her eyes. She felt a constriction around her arms and chest a heartbeat before she was viciously wrenched backward. The reins were torn from her grasp. For an instant she seemed to hang in midair, then she dropped, slamming onto her shoulders.

The world spun. The sky danced. Blue Water Woman forced herself onto her knees and saw the sorrel still running flat out. She tried to stand, lowering an arm to push herself erect, but her movement was hampered by the constriction across her chest. She glanced down.

A rawhide loop explained her fall. Gruff laughter sounded and Rope came alongside her, the other end of the rawhide rope in his hands. His features hardening, he hauled on it sharply, spilling her onto her stomach.

Blue Water Woman tasted grass in her mouth. She attempted to get up, only to be pitched onto her face by a violent thrust forward. The constriction became an iron band that dug deep.

Rope was dragging her! The realization spiked renewed panic into her gut. Blue Water Woman had once seen a white man who had been dragged to his death by Comanches. Every last shred of clothing had been ripped off, including his thick boots. His skin had been flayed to where it hung in thin shredded strips. What was left of his face was horrid to behold. And now Rope intended doing the same to her!

Blue Water Woman attempted to brace her legs, but it was useless. Her strength paled beside the raw power of the speckled horse. Thankfully, they were crossing a grassy tract. The stems lashed and whipped her but did no real harm.

She glimpsed Rope. The Ute wore a sinister expression that did not bode well. Sneering, he cantered to the right. Terrified that he intended to ride into the trees, she redoubled her efforts to slip free of the rope.

The warrior changed direction again, and slowed.

Blue Water Woman momentarily relaxed, assuming the worst was over. She was battered and bruised and her dress was a mess, but she would recover readily enough.

Then Rope yipped in sadistic glee and spurred the speckled horse into a gallop. Blue Water Woman's breath was whooshed from her lungs by the abrupt jerk and the gouging of the rawhide into her chest.

Swiftly, she gained speed. The grass beat at her, lashing her face, her hands. She managed to raise herself high enough to see what lay ahead.

Her heart leaped. A stone's throw away was a broad patch of thorny brush, and Rope was heading straight for it.

Shakespeare McNair wiped his perspiring brow with a buckskin sleeve and walked to a log. Sitting, he placed his right foot on his left knee and examined the sole of the moccasin. As he had suspected, it had a hole.

"Never so weary, never so in woe," he quoted glumly. "Bedabbled with the dew, and torn with briers. I can no further crawl, no further go. Me legs can keep no pace with my desires. Here will I rest me till the break of day."

Chuckling to himself, Shakespeare said, "I wish." He stood and resumed his trek, climbing, always climbing, the going tough, the land uncompromising. He had not done this much walking in ages, and it was telling on him. Every muscle in both legs was inflamed. Every step was an exercise in concentration.

It did not help that the countryside had become more open, making it harder to stay under cover. Ravines and gorges bisected the densely forested slopes. More meadows and open valleys were encountered. Throwing a shadow over him and everything else was Long's Peak, its summit lost amid the clouds.

It was great consolation to him that the trail had grown fresher. He was not far behind Varga's outfit. It was his hope that by nightfall he would overtake them, or at least spot their campfires.

Shakespeare planned to ask for the loan of a horse and go in search of his wife and the Kings. Mounted, it would not take more than a couple of days for him to reach Nate's cabin. His own homestead was twenty-five miles north of Nate's.

He hefted his spear, a lean but sturdy trimmed limb tipped by a fire-hardened point. As yet he had not been able to bring down a deer or elk so he could fashion a bow. If he caught up with the Vargas, there would be no need. Surely, Don Varga would be kind enough to let him use a spare rifle and a brace of pistols.

Things were looking up, the mountain man figured.

Seldom did five minutes go by that Shakespeare did not check his back trail for evidence of the renegades. Jasper Flynt and company had not appeared yet, which was surprising. For all of Flynt's faults, the cutthroat had struck Shakespeare as the kind who did not give up easily.

The mouth of a gorge loomed on the right. Since the tracks led toward it, Shakespeare bent his steps accordingly. He halted on learning that many of the tracks leading in had been partially obliterated by an equal number of tracks leading back out and then bearing westward.

Doffing his hat, Shakespeare scratched his head. Why had the expedition gone in and then come right out again? What was Varga doing in the mountains, anyway? Varga had promised to tell them, but they had been ambushed before they reached his camp.

Sighing, Shakespeare stuck with the prints. Lady Luck had smiled on him in that no rainstorms had materialized to erase the sign. At that time of year, late-afternoon storms were fairly common.

A squirrel appeared, chattering at him from the haven of a limb high in a conifer. For no real reason, Shakespeare helped himself to a palm-size rock, cocked his arm, and let fly.

In his younger days he had been adept at pelting sundry critters. Anything that made the mistake of wandering across his father's acreage became a prime target. Once, he knocked a crow off a fence at forty paces.

It got to the point where animals like deer and raccoons gave the property a wide berth.

Now his rock sailed high and true, crashing into the conifer inches below the startled squirrel. Tail shooting up, the feisty animal spun and fled, negotiating the treeways at a breathless pace, leaping distances that put a human to shame.

Tickled, Shakespeare smiled and moved on. In the vicinity of boulders to his right, chipmunks scampered. A golden eagle soared near Long's Peak. And far up on the mountain tiny white specks crawled across a rock face.

Mountain sheep. Of all the game animals, they were hardest to reach, harder still to kill, so acute was their eyesight and their hearing.

"My home," Shakespeare said grandly to himself. "Paradise on earth."

His left foot was paining him, so he stopped. From under the top of his moccasin he slid a small piece of rabbit meat left over from his supper the evening before. Munching gloomily, he pondered the state of affairs.

"Downright pitiful" was Shakespeare's spoken assessment. He resorted to the Bard. "If there were reason for these miseries, then into limits could I bind my woes. When heaven doth weep, doth not the earth o'erflow? If the winds rage, doth not the sea wax mad, threatening the welkin with his big-swoln face? And wilt thou have a reason for this coil?'' Pausing, Shakespeare took another bite. ''Yes, I would,'' he concluded.

The loss of his Hawken and his pistols he could deal with. They could be replaced. So could the white mare, although she was as fine a horse as he had ever owned. A new possibles bag could be crafted, new flint and steel obtained.

One loss, though, could never be replaced. It tormented his soul day and night. It put lethargy in his stride.

''Oh, William S.,'' Shakespeare said in sorrow. His edition of the complete works of the great playwright had cost him a king's ransom. More than that, it was his treasure, his comfort, his inspiration.

Books were as scarce as hen's teeth on the frontier. Easterners would be surprised to learn that many of the mountaineers were avid readers, especially during those long, cold winter months when deep snow confined them to their dwellings. Books were swapped and traded and read so many times that the spines gave out.

''Nimble mischief, that are so light of foot. Doth not thy embassage belong to me, and am I last that knows it? O, thou think'st to serve me last, that I may longest keep thy sorrow in my breast.''

Sliding what was left of the rabbit meat under his moccasin, Shakespeare tramped on. He shuddered to think of what the cutthroats might have done to his prized volume. Probably used it for kindling, he reflected. Or tore it up for the sheer hell of it and scattered the bits of paper to the four winds.

''Bastards,'' Shakespeare opined.

Talking to oneself was a habit many mountain men acquired. Loneliness was a key factor. When a person was a thousand miles from civilization, adrift in the middle of nowhere, hearing the sound of a human voice was comforting. So what if the voice was their own?

In due course another gorge became visible. Again the Varga expedition had gone into it, but this time Shakespeare could find no tracks leading out. Either they were still in there, or they had gone on through and out the other side.

A knobby spine to the west of the gorge gave Shakespeare a brainstorm. From up there he would be able to see for miles. It took only a few minutes to reach. A well-defined game trail caught his eye, and he was about to start up when the thud of hooves let him know he was not alone.

Shakespeare spun. Out across the valley galloped three riders. Indians, they were. As he looked on, one of them threw a rope over another. Raven tresses identified the figure as a woman. He saw her strike the ground hard, saw her being dragged. The high grass partially hid her. But not her horse.

Shock knifed through the mountain man. It was his wife's sorrel! That could only mean the woman being dragged was—!

He was outnumbered. His only weapon was the spear. His legs were so sore every step was a trial. But he never hesitated. Legs pumping, Shakespeare McNair flew to Blue Water Woman's rescue.

Chapter Twenty-one

A musty scent filled Nate King's nostrils as he cautiously advanced into the ancient mine. Puffs of dust were raised with each footfall. Dust also layered the walls and ceiling. In the light of his lantern, tiny particles could be seen shimmering in the air.

A cool breeze chilled his skin. Nate paused to look back. The Vargas were crowded at the entrance, Ignacio with a leveled pistol. "Keep going, *Americano,*" he said loudly.

Too loudly. Above Nate a timber creaked. The echo rumbled on down the tunnel and was lost in the distance. Extending the lantern, Nate proceeded slowly.

Most of the beams he passed were in dire need of repair. They gave the illusion that if he so much as sneezed, it would cause a massive cave-in.

The iron rails on which the ore carts rode were rusted but serviceable. Here and there lay antique lanterns of a type no longer used, dropped by fleeing workmen, no doubt, when the Utes attacked. Rusted tools were scattered about.

The tunnel was wide enough for four or five men to walk abreast. Nate stayed in the center, where he would have a split second more to react should one of the walls buckle. He brushed the left side with his fingertips and loose dirt cascaded down.

The mine was a death trap, a catastrophe waiting to happen. Shoring the supports would reduce the hazard but not eliminate it. Manuel de Varga was a fool if he persisted in his mad dream. He would be smart to give up and turn back. The vineyard would support his family amply enough if they gave up their lavish estates.

Of course, Varga was not about to listen to reason. Gold fever had the Spaniard in its unrelenting grip. Many a man had become unhinged by lust for the precious metal; many a poor soul had lost his wits, his family and friends, even his life, in the demented quest for riches beyond compare.

Pale objects lying on the ground brought Nate to a stop. He raised the lantern higher but could not quite make out what they were. Tentatively going on, he could not resist a shudder when he recognized them.

A human skull and skeleton were sprawled across the rails. The front of the skull had been caved in by a blow, and the bones of the right arm bore gash marks like those a tomahawk would make. Tattered remnants of clothing and boots littered the dirt. Nearby was a broken lantern.

It was one of the old workmen, slain during the attack. Farther on Nate found more skeletons, eight all told. They confirmed that the Utes had taken the Spaniards completely by surprise. Captain Valdez had been lucky to get out alive.

Nate avoided stepping on the remains. His eye on the rope that was linked to the Maricopas, he moved warily onward. He listened for their voices but heard only constant creaking and furtive rustling.

Their footprints were clearly imprinted in the dust. They had been moving briskly, in single file. As Nate recalled, Chivari had been in the lead, Azul had been last. Studying their tracks, he noticed that Azul's left moccasin had a curious little dent on the heel, perhaps where a stone had gouged the sole.

Suddenly Nate sensed the tunnel was widening. A stronger breeze fanned him, a cold breath of wind such as might emanate from frigid cavernous depths. Hiking the lantern even higher, he discovered a fork. The main tunnel angled to the left while a smaller branch slanted to the right.

The rope lay on the floor of the branch. Why the Maricopas had taken it instead of staying in the main tunnel, Nate could not guess.

A glimmer on the wall arrested his gaze. Moving closer revealed a narrow vein of quartz mixed with gold, a vein that grew larger the farther into the branch he went. He was so fascinated by it that he tripped over something at his feet and nearly fell.

It was a sack, or what was left of one. Large chunks of pure gold formed an irregular pyramid where they had fallen. Another skeleton lay beside them. Evidently a workman had been carrying the heavy burden when he was struck down.

Hunkering, Nate fingered a piece of the precious ore. The surface was smooth and cool to the touch. A deep yellow color lent it an enticing allure. He grinned at the thought that the chunk he held must be worth more money than he made in half a year of trapping. Maybe he should give up chasing plews and take to prospecting!

A sound from farther along the branch brought Nate's head up. It had sounded like a muffled cry of anguish. The hair at the nape of his neck prickled as he set the gold down and rose.

Advancing, Nate probed the shadows ahead. The rope at his feet ran straight and true. The footprints of the Maricopas disclosed that they had been moving along briskly. He wondered what orders Don Varga had given them. Were they to explore all the tunnels they found? Or were they only to get some idea of the condition of the mine, then report back?

The air grew chiller. Nate had taken his eyes off the rope, so he was all the more startled when he glanced down and saw that it was no longer there. Stopping short, he swiveled. The end of the rope was a few feet behind him. But the Maricopas were nowhere to be seen.

That couldn't be, Nate told himself. He picked up the rope, suspecting they had untied themselves. Closer examination revealed that the strands had been neatly severed by a sharp implement.

Nate stiffened. Someone had cut it. Letting go, he turned. Three sets of footprints had gone on unbroken, but the fourth set, the set with the dent in the heel, showed that their owner had stopped at that exact spot and shifted a bit, then continued on after his companions.

Azul had freed himself. His footprints were spaced closer together now, as if he had been taking small steps because he was afraid. Which hardly seemed likely for a grown warrior. The only other possibility was that he had been moving stealthily.

But why? Had he heard or seen something? And if so, why had the others gone on as if nothing were wrong?

Mystified, Nate took four more steps, staring down the tunnel instead of looking at the ground. The first inkling he had that he had made a mistake was when the earth under his right foot buckled under his weight, pitching him forward.

In the dancing glow of the swaying lantern, a gaping black chasm yawned. Frantically, Nate threw himself backward, but he was too late. He started to drop. Twisting, he flung the lantern from him and grasped at the edge of the chasm. His clawed fingers dug into the dirt, stopping his fall, and his body slammed into the side of the chasm.

Jarred, Nate almost lost his grip. He managed to hook both elbows on the rim and hung there, catching his breath. The lantern was an arm's length away, leaning against the tunnel wall, still glowing. The light barely penetrated the inky darkness that shrouded the chasm.

Nate tried to pull himself up. He dislodged a stone that tumbled past, and he listened for it to hit bottom. Seconds elapsed. More seconds. Many more. He concluded that he had missed hearing it strike and he was tensing to try to climb out again, when at long last a faint plink wafted upward.

Nate looked down. The chasm must be hundreds of feet deep. It was an abyss, and it would be his grave if he slipped. A fall that far would smash his body to a pulp. Steeling himself, he pressed his toes against the side and levered upward. He almost made it. Scrambling onto the lip, he hooked an ankle on the rim and was pulling himself to safety when the rim crumbled.

For an awful moment he teetered on the brink of eternity. Then, lunging, he caught hold just as he was falling. Again he slammed against the side. Blood racing, he clung on for dear life.

Nate felt momentarily weak. The close call had sapped his strength, and he feared that he might plummet into the chasm at any instant. Mustering his nerve, he began to inch upward, using his toes to brace himself, his fingers gouging into the dirt like the talons of a great bird.

Down the tunnel, something moved. Nate glimpsed a shadowy crouched form moving toward him. Ghostly images of spectral creatures filled his head. Terror born of childhood tales of ghosts and goblins galvanized him into making a Herculean effort. Flinging his right leg high, he snagged it on the edge, tucked at the stomach, and surged upward.

His shoulder caught on the rim, throwing him off balance. Desperately, Nate grasped at the nearest wall, his fingers wrapping round a stone knob. Clinging to it, he broke out in a cold sweat.

The figure was much closer.

Nate heaved onto his knees and scooped up the lantern. ''Who's there?'' he demanded, prepared to hurl it.

Uncoiling, the figure stepped into the light. ''Only me, white-eyes,'' Azul said.

Nate did not know which shocked him more: that Azul had been lurking somewhere in the tunnel all along, or that the Maricopa spoke English. Somehow he had gotten the notion that only Chivari did. ''Where did you come from?'' he demanded. ''What happened to the others?''

''Me lost,'' Azul said with a vague motion behind him. Coming forward, he stood and peered into the abyss. ''Others there,'' he said, pointing.

''What?''

''Them fall. All stand at edge. Ground give way,'' Azul said. ''Me cut rope or me fall too.''

Nate stared into darkness. The three warriors were beyond help. That anguished cry he had heard earlier must have been made by one of them when the rim gave out from under them. He backed away, not wanting to share their fate.

A disturbing suspicion flared. If the mishap had

happened exactly as Azul claimed, there would not have been time for him to cut the rope. It had to have occurred in the blink of an eye. The others would have dragged him down with them.

Nate stopped where the rope ended. The only explanation was that Azul cut the rope before his companions fell. If so, why had he snuck toward them?

A keg of black powder went off in Nate's mind, and he shifted to regard Azul closely. What if Chivari and the other two had *not* fallen? What if they had been *pushed*?

The notion seemed ridiculous. What possible motive could Azul have for killing his friends? They were leagues from home, virtual slaves of the Spaniard. It made more sense for them to stick together, not slay one another.

"We go back?" the Maricopa asked.

Nate nodded. "You first," he said. Azul moved on by, and Nate followed. "I'm sorry about your friends," he said.

The warrior gave a toss of his head. "It's life. Some live, some die."

Now, there was a philosophical outlook for you, Nate mused. His suspicions firmed. Azul displayed no remorse whatsoever. Had he killed the others on Don Varga's orders, perhaps?

The answer to that question was a resounding No! On hearing the fate of the three doomed men, Varga stepped back, sincerely stunned. "It can't be!" he blurted. "I told Chivari to be careful! I told him not to take any undue chances!"

Ignacio tucked a thumb under his red sash. "It is no great loss, *padre*. We did not need them anymore, anyway." He regarded Azul. "What happened to your lantern, Indian? We gave Chivari and you each one."

"Me lose it," the Maricopa said. "It drop in big pit."

"Is that so? Well, lanterns are not cheap," Ignacio said. "I'll deduct the cost from the money we pay you when we reach Santa Fe."

Diego, normally the quiet one, declared, "Brother! How can you be so heartless? His *amigos* have just died. Now is hardly the right time to bring up so trivial a matter."

"Trivial, little brother?" Ignacio responded. "Allow an underling to get away with something like this once, and he will think he can lose things any time he wants. When you are older, when you have your own estate to run, you will remember this day and see that I was right."

Nate had heard enough. Stalking down the incline, he rejoined his family. As his wife rushed to embrace him, he saw Azul and Martin off by themselves, shoulders bent, talking in secret. *What was that all about?* he wondered.

Winona was overjoyed to have her man back alive and well. Dread had numbed her every second he was gone. Dread that she would hear an ominous rumble, and the roof of the tunnel would come crashing down.

Losing Nate would devastate her. She would not remain in their cabin if that ever happened. The memories would be too painful to bear. She would burn it down and go live with her own people. Zach could become a full-fledged warrior, if that was his wish. Evelyn would one day marry the man she desired, and be master of her own lodge.

As for Winona, there would never be another mate for her. In her heart of hearts she knew that Nate was the only one she could ever love. Without him, she would rather live her days out alone, treasuring fond memories of their happy years together.

"Husband," Winona said softly, wrapping both arms around his waist.

"Wife," Nate said, reciprocating.

Evelyn was all smiles. "What was it like in there, Pa? Did you see any gold?"

"It was scary," Nate admitted. "And yes, I did. Lots and lots of it. Enough to make Varga one of the richest men in the world."

Zach hung back, uncomfortable with making a public display of his affection. "I hope Varga chokes on it," he said bitterly. He was sick and tired of being held captive, of being told what to do and when to do it. Most of the Vargas treated him as if he were the same age as his sister. Diego was the exception. They would talk on occasion, whenever Ignacio and Don Varga were not around to shoo Diego away.

By coincidence, the youngest Varga was hobbling toward them on his crutch. Sheepishly, he said to Nate King, "Forgive the intrusion, *senor*, but my father sent me to get the lantern."

Nate had forgotten to hand it over. Untangling himself from his wife, he said, "Here. Take it."

Diego propped himself on his crutch, raised the glass, and blew out the wick. "I am sorry for what my *padre* forced you to do," he mentioned. "It was not right that he make others do something he would not do himself."

"Too bad your father doesn't share your sentiments," Nate said.

"He is not himself, *Senor* King. Before we sailed from Spain, he was always kind and considerate of others. This gold business has changed him." Diego turned to go, then faced Zach. "Were it up to me, my friend, I would free you. But I dare not help you. My father would never forgive me."

Zach's bitterness spilled over. "It seems to me that

your family is always making excuses. When are you going to stand on your own two feet?"

"It is not that simple."

"Another excuse," Zach said. "But that's okay. You go on fooling yourself. And when your pa gets around to having us killed, it will be on your shoulders."

"*Mi padre* will not harm you. Hasn't he told you as much?"

Nate had been listening and interjected a remark. "I wish I shared your confidence, Diego. But you just said yourself that your father has changed in the past few months. And not for the better."

"Why would he hurt you? Once he has the gold, he will have no cause to."

"He'll have all the reason in the world," Nate disagreed. "You're forgetting that you are on American soil. If the American government were to learn what he has done, there would be hell to pay. Remember, he doesn't have official approval to be here."

"Why would they be upset? He has done nothing wrong?."

"Hasn't he?" Nate countered. "Your father has held us against our will. He's provoked a war with the Utes by wiping out a Ute hunting party. He's violated American sovereignty. I'd bet my poke that he'll be in hot water if word gets out." He stared at the boy's father, who was conferring with Azul and Martin. "The only way for him to make sure that it doesn't is to dispose of anyone who might raise a fuss."

Diego gnawed on his lower lip. "My father would not do such a thing," he insisted, but his tone lacked conviction.

Zach got in the final word. "After what he did at Sandy Lake, how can you be so sure?"

The youngest son hobbled toward his family, his

head bowed in thought. At the ramp he looked over his shoulder, apprehension caking his features like so much icing. His father called his name and he hobbled on, his shoulders stooped.

"I feel sorry for him," Winona said. He was a good boy caught in a bad situation, his manhood hanging on the decision he must make. Would he be true to his own convictions, or would Diego go along with his father no matter who suffered?

"I feel sorrier for us," Nate commented, sitting.

Evelyn had lost interest in the discussion. What would be, would be. No amount of fretting could change that. So she stepped to a low boulder and hopped on top of it to see if she could spot her horse among the string. Instead, she caught sight of a heavyset figured shambling toward them. "It's Rosa!" she cried.

Of all the servants, Rosa the cook treated them the best. Twice a day she brought food. Sometimes, like now, she would bring a water skin. She also held a loaf of bread.

Nate had a hunch that the cook had taken a shine to his daughter. On several occasions Rosa had slipped Evelyn sweetcakes when no one was looking. Rosa also liked to ride beside Evelyn, although Don Varga frowned on it.

The trapper had not been surprised to learn that she had a husband and four small children in Mexico. Evelyn must remind her of her little ones, he had concluded.

The cook did not speak a lick of English. But her cheerful nature and ready smiles more than made up for it. She was partial to bouncing Evelyn on her knee, the two of them laughing and having a grand old time.

Winona was glad for the water. She passed the skin

to her children, then to her husband, and finally took a deep drink herself.

Nate held out his hand for the water skin. Leaning closer, he said quietly, "Tonight is the night."

Fueled by the massacre, for days they had been plotting an escape. Both of them were keenly aware that they must get away before it was too late. Soon the Utes would show up in force, and Varga would rue the day he entered their territory. There would be no reasoning with the Utes, no parleys, no truces. Swarms of warriors would descend on the expedition like a swarm of locusts on a ripe field of grain, and by the time the Utes were done, not a single Spaniard or Mexican would be left standing.

"Tonight," Winona said. What they were planning might cost their lives, but it was better to be slain fighting for their freedom than to be slaughtered like buffalo in a surround.

Nate wagged a finger at his son, and when Zach came over, he repeated what he had told his wife.

"At last!" Zach exclaimed. Since the day they were taken captive he had been itching to do something. "But I wish you would let me trick the guards instead of sissy."

"They'll never suspect Evelyn" was Nate's reply, praying he was right. Putting his daughter in danger went against his grain. Should she be harmed, he would never forgive himself.

Winona could read her husband's features as easily as he read books. "Trust her, husband. She is young, but she can do what has to be done."

"It's not her I fret over," Nate said. It was one of the guards proving too quick on the trigger. It was the innermost fear of every parent made real: losing a child.

Watching the cook play with Evelyn, Zach said, "What about Rosa and Diego and the others who have been kind to us? Is there anything we can do to save them, Pa?''

"We've warned them. That's all we can do."

"Why not offer to take them with us?"

"Be realistic, son. How many do you honestly think will go? Most of them are convinced that we've exaggerated the danger. Maybe they like us, but they trust their *patrón*'s judgment more than they do ours. Our hands are tied.''

Zach glanced at Varga's daughters. Seated on folding camp chairs, with servants behind them holding brightly colored umbrellas to protect them from the sun, they chattered merrily while snacking and sipping drinks. In his mind's eye he saw fair Luisa, her trim body riddled by bloody ash shafts. A lump formed in his throat. "There must be something," he insisted.

Nate shared his son's yearning. It was perfectly human, perfectly understandable. But the four of them could no more prevent the wrath about to fall on the expedition than they could stop a raging storm or block the path of a towering tornado. Manuel de Varga had set forces in motion no one could withstand.

"It's a crying shame," Zach said.

That it was, Nate conceded. He sought words to console his son, but what could he say? Everyone had to pay for their mistakes. It was the first law of the wild. Neither humans nor animals were immune. A buck that went on grazing when the scent of painter was heavy on the wind paid for its lapse just as assuredly as Varga would. A quote came to him, one from his childhood, one as true then as it had been when it was uttered centuries ago: "As we reap, so shall we sow."

Chapter Twenty-two

Blue Water Woman closed her eyes, lowered her chin to her chest, and braced for the worst. Grass lashed her. Weeds battered her. Any moment that would change. She would be in the thorny brush and it would rip her to ribbons.

Loud crackling arose. They were there. A cry escaped her as lancing pangs seared her shoulders, her arms, her legs. It felt as if she were being cut by dozens of knives, all at once. She kept her head down, her eyes closed to protect them. Yet that did not spare her face. A stinging pain in her left cheek, another in her forehead, produced trickles of blood.

She could feel her dress being torn and rent. Her thigh flared with anguish. Her left forearm throbbed. The drumming of the speckled horse, the crunch of brush, were loud in her ears. Suddenly the crunching stopped. She was being lashed by grass instead of being slashed and gouged.

Blue Water Woman looked up. They were through

the patch of brush! She had survived, but it was only the first pass. Rope was looping around to plow through again.

She strained against the rawhide that was digging into her chest, but it was hopeless. She could not loosen it or burst it. Suddenly rolling to the right, then back to the left, she tried to gain enough momentum to maybe be wrenched free.

Rope saw what she was doing and laughed. Out of the corner of an eye, she spotted Hook Nose about sixty yards away, observing. He made no attempt to stop Rope. With Stout gone, her fate was sealed.

Unknown to her, though, a white-maned figure was sprinting madly toward them. Shakespeare McNair ran as if he were running a footrace with death—which he was. His blood had stopped in his veins at the sight of his wife being dragged through the brush. He was not going to let it happen twice, not if he could help it.

Shakespeare closed on the warrior who was watching the torture. The Ute's back was to him. He had to get near enough to cast his heavy crude spear, no more than ten feet, preferably less. But he could not help making noise, as fast as he was running. He was still thirty feet away when the warrior glanced over a shoulder.

The Ute's eyes widened in surprise. Recovering, he wheeled his mount and grabbed a bow that was slung over a shoulder. His other hand shot to the quiver on his back and he snatched at an arrow. In his haste, he gripped two. He had to transfer the extra shaft to the hand that was already holding the bow, and that took precious seconds. Swiftly, he nocked the arrow he intended to use to the sinew string.

Shakespeare was fifteen feet out. Much too far to make a successful cast. But he threw the spear anyway, without breaking stride. It arced high, but not high enough to impale the warrior in the chest. It would hit his horse.

The Ute had a choice to make, and only a heartbeat in which to make it. Unleash his shaft or save his warhorse. Jerking on the reins, he brought the animal around in a tight half-circle. The spear went flying harmlessly past. Quickly, the warrior brought up his bow.

By then, Shakespeare was close enough to fling himself upward. His arms wrapped around the Ute's waist, batting the ash bow to one side. Clamping hold, Shakespeare twisted and heaved, flinging the warrior as if the man were a child's rag doll. The warrior crashed to earth with such force that the bow went flying and the Ute lay momentarily insensate.

Shakespeare twirled. The other warrior was nearing the brush. Blue Water Woman was striving mightily to break loose, but she could not possibly do it before she was subjected to another harrowing ordeal. He turned to the horse to mount and fly to her rescue.

Hands gripped his ankles. Shakespeare looked down. The Ute on the ground had recovered and was clawing at a knife in a beaded sheath. Shakespeare kicked to break the man's grip, but the warrior held on and yanked, spilling him to the turf. The knife sheared at his throat and he flipped backward, pushing into a crouch even as the Ute did likewise.

The warrior stabbed, down low. Shakespeare grabbed the man's wrist. The Ute gripped his other arm. Locked together, they grappled. They were evenly matched; neither could gain the upper hand. And every moment they struggled brought his wife that much closer to the thorny brush. A bestial growl of frustration passed his lips.

At that very instant, Blue Water Woman saw the brush appear and tucked her head as she had done before. None too soon. It felt like a red-hot poker was plunged into her right shoulder. Another gashed her ribs. A third pierced her thigh. She was ripped across the chin and mouth. Her forehead was opened.

She realized that Rope was dragging her through the thickest part. Her knee was spiked by exquisite agony. Her back was cut. She knew that she was bleeding profusely, that even if she lived through this second pass, she would rapidly weaken. There would be no surviving a third time.

The brush gave way to grass. She sagged, as much from relief as from fatigue and pain. Rope was grinning wickedly and swinging wide to approach again.

Blue Water Woman sobbed. She did not want to die like this. It had been her dream to live a good many years yet, to enjoy McNair's company for as long as the Great Mystery was willing. Now that dream was dashed. And the saddest part of all was that her husband would never know what had happened to her. His torment would be worse than hers.

Sixty yards away, the man that she valued more highly than her own life was flat on his back, the young Ute on top, the Ute's keen blade lowering slowly but steadily toward his throat.

The Ute's face was beet red, his veins bulging. He was exerting every ounce of energy he possessed.

Shakespeare was barely able to hold the knife at bay. He tried to push the warrior off, but the man clung tenaciously to him. Shifting his legs, he hooked his right one under the Ute's left shin. Then, bending upward at the hips, he flipped the warrior to the left and rolled with the motion so that he wound up on top and the Ute was on the bottom.

The warrior snarled and strove to thrust his weapon into Shakespeare's jugular. Shakespeare drew his head back. In doing so, he spied an object lying on the ground close to them. In a twinkling, he released the Ute and dived, grasping it and spinning back again.

The Ute had come up off the ground in a rush, his arm hiked to deliver a fatal blow. His eyes were ablaze with bloodlust. A split second later, the right one was filled with something else.

Shakespeare McNair drove the arrow he held up and in. The barbed point sliced into the Ute's pupil, rupturing the eyeball and tearing on through into the brain cavity.

As if jolted by a bolt out of the blue, the Ute went as rigid as a broom handle and staggered backward. Feebly, he gripped the arrow and tugged. His shattered eyeball slid down the shaft, oozing gore in its wake. Like a poled ox, he fell onto his backside and sat, his lips moving but no words coming out.

Shakespeare did not waste another second. Darting to the man's mount, he seized the reins before it could run off, vaulted on top, and sped toward his wife.

Blue Water Woman felt herself going faster. Rope was gaining speed to drag her through the brush for the third and final time. She was so weak, she could barely raise her head. Blood from her forehead had seeped into her eyes, and she blinked to clear them.

A strange thing happened. Rope glanced at her and smirked, knowing as well as she did that he was about to finish her off. But his smirk died when his gaze drifted past her.

A look of baffled rage came over him. He hauled on the reins, bringing the speckled horse to a stop. Wheeling, he flung the rawhide rope to the ground, or tried to, for he had wrapped it around his right wrist and it would not come off. He had to unwind it first.

Hammering hoofbeats approached. Blue Water Woman figured it must be Hook Nose. Yet if so, why was Rope frantically tugging at his bow? It was slung across his chest and had caught on his quiver.

A piercing war whoop rent the air. Not a Ute war whoop, or the peculiar yipping cry of the Sioux, or the bellows of the Blackfeet. It was a war whoop unique unto itself, one she had heard before, one that set her heart to fluttering and her hopes to soaring.

Flashing into view came Hook Nose's mount. But Hook Nose no longer rode it. A berserk buckskin-clad avenger with hair the color of snow bore down on Rope like a charging bull buffalo. Rope gave up trying to unlimber his bow and started to turn the speckled horse. He never made it.

Shakespeare McNair rammed into the warrior's mount broadside, at a full gallop. There was a rending crash and both animals went down, squealing and flailing. Shakespeare jumped clear, rolling when he hit. Catlike, he was on his feet before the Ute. Lowering his shoulder, he catapulted into the warrior's chest, bowling him over.

Rope groped for the hilt of his knife. He was shaking his head, blinking furiously. Snaking backward, he scrambled onto one knee.

Shakespeare would not be denied. His foot caught the Ute flush on the jaw. As the warrior struggled to stand, Shakespeare scooped up the rawhide rope that was still attached to the man's wrist. Holding it in both hands with a foot or so of rope between them, Shakespeare bounded behind his foe. A deft flip, and a loop settled around the warrior's throat.

Rope clutched at the rawhide, his fingernails scraping his neck raw.

Ramming a knee into the Ute's spine, Shakespeare crossed his forearms and pulled. The warrior broke into a frenzy of clawing and twisting and thrashing. Using his knee for leverage, Shakespeare heaved backward, throwing his entire weight into it. The rawhide was digging so deeply into the Ute's flesh that it was covered by folds of skin.

Rope's right hand dropped to his knife. He pulled the blade out, but as he raised his arm to hack at his rope, his limbs drooped. His head lolled forward.

"For what you did, you bastard!" Shakespeare hissed, pulling harder. The warrior gave a few wheezing pants, then collapsed like a deflated balloon.

Shoving the body, Shakespeare dashed to Blue Water Woman. She was covered with cuts and welts, her buckskin dress half gone, her body smeared red. "Oh, God," he said. She was so still, but her eyes were open and fixed on him in radiant joy. "You're alive!"

Blue Water Woman had to swallow several times before she could speak. "Husband," she said fondly.

Kneeling, Shakespeare tenderly placed her head in his lap. "Wife," he choked, stemming a flood tide of tears.

"I came to save you, and you save me," Blue Water Woman joked. Her laugh was more a brittle cough. Weakness pervaded her every pore.

"Hush, woman," Shakespeare scolded. "I'll get you up in the hills somewhere safe and tend you night and day until you're back on your feet." He started to rise so he could lift her, but she entwined her fingers in his.

"No!" A wave of dizziness made it difficult for Blue Water Woman to form coherent thoughts. But she must. "The Kings—" she croaked.

"We'll go to their cabin once you're fit enough," Shakespeare promised.

"You—do—not—understand," Blue Water Woman said, every syllable a labor of effort. The dizziness was worse, much worse. She licked her lips and opened her mouth to tell Shakespeare that the Kings were being held captive by Manuel de Varga, and about the slaughter at the lake. They must save

Nate and Winona before it was too late.

"Don't fret yourself," Shakespeare said, gently caressing her cheek.

"But—" Blue Water Woman could barely say. She fought to stay awake and alert, but a roiling black cloud sucked her into a spinning vortex and consciousness dimmed.

It would soon be dark.

Nate King took a sip of coffee while surveying the encampment. Four roaring fires lit up the scene. The horses and pack animals were tethered at the north end, grazing on grass brought in earlier. Cooking pots hung from tripods. Rosa and another woman were carving a deer haunch. A handsome *vaquero* strummed on a guitar.

To the right of the mine entrance lay a pile of timber that would be used to shore up the mine in the morning. The ore carts had been rolled down the incline and were being repaired by an older man and several helpers.

The Vargas had one of the fires all to themselves. The men sat on one side, the women on the other. Most of them were merry and talkative, buoyed by their newfound riches. Even Don Varga was in good spirits. Gone was the gloom that had oppressed him for days. He joked and laughed along with his children.

Martin, oddly enough, was quiet and reserved. He did not take part in their discussions, and when the others broke out in peals of mirth, he merely smiled.

"How soon, Pa?" Zach asked.

Nate faced his loved ones. "Not until everyone is asleep except the guards," he whispered.

"That could be well past midnight," Zach grumbled, boiling with impatience.

"We'll only get one crack at this," Nate reminded

him. "We must do it right, or else." He did not elaborate. Each of them knew what the "or else" implied.

Evelyn was picking up handfuls of dirt and letting it sift through her fingers. "I know what I'm supposed to do, Pa," she said excitedly. Her parents had never entrusted her with anything so important before, and she was eager to show that she could be counted on.

"Whatever happens, do not be afraid, little one," Winona said. "We will not let them hurt you."

"I'm not scared, Ma," Evelyn declared with the cheery innocence typical of someone her tender age. "Not one little bit."

The aroma of roasting deer meat made Nate's mouth water. Most of the *vaqueros,* he noticed, had gathered around the fire closest to the horse string. Usually they were spread out at several fires.

When Martin rose and moved toward them, Nate's interest was piqued. Martin spent more time with the *vaqueros* than any of the Vargas, including his father and older brother. It was safe to say that the *vaqueros* were more fond of him than their *patrón.*

Azul drifted over to the group. Normally, the Maricopas kept to themselves, so this was equally unusual. The warrior hunkered beside Martin and a stocky *vaquero* named Pedro. They talked in whispers, Martin gesturing as if giving instructions.

At the fire nearest the mine, Maria was pouring more coffee for her father. Ignacio was polishing a pistol. Diego examined the bandage on his leg. Francisca and Luisa had broken out knitting needles and yarn, a favorite pastime of theirs.

Against the far wall were stacked the expedition's supplies, tools, ammunition, and sundry items. Somewhere among that huge pile were two bundles Nate must retrieve: a blanket wrapped around their rifles, pistols, powder horns, and ammo pouches; and another in which his possibles bag and Winona's large leather pouch had been placed.

"Say, Pa, what do you reckon that bunch is up to?"

Martin, Azul, and the *vaqueros* with them had risen and were moving in a body toward the fire ringed by the Vargas. The three men assigned to guard Nate's family turned, one of them swearing under his breath in Spanish.

Nate recollected that the skinniest of their guards spoke a smattering of English. "What is it, Ramirez?" he asked. "What's happening?"

"Silencio, Americano."

Don Varga had seen his middle son approaching. He rose, a coffee cup in hand, his brow knit in perplexity. In Spanish he said something that provoked a curt response from Martin.

Ignacio stood, pistol at his side. Diego glanced up but did not stand. The sisters shared confused looks, Luisa edging toward Francisca.

"What is going on?" Nate pressed.

Ramirez swore again. "This *mucho* bad, *gringo*. There was talk. But I never believe him do it."

Nate stepped closer. "Who? Do what?"

Martin had halted a few feet from his father. Planting himself, his thumbs hooked in his sash, he addressed Don Varga at length. And the longer he talked, the angrier his father grew.

"Tell us, please," Nate said, his intuition warning him that whatever was about to occur did not bode well for his family.

"Martin be long time mad," Ramirez translated as best he could. "When little, him always second best. Father always like Ignacio more. Then Diego born. Father like Diego more than Martin, too. Martin be madder."

It shed new light on a lot Martin had done that Nate

289

David Thompson

had been puzzled by. "Why is Martin bringing it up now?"

Ramirez motioned for him to be quiet. The middle son had stopped talking and was awaiting his father's reply. It came in the form of hot coffee, flung in Martin's face when Don Varga hurled the cup. Martin calmly wiped himself with a sleeve and made a remark that enraged his father. Clenching his fists, Manuel stalked forward, only to abruptly halt when half the *vaqueros* backing Martin leveled guns.

The gorge crackled with tension. Ignacio, Diego, and ten or eleven *vaqueros* moved to Don Varga's side. Rifles and pistols were fingered. Knives and daggers were fondled. All it would take was a tiny spark to inflame them and incite a bloodbath.

Don Varga jabbed a finger at Martin. Now it was the middle son who flushed and glowered.

"What is your *patrón* saying?" Nate prodded.

Ramirez was a study in confusion. "Him say Martin always worthless. Him say Martin never like work. Always want do things easy way. Always care more for what he want than what others might want." Ramirez paused, becoming more nervous. "*Patrón* say Ignacio good worker. Diego always try hard."

Martin's remark to his father caused Maria, Francisca, and Luisa to leap to their feet. Ignacio started to push past his father, but Don Varga stopped him.

"This bad, bad, bad," Ramirez said. "Martin say him tired way things are. Him want be head of family. Him want gold for his own."

Don Varga did the absolutely worst thing he could have under the circumstances: He laughed, long and hard. Hands on his hips, he chided his middle son, then barked commands at Pedro and the *vaqueros* with Martin.

"*Patrón* say Martin get gold over *patrón*'s dead body. Him tell men go sit down," Ramirez said.

290

No one moved.

Martin imitated his father, draping his hands on his hips and using the exact tone of voice Don Varga has just used.

Ramirez appeared ready to bolt. "Martin say those men *his* men now. Him pay them more, treat them better. They take orders from him alone. Him tell *patrón* to drop weapons."

Decades of pent-up hatred were etched on Martin's contorted features. Years of being the black sheep of the family, of being treated as if he were less than the dirt under his feet, had taken a terrible toll. He was a lit cannon waiting to explode. Which he did the next moment, when Ignacio snarled and elevated his pistol.

A few seconds earlier, Winona had clasped Evelyn to her and retreated toward a boulder that would offer sanctuary should shooting break out. None of the guards stopped her. They were as mesmerized by the impending clash as everyone else. None of the three seemed to know whom they should support. It was the same with a dozen or so others.

Suddenly Martin roared. Pedro shot Ignacio, and wholesale carnage erupted. *Vaqueros* on both sides opened fire. From other points in the camp men rushed to take part. Most, Nate noted, backed Martin.

More than half of Manuel de Varga's *vaqueros* were down, dead or writhing in their own blood. Six or seven of Martin's men had also taken lead balls. At an order from Martin, the rest charged. The battle became a whirlwind of confusion, shouts, and screams.

Nate saw Ignacio on his knees, a scarlet stream staining the firebrand's fancy white shirt. Ignacio had dropped the pistol and had his left arm tucked to his side. His right hand dipped under his sash and reappeared flourishing his dagger. It sank to the hilt in the gut of one of Martin's men, then flicked upward, slitting the throat of another.

A third *vaquero* raised a rifle butt to cave in Ignacio's skull, and was stabbed in the groin. The man staggered back. Losing his grip, Ignacio snatched up his pistol and looked around.

Don Varga was wounded in four places, but still he fought on. He punched a *vaquero,* kicked another. As he drew back his arm, Martin stepped in front of him, a pistol ready to fire. The middle son showed no regret, no remorse, no hesitation. He shot his father squarely in the face.

Maria screamed. Ignacio raised his pistol to shoot Martin and was smashed to the earth by three shots from three different *vaqueros.*

Just like that, it was over. Manuel de Varga and all those who had sided with him were dead.

Aglow with vicious glee, Martin lowered his smoking flintlock and scanned the broken, blasted bodies. His sinister gaze drifted from spot to spot—and centered on the Kings.

Chapter Twenty-three

Nate King felt his insides shrivel as Martin Varga, accompanied by ten or more loyal *vaqueros,* came toward those who were everything to him. Winona and Evelyn emerged from behind the boulder, and Nate automatically placed himself between them and Martin.

Seeing what his pa had done, Zach stepped to Nate's side and said so only his father could hear, "Just let him try to hurt us. I'll hold his legs while you rip his throat out."

Nate tore his eyes from Martin. Was that his son talking? The boy who had once cried and cried when Nate put a deathly sick pony out of its misery? The same boy who had been heartbroken for weeks when Apaches killed the family dog? He reminded himself to have a long talk with Zach after they got back home. That was, *if* they lived long enough to reach it.

"Well, *Senor* King," Martin said as suavely as if

they had just met at the theater. "The situation is changed, no?"

"Did you have to do that?" Nate said, nodding at the bodies being checked by *vaqueros* for signs of life.

"*Sí, senor.* I did." Martin faced Ramirez and the other two guards. "But first, what of you three?" he said in English. "You did not help *mi padre.* But neither did you help me. Where does your allegiance lie?"

The tip of Ramirez's tongue rimmed his mouth. "You are the new *patrón.* What you say, we do."

Martin was pleased. "You will not regret it, *amigo.* Those who side with me will be amply rewarded. You will make more money on this journey than you would make in a lifetime. I am not stingy, like my father. My wealth will be freely shared."

Nate was tempted to comment that it sounded to him as if Martin was buying silence with gold, but he did not.

"Now, where were we?" the betrayer said, turning. "Oh, *sí.* What to do with you and your *familia*? Can you give me one good reason why I should not have you shot where you stand?"

"What have we ever done to you?" Nate retorted. "Haven't we always been friendly? Have we treated you any differently than we treated Ignacio or Diego?"

At the mention of the youngest son, Zach looked toward the fire. One of those bodies lying lifeless was Diego's. A ball had splintered his cheek and blown out the rear of his cranium. Nearby were the three petrified sisters, Maria doing her best to console Francisca and Luisa.

"No, you have not," Martin was saying. "It is to your credit, but it is not enough to keep you alive."

"Then how about this," Nate said, and paused,

anxiously seeking a valid excuse Martin would buy. Something. *Anything.* The sight of Azul, crumpled in a miserable heap, was the inspiration he needed. "You've already tangled with the Utes. And you're smart enough to know that they're not the only tribe you might meet up with. I can be of use if that happens."

"How, *senor*?"

"I know sign language," Nate said, and to illustrate, he gestured with his fingers and hands, saying, in effect, "You man with bad heart."

"I know of this finger talk," Martin said. "Jasper Flynt was fluent in it. A small band of Pawnees visited our camp once, and he talked with them by signs." He tapped his chin. "Very well, *senor*. You get to live. But only so long as it suits me." Pivoting, he told Ramirez, "Tie them hand and foot."

"What?" Nate blurted. Seeing their chance to escape ruined, he grabbed Martin. "I gave your father my word that I'd behave."

Martin jerked his arm free. "I am not my father, *gringo*. Never lay a hand on me again." Brushing his sleeve where the mountain man had gripped it, he left.

Covered by pistols, Nate and his family were securely bound. Winona sought to soothe him by saying, "Look at the bright side, husband. At least they did not gag us."

"Don't give them any notions," Nate spat. Now it would be ten times as hard to flee before the Utes came. He had waited too long to make his bid, and his wife and children would pay for his oversight. "Damn!"

The eternal optimism of youth prompted Zach to say, "We'll turn the tables yet, Pa. Just wait."

Would they really? Nate wondered. Or were they deceiving themselves?

The next morning, Martin oversaw a mass burial.

His father and brothers were laid to rest in individual graves, but the *vaqueros* who had perished were dumped in a mass unmarked hole. That afternoon, under Martin's direction, the work on the mine began in earnest. The timbers were replaced one by one, from the entrance on back. Practically every last *vaquero* was pressed into service.

A single guard watched the captives. Five others were off felling trees. Unlike his father, Martin did not see fit to post sentries at the gorge mouth.

Toward evening Martin assembled the expedition members. His speech was in Spanish, so Nate caught only bits and pieces, enough to glean that Martin had promised them all they would be well set for life if they obeyed him as diligently as they had obeyed his *padre*.

The *vaqueros* cheered their approval. But many of the family servants were downcast, especially Rosa. Formerly so full of zest and cheer, she went about her duties as one half dead.

By the evening of the second day, digging was under way. The first cartload of ore rattled down the incline shortly before sunset, to another resounding cheer.

By the evening of the third day, a pile of pure gold as tall as Zach lay gleaming and glittering in the firelight. Martin spent hours touching and rubbing the ore, and took a piece with him to his blankets when he turned in.

The fourth day began no differently than the others. The Kings were untied so they could eat breakfast and briefly stretch their legs under the watchful eyes of four *vaqueros*. Afterward they were tied and left to bake in the hot sun. At noon Martin ambled over and sat on a boulder. "It goes well," he gloated. "We will have more gold than we can transport by the end of the month."

"And what then?" Nate quizzed him. "What will you do with us?"

"I do not think you truly want to know, *senor*. Suffice it to say, you should enjoy life while you have it, eh?" Martin chortled lightly.

Nate had been meaning to ask another question. "I'm curious. I know that Azul killed Chivari and the other two Maricopas. Did you have a hand in that?"

"Of course," Martin crowed. "Chivari and the others would not turn against my father. They wanted no part of it, and they gave me their word that they would not interfere."

"But you had them murdered anyway."

"I do not take undue risks, *senor*. Azul agreed to dispose of them when he could. The chasm in the mine was most convenient."

"Won't the Spanish authorities be suspicious when you show up in Santa Fe without your father?"

"Not at all. Are we not in hostile country? The Utes wiped them out, without provocation."

"So that's your story. What about your sisters? How do you plan to keep them quiet?"

For once a flicker of sadness lined Martin's countenance. *"Mi hermanas,"* he said softly. Maria, Francisca, and Luisa were seated in the shade of the high wall, a portrait in misery. "They can be so stubborn. Why can they not see that what I have done was for their benefit as much as mine?"

"So you're fixing to make worm food of them, as well." Nate had never despised anyone as much as he did this man at that moment.

"You bore me," Martin stated stiffly, rising.

"One last thing," Nate said. "The attack on my cabin. Was that your doing?"

Martin shook his head. "Jasper Flynt is to blame. Why, I know not." He adjusted his *sombrero*. "I learned later that Azul helped him in exchange for a new knife.'' Martin snickered. ''That Azul. He would kill his own *madre* for trinkets.''

Nate could only stare. Martin was no better. Whether a trinket or a fortune in gold, no reward was worth becoming a Judas.

For the next few hours they were ignored. Then Evelyn called out to Winona, wishing she could wet her parched throat. Not two minutes later, Rosa was there with a pitcher full of water. The guard blocked her way, but Rosa brushed past him as if he were not there. She gave Evelyn a drink, then each of them in turn.

Nate was last. As the kindly matron tipped the pitcher to his lips, she leaned low to whisper, *''Resignarse. Esta noche. Trinchante.''*

Before Nate could say that he did not understand, Rosa stood, smiled at Evelyn, and was gone. He rose on an elbow to call out, but the guard was regarding her suspiciously. Sinking back, he sorted through his meager store of Spanish. *Noche* was ''night,'' if he recalled correctly. *Esta*? Didn't that mean ''steak''? Had she told him that they were to have steak for supper?

No, no, no, he had it all wrong. *Estaca* meant ''stake,'' the kind that had nothing to do with food. *Esta,* now that he thought about it, meant ''this.'' *Esta noche. This night.* So she had hinted that something was going to happen later on. But what?

Try as he might, Nate could not think of the meaning of *resignarse*. Did it mean ''resign,'' maybe? And what about *trinchante*? He was sure he had never heard the word before. Sometimes, though, Spanish words were a lot like their English counterparts.

Take ''doctor,'' for example. It was the same, only pronounced differently. And what about *mula*, or ''mule''? Or *centro*, or ''center''?

So maybe *trinchante* was one of those. But if so,

what in the name of creation was a *trinchant*? Did it mean "trench"? Had she warned him that they were to be killed during the night and dumped in a trench? Was that it?

More worried than ever, Nate counted every second until sunset. It was business as usual in the encampment. Cart after heavily laden cart clattered out of the mine to deposit its loads of rich ore. More trees were brought to further shore up the tunnel.

The camp, though, was not as noisy as it usually was. All the *vaqueros* and the servants were uncommonly quiet, many deep in thought. Nate's hunch was that the atrocity committed the other day had caught up with them. They were finally fully realizing just what they had done, and the burden they must bear for the rest of their lives.

Presently the sun relinquished the heavens to the first stars. Four fires crackled and danced. The evening meal was being prepared. A buck, a doe, and several rabbits were the fare. Rosa skinned most of them herself. Nate saw her butchering the buck, her carving knife peeling succulent flesh with practiced strokes.

About half an hour after everyone else had eaten, Rosa brought a tray to the Kings, just as she did each and every evening. Extra *vaqueros* came over to untie the captives, then to help stand guard while they ate. As Martin had boasted, he did not take undue chances.

The guards had become so accustomed to the routine that they hardly paid any attention to the cook. Sinking onto her left knee, Rosa set the tray down and handed plates to Winona and Evelyn. She ladled out thick stew and gave each a spoon and a buttered roll.

Next it was Zach's turn. He was so hungry, he wolfed the roll in two chomps.

Nate leaned forward. "I didn't understand earlier," he whispered. "What was that all about?"

Rosa's blank look was added proof, as if any were needed, that she did not speak English. Smiling sweetly, she put her right hand on the ground and pushed herself up. Her smile widened, and she winked.

Mystified, Nate dared not so much as gesture to let her know how confused he was, or one of the guards might notice. Rosa turned to leave, and as she did, her right thumb, which was close to her dress, jerked toward the ground.

Nate glanced down. Lying at the exact spot where she had put her hand was the large carving knife. She had hid it up her sleeve! Tingling from head to toe, he casually shifted his leg to cover it. His eyes had to express his gratitude, since he could not do so with words or signs.

Rosa sighed with contentment. She beamed at Evelyn one last time, and walked off.

Nate ate slowly. Each of them always did, to delay being trussed up again. It gave him plenty of time to slide the knife high up under his thigh. When he was done, he lay flat, as the guards required, and extended both arms, his wrists together.

It was the cue for one of the *vaqueros* to tie them. For once, Nate did not mind. He had a nervous moment when the *vaquero* hiked his legs a few inches to bind his ankles, but the man did not raise them high enough to spot the knife.

Winona had seen what the cook did. She watched Rosa go about her regular routine, marveling at the risk Rosa had taken on their behalf. Should Martin find out, his rage would be terrible.

Now the minutes were endless. Nate feigned drifting to sleep but cracked his eyelids. All the guards but one went elsewhere. Activity gradually tapered

off as more and more weary expedition members re-
tired. By midnight only Martin and a few others were
up.

Soon it was just Martin, sipping coffee and gazing
in entranced rapture at the huge pile of gold, much
like a man would stare at a love.

By one A.M. or so, Martin turned in. That left a
guard at each of the two fires still burning, another
over by the horses, and the man who sat on a boulder
a few yards from the trapper and his family.

Nate contrived to roll onto his side, facing the *vaquero*. The man was tired. Repeatedly, he yawned.
Twice he stretched. Eventually his chin drooped. He
snapped it up again, but his eyes were so heavy that
they kept closing of their own accord no matter how
many times he tried to keep them open.

By two in the morning, the man dozed. So did the
men at the fires. Small wonder. From dawn until dusk
Martin had them perform grueling labor, then he had
the gall to expect them to stay up half the night keeping watch.

It would be another hour before the guards were to
be relieved. That did not give Nate much time. Easing
off the knife, he twisted, gripped the hilt in both
hands, and slowly bent until he could slice the rope
around his ankles. The razor-sharp steel parted the
strands as if they were paper.

Reversing his grip, Nate sliced the loops securing
his wrists. The moment they separated, he was in a
crouch and stalking the guard. A glance revealed that
Winona and Zach were awake. Their eyes glinted in
the starlight. Each of them knew that this was their
only chance. They must not fail.

Nate's moccasins made no sound on the bare earth.
He could hear the *vaquero* snoring softly. His next
move was critical. It must be done swiftly and silently.

Throwing his left arm around the Mexican's throat, Nate clamped down, cutting off the guard's breath and stifling any outcry. Even as his left arm constricted, his right drove the carving knife into the *vaquero*'s back, the long blade sliding between ribs to pierce the heart.

It was over astoundingly quick. The guard stiffened, gasped, and was still.

Neither of the men at the two fires lifted their heads. Of the *vaquero* by the horses, there was no sign. But no shouts rang out.

Nate steadied the body, arranging it so it would not slide off to give the illusion all was well. Hurrying to his loved ones, he freed his son, who was nearest, then his wife and daughter.

Zach was up off the ground in a flash. Gliding to the guard, he helped himself to the man's personal arsenal. It consisted of two fine pistols, a rifle, a dagger, a powder horn, and an ammo pouch.

Winona held Evelyn close. The poor child was sluggish and drowsy and might give them away.

"Here," Zach whispered, giving his mother a pistol and his pa the rifle.

Nate was impressed by how competent his son had grown. Motioning for them to stay where they were, he returned to the dead *vaquero* for two more items they needed. One was the man's *sombrero*. Nate also peeled off his jacket.

"Stay low," the mountain man reminded his family as he guided them toward the east wall. Slinking from boulder to boulder, always in the deepest darkness, they were not discovered.

"What now, Pa?" Zach asked.

"We wouldn't get very far without mounts," Nate whispered, giving his beaver hat to his son and donning the wide-brimmed *sombrero*. It was too small, but by mashing it down he made it stay on. The jacket was also several sizes too little. By slicing the seams at the sides and partway up the back, he could shrug into it. From a distance, he might pass for a *vaquero*.

"If something goes wrong, get out while you can," Nate advised. Shouldering the rifle, he headed for the horse string. Once in the open, he slouched to disguise his height and bulk.

The guards by the fires had not stirred. A chorus of snores and grunts rose from scattered sleepers. One man muttered in his sleep. Another tossed and turned restlessly.

Most of the animals also slept. A few raised their heads as Nate came up, but none whinnied or shied. He walked briskly down the line to where the stallion, his wife's mare, Evelyn's pony, and Zach's horse were tethered together.

"Quien es?"

Nate froze. Shuffling sleepily toward him was the horse guard.

The man rubbed his beard and yawned. "Estrada, is that you?" he asked in Spanish. "Are you here to relieve me already?"

"Sí," Nate said to lure him closer. But the guard abruptly realized the trapper was not Estrada, and halted.

"Wait. Who are you? I have never seen you—"

With pantherish speed, Nate whirled. The carving knife was almost impossible to see, so fast did it span the six feet between them. There was a thunk, and the *vaquero* gaped dumbly at the hilt that jutted from his chest. He took a faltering step, lips gaping to yell.

By then Nate reached him. A brawny hand clamped over the guard's mouth smothered the alarm. Limply, the *vaquero* sagged, and Nate slowly lowered the body.

Some of the horses were agitated. Don Varga's

Arabian was sniffing loudly. Nate prayed it would not catch the scent of blood.

He untied the stallion first and led it to their hiding place. Every clomp of a hoof was like a peal of thunder to his edgy mind, but none of the sleepers awakened. Handing the reins to Zach, he went back for another animal.

It took longer doing one at a time. To lead all four at once would make so much noise that someone was bound to hear. The pony was last. Evelyn hugged it and lavished kisses on its neck, whispering, "Are you ready to go home, precious?"

"Let us go," Winona said, gripping the mare's mane.

"What's your rush?" Nate asked. Their luck had held so far. Why not a while more? "Come with me," he said to his son, and padded to where the provisions were piled. Locating the blankets bound by cord was not the challenge he feared it would be. The bundles lay in plain sight, toward the back. Giving one to Zach, he carried the heaviest.

They started for the east wall. Zach was in the lead, about to pass the last of the horses, when a man sleeping twenty feet away sat up and looked right at them.

"Keep going," Nate whispered. Smiling at the Mexican, he stopped and nodded. The man blinked, scratched himself, then sank back down with a low snort and a cough. Nate walked on.

Now they had their mounts, and they were all armed. "What about our saddles?" Zach asked. His had been a gift from a Shoshone uncle, and he was loath to part with it.

"We ride," Nate said. They had tempted fate long enough. Boosting Evelyn onto her pony, he forked the stallion. Riding bareback came as naturally to him as breathing, as it did to all of them.

Shoshones relied on saddles only for special occasions. Winona had ridden without one from an early age, and she had taught her children to do the same.

In single file, the Kings headed for the mouth of the gorge. Nate brought up the rear to cover them. He had just flung the *sombrero* down and was adjusting his beaver hat when the *vaquero* by the fire nearest to the edge of camp stood and stretched. The man was facing Nate. In the rosy glow, the guard could not help but notice him.

Recognition jolted the *vaquero* into action. *"Los Americanos!"* he bellowed, sweeping his rifle to his shoulder.

Nate's shot was a shade sooner. The impact tumbled the *vaquero* into a row of sleeping forms. Angry yells and lusty curses added to the mass confusion as people stumbled from their blankets groping for weapons.

"Ride!" Nate bawled, and spurred the stallion into a trot.

Winona was in the lead. She verified Evelyn was right behind her as they wound southward, the hammering of hooves on the gorge floor echoing off the high walls. At the entrance she reined up to learn which direction her husband intended to go.

From deep in the defile came jumbled voices and the nicker of horses. Martin was organizing pursuit.

"This way," Nate said, bearing to the northeast. Riding in the dark was always a perilous proposition, what with logs and boulders and trees to be avoided, clefts that could swallow horses and riders alike, and more wild beasts than a man could shake a stick at. Nonetheless, they had to do it.

For more than half an hour they climbed, traversing slope after slope. On a crest dotted by stunted trees, Nate stopped to give their animals a breather. Over a mile below, pinpoints of light flickered, crisscrossing back and forth.

"They're using torches to try and track us," Zach guessed.

For even the best of frontiersmen, that was a formidable feat. For the Spaniard and his men, who were fair trackers, at best, it was akin to searching for the proverbial needle in a haystack. In a short while the torches converged and headed down the mountain. Martin had given up.

"We've seen the last of them," Nate predicted. "Martin won't waste any more time chasing us."

The trapper and his family rode on, northward. Nate would not feel completely safe until they were in their secluded valley. Dawn found them on a high ridge. The gorge was visible, a slash in the earth, bathed in shadow.

"Do we rest a spell, Pa?" Evelyn asked. She was so weary, her eyelids weighed more than her pony. "Please," she added. "I'm plumb tuckered out."

To the west and north were wooded slopes. To the east, an aspen grove. It seemed all right, so Nate nodded. Dismounting, he moved to a spur that overlooked the gorge. Tendrils of smoke curled lazily above it. But of Martin and the others, he could see no sign; it was simply too far.

Zach hopped down and pumped a leg to relieve a mild cramp. He happened to be facing the aspens, so he was the first to spy the grungy riders who filtered out of the trees. "Pa!" he exclaimed, bringing his Hawken up.

Nate pivoted, afraid that a party of Utes had stumbled on them. But it might have been better if they *were* Utes. For spreading out into a skirmish line, savage glee rampant, was Jasper Flynt and twelve of the most venomous characters Nate had ever set eyes on. "You!" he blurted.

Flynt and his men had their rifles resting across their thighs. Some ogled Winona, others smirked and chuckled as they drew to a halt not fifteen feet out.

"Well, ain't life grand!" Flynt declared. "Here we were, hidin' in those aspens yonder, bored to death waitin' for the Vargas to get done minin' so we can steal all their gold, and look who wanders by! It's almost enough to make a body believe in the Almighty."

Winona had her finger on the trigger of her rifle. There would be no quarter given, none asked. The outcome, sad to say, was inevitable.

"So that's what you're up to," Nate said, masking the fear for his family that threatened to render him as weak as a kitten. Angling toward a spot in front of Winona and Evelyn, he remarked, "You're in for a surprise. Don Varga is dead."

Flynt's eyes narrowed. "What sort of trick are you tryin' to pull, pup? How'd he die?"

Nate kept sidling to his left. "Martin. He wants all the gold for himself, the same as you."

"Well, I'll be," Flynt said. "I reckon that jackass has more gumption than I gave him credit for."

"Ignacio and Diego are also dead," Nate disclosed to keep Flynt talking. "About a third of the *vaqueros,* too."

"You don't say?" Laughing, Jasper Flynt smacked his leg and glanced at his men. "Did you hear that, boys? Our job just got a heap easier!" He paused. "Thanks for the good news, King. In return, we'll make this quick and painless. How would that be?"

Nate stopped, the Hawken in his right hand, his left hovering above a pistol. The cutthroats would come out on top, but they would know they had been in a scrape. Suddenly he noticed that a man on the far left held the lead rope to a familiar white horse. "That's Shakespeare McNair's mare!"

"Sure is," Flynt confessed. "Seems your mentor didn't have no more need for it."

"You killed him?"

Flynt chuckled. "Sure did, pup. I hacked off his oysters and made him eat 'em."

Just then, from the fringe of the pines to the north, an equally familiar voice hollered, "Liar! Say hello to a ghost, you son of a bitch!"

Everyone shifted toward the slope. Shakespeare McNair and Blue Water Woman were side by side, arrows notched to drawn bows.

Jasper Flynt was not flustered one whit, but many of his men fidgeted in their saddles. So long as they held the upper hand and there was little chance of being wounded or slain, they were full of courage and confidence. But now that the odds against them had risen, they showed their true natures.

"This is some reunion we're havin'," Flynt joked. "Next thing, Manuel Varga himself will rise up out of the ground to join in the frolic." And as he finished speaking, he snapped his rifle to his chest.

Nate fired the Hawken with one hand, the recoil kicking the barrel skyward. The ball penetrated Flynt below the sternum, smashing him from his horse. Simultaneously, Nate yanked a pistol clear, cocked it as he drew, and squeezed off a shot at the renegade on Flynt's right.

Behind Nate, Winona and Zach cut loose, their rifles booming in unison. Evelyn, unarmed, stuck her fingers in her ears and scrunched low over her pony.

Four of the killers had gone down in half as many seconds. Belatedly, the others brought their weapons into play. A man on the left was taking aim at Winona when an arrow transfixed his neck. Screaming, he threw up his hands and toppled. Another ruffian kneed his mount toward Zach, only to be tumbled off it by a whizzing shaft that caught him high in the chest.

The renegades finally got off a ragged volley, but

most fired without taking deliberate beads. Half of their number were now on the ground, and those who were left had no desire to end up the same. Four of the remaining seven whirled their animals to flee.

Zach centered on a cutthroat who was elevating a pistol. His own flintlock blasted first. The man's left eye dissolved; he melted to the earth.

Winona snapped a pistol up. She was centering on an onrushing figure when a glittering shaft sheared into the man's torso.

Nate had traded his spent pistol for his other flintlock. He took a step to the left to get a clear shot, but there was no one to shoot. The brigands who were left were racing pell-mell for the aspens.

The mountain man rotated. His wife, son, and daughter were as amazed by their deliverance as he was. Not one of them had been so much as scratched. Winona abruptly gazed past him in horror.

Jasper Flynt was on his knees, steadying a pistol with both hands. Flynt's mouth curved in a froth-covered grin; he had Nate dead to rights, and knew it. But at that juncture an arrow impaled him above the ear. The leader of the renegades flopped like a headless chicken for a few moments, expiring with a gurgled whine.

In the heavy silence that followed Flynt's death, the faint, distant crack of shots was like the popping of corn kernels in a hot pan. The gunfire punctuated a melody of screams and screeches that went on— and on—and on.

They all knew what it meant.

Twenty-four hours later, six riders stared down from the east rim of the gorge. For the longest while no words were uttered. None were necessary. To call what they saw a slaughterhouse would not do the butchery justice.

"I tried to warn them," Nate said.

Winona could not bear to look any more. "You did what you could, husband. They brought it on themselves."

"I wish we could have saved Rosa," Evelyn remarked. "She was awful nice."

"And Luisa," Zach said, pricked by the image of her radiant features.

Blue Water Woman pointed at an object being pecked at by a big raven. "I believe that is the young girl's head."

Zach shivered, even though the day was warm. "Shouldn't we bury what's left?"

"I'd like to, son," Nate responded, "but the Utes might still be in the area. We took a big risk checking for survivors. It's best if we light a shuck while we can."

"Amen to that," Shakespeare McNair declared, backing the white mare from the brink and turning homeward. "As old William S. once put it, now the play is done. All is well ended, if this suit be won."

Off they rode, family and friends, into the bright light of a new morning.

WILDERNESS

VENGEANCE TRAIL
DEATH HUNT

The epic struggle for survival in America's untamed West.

Vengeance Trail. When Nate and his mentor, Shakespeare McNair, make enemies of two Flathead Indians, their survival skills are tested as never before.

And in the same action-packed volume....

Death Hunt. Upon the birth of their first child, Nathaniel King and his wife are overjoyed. But their delight turns to terror when Nate accompanies the men of Winona's tribe on a deadly buffalo hunt. If King doesn't return, his family is sure to perish.

___4297-5 $4.99 US/$5.99 CAN

Dorchester Publishing Co., Inc.
P.O. Box 6613
Edison, NJ 08818-6613

Please add $1.75 for shipping and handling for the first book and $.50 for each book thereafter. NY, NYC, and PA residents, please add appropriate sales tax. No cash, stamps, or C.O.D.s. All orders shipped within 6 weeks via postal service book rate. Canadian orders require $2.00 extra postage and must be paid in U.S. dollars through a U.S. banking facility.

Name_____
Address_____
City_____State_____Zip_____
I have enclosed $_____ in payment for the checked book(s).
Payment <u>must</u> accompany all orders. ☐ Please send a free catalog.

WILDERNESS

GIANT SPECIAL EDITION:
HAWKEN FURY
by David Thompson

Tough mountain men, proud Indians, and an America that was wild and free! It's twice the authentic frontier action and adventure during America's Black Powder Days!

AMERICA 1836

Although it took immense courage for frontiersmen like Nathaniel King to venture into the vast territories west of the Mississippi River, the freedom those bold adventurers won in the unexplored region was worth the struggle.

THE HOME OF THE BRAVE

But when an old sweetheart from the East came searching for him, King learned that sometimes the deadliest foe could appear to be a trusted friend. And if he wasn't careful, the life he had worked so hard to build might be stolen from him and traded away for a few pieces of gold.

_3516-2 $4.50 US/$5.50 CAN

CHEYENNE

DOUBLE EDITION
JUDD COLE

One man's heroic search for a world he can call his own.

Arrow Keeper. A Cheyenne raised among pioneers, Matthew Hanchon has never known anything but distrust. The settlers brand him a savage, and when Matthew realizes that his adopted parents will suffer for his sake, he flees into the wilderness—where he'll need a warrior's courage if he hopes to survive.

And in the same volume...

Death Chant. When Matthew returns to the Cheyenne, he doesn't find the acceptance he seeks. The Cheyenne can't fully trust any who were raised in the ways of the white man. Forced to prove his loyalty, Matthew faces the greatest challenge he has ever known.

___4280-0 $4.99 US/$5.99 CAN